I0823966

BY CALLIE KAZUMI

Claire, Darling

Greedy

GREEDY

GREEDY

CALLIE KAZUMI

BANTAM
NEW YORK

Bantam Books
An imprint of Random House
A division of Penguin Random House LLC
1745 Broadway, New York, NY 10019
randomhousebooks.com
penguinrandomhouse.com

Published in the United Kingdom by Penguin, a division of
Penguin Random House UK, in 2026.

Hardcover ISBN 978-0-593-87166-9
Ebook ISBN 978-0-593-87166-9

Printed in the United States of America on acid-free paper

1st Printing

First US Edition

BOOK TEAM: Production editor: Cindy Berman •
Managing editor: Saige Francis • Production manager: Ali Wagner

Book design by Debbie Glasserman

The authorized representative in the EU for product safety and compliance is
Penguin Random House Ireland, Morrison Chambers, 32 Nassau Street,
Dublin D02 YH68, Ireland.
https://eu-contact.penguin.ie.

FOR STEVEN, WHO IS FOREVER GREEDY

Solitude produces originality, bold, and astonishing beauty, poetry. But solitude also produces perverseness, the disproportionate, the absurd, and the forbidden.

—THOMAS MANN

STARTER

HE IS NOT A MONSTER

T*hey will kill me soon,* he thinks to himself. Another hard kick comes, a firm leather toe cracking into his rib cage. He grunts and keeps his eyes closed. The thought of dying doesn't bother Ed as it once would have; he can't see another way out of his current predicament. Death would only resolve the problem. An easy exit for himself, eternal rest after so many sleepless weeks. There's a viciously sharp kick to his shoulder, and he curls tighter into himself, knees to chin. He's toyed with the idea of joining the ghosts of the Aokigahara suicide forest, of swinging from a hooked branch out of this life and into the next, but he knows it isn't an option. When Ikagi and his troop of Yakuza grunts are unable to collect what they are owed from his cold corpse, they'll turn to his innocent wife and child for payment. *Sayuri.* The thought makes Ed's stomach clench with guilt-rusted fear. A glob of spit lands on his arm, hocked up by one of the gangsters booting him in the alleyway where he was jumped.

"Let this be your final reminder. Your payment is due soon. Aniki is waiting," one of the thugs warns, referring to their boss, Isamu Ikagi. Then, he takes a tanto knife from his pocket, the curved point glinting sharply in the autumn sunlight. He wags it playfully right beside Ed's nose, which twitches nervously. "Next time you can't cough up anything of value, we'll be leaving with your pinkie finger." He grins, showcasing a silver canine.

Ed curls his hands into fists reflexively and manages to grunt an affirmation. He understands. He knows his time is running out, the interest rate escalating with every breath he takes. The second man throws one final blow to Ed's side, and he groans, watching as they both stroll away together, leaving him shivering in the fetal position. He needs to bring in some cash, fast. Everyone knows Ikagi always collects his debts, and boy, does Ed owe some debt.

Everyone local has heard about Missing Ricky, the loudmouth American expat who got in too deep with Ikagi and hasn't been seen since. The rumors say he's ten feet under the Sumida River, rocks tied to his ankles. Ed laughed about it over pints, made jokes and blamed Sticky Ricky for getting into such a bad deal with such a bad group of guys. But then two short months later, he somehow found himself in the exact same position, driven by insatiable greed and an embarrassingly inaccurate ego informing him that he would be different. He wasn't. He owes money to Isamu Ikagi, money he cannot pay off, and now he's waiting to join the fishes with Dead Man Ricky.

After a while, Ed collects himself and slowly rises up off the ground. He winces at the pain in his side and knows that a black bruise will quickly bloom there as evidence of his alleyway dance. Another thing he will have to hide from Sayuri, his wife. He sighs and dusts himself off, picks up his empty wallet and looks down at the photograph on the ID card staring back at him. The man in the photo is young, a twenty-nine-year-old newlywed excited to be the owner of a Japanese ID card, to be pivoting from the dreary suburban UK life he was so bored of to an exciting, new, and flashy life in Tokyo. How things have changed in just eight years.

Ed pockets his wallet and straightens, forces himself to walk without a limp—practice for when he returns home. He finds he can manage it if he breathes slowly and carefully. But he is not yet home, so he allows himself to hunch over, to relish the slight relief of pain that his cragged posture brings, and waddles slowly to the subway, pausing several times and holding on to walls for support as he rests his aching body.

Once outside his front door, he steels himself, ready to perform once more. He lets himself in, removes his shoes, and is immediately met by the sight of Sayuri, who is bustling around the kitchen with Kaori perched on her hip. Ed's toddler emits a joyful shriek at the sight of her father, and reaches out to him, her little fingers twitching.

"Any luck with the job search?" Sayuri asks as soon as he enters the kitchen. The same automatic six words of greeting that he has heard on repeat for months, her tone bland and bored, not a taste of hopefulness behind them.

He flinches, but quickly recovers. "No, but I'm going to check the papers again," he assures her, sticking his tongue out at Kaori in exchange for a giggle.

His wife sighs, but says nothing. She doesn't have to—the disappointment was evident the first time he came home unsuccessful, and the second and third times, too. Now he expects it, and she knows she doesn't need to bother vocalizing her frustrations. He is letting her down as an unemployed husband enough already, and she doesn't even know the full extent of their troubles. When they married, he was a shiny promise of security for Sayuri, who had been brought up in a poor household in the outskirts of Osaka before managing to turn her life around, work her way up in hospitality, and get a job managing a hip coffee joint in Shinjuku. Ed was handsome, tall, white, intelligent, and swept her off her feet with promises of a happy, stable life together. It was a whirlwind romance built on the foundations of lust, but quickly became something deeper as they each found hopes of a better life within each other.

Despite their worries about his ability to get a job while not being fluent in Japanese, he quickly managed to get a decent-paying sales job at an English-speaking recruitment company that placed employees in hospitality roles, and for many years they were blissfully stress-free in their easy, comfortable marriage. Now, Ed can feel that just his presence in the kitchen is irritating Sayuri, and she huffs as she places Kaori gently down on the floor to crawl around while she begins to prep dinner. A welcome-home kiss is clearly not in the cards. Not too long ago, she would have glided over to him, taken his jacket, kissed him on the cheek and told a joke, so that the first sound from his lips on arriving home was a laugh. His eyes drop to the ground in guilt. She is not the problem. It's him, and all his secrets.

Kaori crawls over to her father, grabbing at his trouser hems with pudgy fists. He pats her on the head, and for just a moment is reminded of how he would pat his childhood dog. Embarrassed, he squats down, peers into her smiling eyes and searches inside himself for a spark of paternal instinct. Nothing. He holds his hand out to her and she grabs it. For a moment, Ed is comforted—his child is reaching out to him with trust and love. Then she spots her chicken-shaped Kokeshi doll beneath the table and any interest in Ed is dead, her little bottom wiggling furiously as she tears toward the wooden toy.

"You haven't been down at the pachinko parlors again, have you? Or betting on those horses?" Sayuri asks, her voice deadpan.

Ed flinches. If only she knew the worst of it. "No, I've been looking for a job," he replies through gritted teeth.

She doesn't respond, and Ed slinks out of the room, reverting to his hunched posture as soon as he is out of sight, and limps over to the bathroom cabinet. There, he procures three painkillers which he swallows dry, the third tablet sticking to his gullet and causing him to gag silently. He forces it down by slurping directly from the tap, and then goes to sit down at his desk, which is tucked into one corner of the main family room. The floor surrounding him is littered with secondhand toys, and an open packet of rice crackers is lying on the table. He hopes Sayuri had time to cook lunch for herself, that she wasn't wasting away on rice crackers while Ed sauntered around halfheartedly looking for work all day, approaching businesses with his accented Japanese while frequently checking over his shoulder for Ikagi's henchmen.

Ed twitches at his desk, looking down at his latest bank statement. He's run himself dry.

He wipes his brow with the back of his sleeve and thrusts the paper into the bottom drawer of his desk alongside the rest of the evidence, the envelopes piling up. God, if Sayuri were ever to find it all . . . He brings his hands up to his head and cradles himself woefully, allowing himself a rare and private moment of utter despair. She would leave him. He is surprised that she has put up with his six-month unemployment stint as it is. The first few months, she was understanding. The virus hit all industries hard, but especially hospitality. Her café closed for weeks, and she relished the time at home with Kaori. When Ed lost his job, they spent a workless month at home together enjoying their little family unit, taking trips to the park and watching their two-year-old discover the world with eager enjoyment. But after a few months—the borders still closed but the rest of Japan plowing on diligently—she pushed him to find a new job. He was the man of the household, and had to provide. And Ed was not providing. He understands her fear, listened carefully when they were first dating and she explained her childhood and upbringing, working from a young age to help keep the household afloat, picking up odd jobs whenever possible to help her parents pay the bills. She was a woman used to living on the bare minimum, to making do and rationing. She does not want to live that way again, and Ed does not want to be the cause of it.

Ultimately, his lack of a job is temporary, something they can ride out, likely quickly forgotten once regular paychecks reappear. The secret debt he has accrued is not, and he is under no illusion that she will forgive him.

Things have been tense between them recently, of course. When Ed has returned home in the evenings with blood down his shirt and mottled bruises flowering around his puffy eye sockets, he knows she doesn't believe his lies. That he was mugged, fell down on the rail tracks, got into a bar fight. His wife knows that he is lying and she will bristle, turn her back to him and look to the ground. But Ed is too ashamed to admit the truth, unwilling to burden his wife with the anxiety that rots his everyday life. That he has squandered their savings and become tied up with the Yakuza. That he has put her life in danger as well as his.

He is not a monster. He is a man of addiction, and his addiction has cost him. Sayuri and Kaori will soon be all that is left, though when Sayuri realizes the mess he has got them into, he is sure that she, too, will leave him. It's the reason he hides it all from her. He cannot allow this to happen. To lose Sayuri would be like losing all of his limbs. She is his world. She would probably return to living with her parents, Kaori carted away with her, to the safety that his daughter's grandparents can offer. Sure, his in-laws are poor, but at least they aren't being harassed by the Japanese mafia. At least they know how to raise a child: Sayuri, sweet-mannered and kind, proof of their skills. He wouldn't even blame Sayuri if she left him; it is only a matter of time before they lose their home, if the red-lettered notices of eviction piled up in the bottom drawer of his desk are anything to go by. He's thought of leaving, of fleeing back to Britain, but Sayuri would never leave Japan. It's her home, all her friends and family are here. And if Ed were to disappear, to leave her alone, Ikagi's henchmen would try to collect their dues from her instead. He can't let that happen, will never abandon her in such a way. And running isn't an option anyway—he can't even afford a plane ticket.

When his eyes open, he finds them drawn to a job ad in the local paper. It is as though fate has brought them together, the paper open on the ad which seems to pop, looking directly at him. He frowns, sitting back and lifting the newspaper to read the text.

It's odd, and something about it raises the hairs on the back of his neck. It feels off. But if it is all aboveboard . . . Well, it could just end up being Ed's best gamble yet.

INNOVATIVE AND UNUSUAL

CHEF WANTED!

Private chef wanted for a high-profile businesswoman. Does not need professional training or Michelin stars but must have a knack for good flavoring and an experimental disposition. The right character is as important as the cooking for this particular role. Application process will require a sit-down interview and a paid two-day trial, including an overnight stay. Successful candidate will be required on-and-off, long-term, for private dining, and will be paid handsomely for discretion. The potential for a full-time, live-in role is not out of the question for the right person at the right time. The client speaks both Japanese and English, so a chef with fluency in either language is required. An NDA will be necessary before the interview. Salary from one million yen per day for the right person.

One million yen per day. Two million for just working the two-day trial period would give Ed enough to pay off the first installment that the Yakuza are after. Ed runs a hand through his thinning hair, considering the ad carefully, though deep down he knows that really, there is no question. This is the Hail Mary he has been waiting for.

He is not a trained chef, but he has more experience than the average Joe from his time as a sous chef—even if that was some time ago now. Instead of going to university, he wasted almost a decade of his youth frying food at fast-food joints, eventually upgrading to sous chef at several terrible restaurant chains in a depressingly gray Home County. He was desperate for change, and his savings took him from Heathrow to Haneda, and two months later he found himself head over heels for Sayuri. So, it has been a long time since he's set foot in a kitchen in any professional sense, but he likes to think that it will be like riding a bike, all of it flooding back to him instantly and without effort.

His time working in kitchens taught him good basic skills, such as impressive dicing techniques that might help him pass as more professional than he is. He has never made anything more extravagant than a Christmas dinner for six, but he is far from a terrible cook. He knows his way around a kitchen well enough, grew up with a mother who loved to cook meaty, flavorful meals for the family, and his wife has taught him traditional Japanese cuisine and techniques. (He could never go back to using British knives, for example.) Besides, he only needs to blag his way through the two-day trial period. And, as an ex-salesman, blagging is at the top of his résumé. He knows how to craft a brilliant CV; his career in recruitment made sure of that. He will be able to frame himself as highly employable, and knows the terminology they will be searching for. Hell, he has previously placed exclusive chefs in some of the top restaurants in Tokyo! He will definitely be able to place himself—to get through to the interview stage at the very least. Plus, he has both languages, which may give him an edge. He could speak with suppliers and other employees in Japanese, reverting to English as needed for the employer. It all seems too easy, too good to be true.

Once he is through, he'll get the two million yen regardless of whether or not he is kept on, and it will tide him over until he can make a better, long-term plan to pay his debts. He needs Ikagi off his back for a while, and this opportunity is too good to dismiss.

He chews on his lip, but realizes that he has no choice. He doesn't even know what he is considering. The run-in today left him with a near-broken rib and the promise that, if he doesn't cough up some money by the end of the month, things are going to get messy. He doesn't have time to waste right now, or other options, and so Ed pulls out his battered, dented laptop, and after mocking up a CV filled with culinary lies, he emails his application to the address on the ad.

From: edward.cook@mailer.jp
To: chefwanted@jobad.jp
Subject: Private Chef Application

Haikei,
I came across your ad searching for a private chef in the local paper. Native to the UK but fluent in Japanese, I am a seasoned cook with great experience in everything from fine dining to casual suppers. I have catered for events feeding guest lists of up to one hundred and have an extremely unorthodox and alternative approach to the art of cooking. Innovative and unusual, you won't come across another chef like me, rest assured.

I am also extremely discreet and am happy to sign any NDA as needed.

I would be more than happy to showcase my skills to you during the two-day trial and can guarantee you a mouthwatering meeting. My résumé is attached for due consideration.

I look forward greatly to hearing from you.

Keigu,
Edward Cook

He smiles as he hits Send, leaning back in the chair and resting his hands behind his head. Then, he begins to pack Kaori's scattered toys away into the kiddie chest where they belong, moving the table to the edge of the room to allow for space for their tatami mats. In the other room he can hear Sayuri running the tap and feels a stab of affection for both of his girls. He wants to be a better husband. He wants to rewind, to be the Ed of last year, to be a doting father working a decent job and providing for his hard-working wife.

It all began when he was laid off from his job. He had worked so hard to get to where he was, and it was all taken from him in the blink of an eye. After the virus, a large company restructure took place. There were widespread redundancies. Six in the recruitment department emerged from the HR room with their heads hanging low in defeat, and all of them left the office and went to drown their sorrows together at a local train station bar. Ed was one of them. After many hours, and many drinks, they ended up inside a pachinko parlor, where Ed discovered a penchant for the arcade-style game. He went home that night with over ten thousand yen in his pocket. Then, instead of searching for a new job, as Sayuri thought he was, he became addicted to the quick hit of cash he could take home from a decent win. It quickly morphed into weekends spent at the kiosks betting on horses, powerboat racing, motorcross, whatever sport was going at the best rate. He would win and feel that sweet rush of pleasure, satisfaction warming his spine as he crammed wrinkled bills into his back pocket. The online offshore casino websites opened his world even further. The cash was hard and fast; he felt as though he was losing his virginity all over again.

Whenever he lost he'd think, *I'll make it back. One more game, and I'll earn it back.* He started gambling away Kaori's tuition pot; the money he and Sayuri had been putting aside each month for two years in the hopes of sending her to a prestigious university without worry one day. But she was only a toddler, he had time to win it back. Then he gambled their car away, telling Sayuri it had been written off in an accident. The mistakes piled up and Ed could see no way out other than continuing on—surely you had to take a fall before you could climb to the top? He had to be due a big win soon. It was the law of odds, wasn't it?

Unsatisfied by the limitations of Japan's laws, Ed went down the less-than-legal route, gambling—and incurring debts—with the Yakuza. It was stupid then, and it is stupid now. He knows he got too big for his boots; believed he could outsmart them. He was on a winning streak and wanted bigger payouts than the legal parlors and offshore websites could offer him. And so he got involved with Isamu Ikagi.

Ed is pulled from his thoughts by the ping of an email, and he races back over to the laptop, heart thudding with hope.

From: chefwanted@jobad.jp
To: edward.cook@mailer.jp
Subject: RE: Private Chef Application

Mr. Cook,

Your application piqued my interest indeed. You sound like you may be just the person I'm looking for. Attached is the required NDA for the interview process. On receiving a signed copy I will forward you the address for an interview on September 14th at 9 A.M., which will be immediately followed by the two-day trial, assuming that we get on well enough during our initial conversations. This practical trial will run from September 14th to 15th. You will be expected to cook one lunch, one dinner, and one breakfast before leaving, all to my stated preferences:

Lunch—A meat-based meal

Dinner—A light dinner. Lighter than lunch

Breakfast—A Japanese-style breakfast

Please email back with the attached document, signed. You will receive payment for the trial in cash, assuming you stay on after the interview portion and complete the full weekend. I greatly look forward to dining with you.

Many thanks.

H

Ed is too relieved to smile, his shoulders dropping with the realization that he has bought himself another month or so. He barely skims the NDA before sending a signed copy back, anticipating receiving the money soon—so soon it sends a rush of blood down to his dick.

"And you don't know who you'll be working for?" Sayuri asks, her back to Ed as she washes up dinner plates. He eyes the cluttered countertops, the mess of kitchenware and distractions for Kaori littering the surfaces. He has been trying to airplane a spoonful of rice into her little mouth for minutes, but she seems intent on looking at anything other than the mound of food being waved in front of her, instead pointing at a stack of drying bottles and screaming with unwarranted enthusiasm.

Ed sighs. "No. It seems that my interviewer wants to keep their identity hidden until meeting in person," he explains, wiping a thick glob of sauce from Kaori's cheek as she waves her chubby arms ecstatically in the air from her high chair. With her distracted for a moment by the facial contact, he manages to cram the spoon into her mouth and she chews happily, banging her fists on the tray. He feels a flare of victory.

"How peculiar," Sayuri comments, her tone causing his mood to plummet as quickly as it rose.

Ed bristles, wishing that she would shut up and be happy with him. When he first got his job at the recruitment company, even though it was entry-level and poorly paid, the pair of them danced around their apartment joyfully, Ed swinging Sayuri around as she shrieked, her arms wrapped around his neck. She was so proud of him—the hours spent teaching him Japanese in the evenings having helped him to pass the required language test with flying colors. But now, she simply eyes him, one hand on her hip, still holding the dishcloth. Why does she look so furious? He thought she'd be happy for him; this is the most progress he's made in any of the job applications he's submitted so far.

Of course, she doesn't understand the level of debt they are in; of course, she doesn't realize that by getting this bizarre two-day interview he is potentially saving her life as well as his own. Her ignorance sends a flare of unjust anger through Ed, who crunches up the baby cloth he is holding in a tight fist.

He pauses. Collects himself. Breathes out. He is just jealous of her naïveté, of her ability to be sensible rather than desperate.

"Yes, a lot about the ad was strange, but . . . it may help to get me back on my feet," he says carefully.

"Look, don't get me wrong, I'm glad you're getting an interview, especially after turning down my offer to help you search. Interesting for you to switch to a cooking job," she says, swinging around to face her husband. Her thin brows are tilted in the frown that Ed has begun to recognize as her default feature, and her tone is bitter.

He feels a stab of shame. A short while ago, she offered to help him find a role, started telling him about something a friend could refer him for, but he felt a flood of embarrassment that she'd been speaking with her girlfriends about his failing job hunt and he snapped at her to stay out of it. He knows she was only trying to help, but he couldn't bear the pitying looks from her.

"Well, looking for a sales job hasn't exactly been going swell for me," he huffs back. She frowns, and he realizes she probably doesn't know what the word "swell" means. He softens immediately, switching to Japanese for her. "I love cooking," he tells her. The words sound hollow, even to his own ears. "I cooked loads before I met you, in those restaurants."

She rolls her eyes and turns back to the sink, and he can tell she is counting to ten in her head before responding. When they first met, he told her about his life back in England, how he had sweated over steaming hobs and taken orders from angry, underpaid chefs restricted by chain menus, and how he'd hated it. She laughed, delighted by his dramatic storytelling. Looking at her rigid posture now, he knows Sayuri remembers these exchanges, too.

"Whatever, Ed," she says after a pause.

Her voice drips with contempt. She probably thinks he's a waste of space. She probably regrets marrying him, now stuck with an unemployed, useless, *gaijin* husband.

He flexes his fingers into a claw, thinks of the unpaid bills in his desk drawer, and forces a smile at his wife's back, his lips peeling back grimly on his face.

Kaori screams, smiling back joyfully.

MASTER CHEF ADULT MALE

Ed was up at the crack of dawn, leaving Sayuri asleep before making the long train journey from Tokyo to Yamanashi prefecture. Now he finds himself traveling farther from the station—and civilization—as he follows the directions that were emailed to him. Mountain ranges kiss the clouds and lakes reflect the sky, light ripples dancing with the wind. It's beautiful. Eventually, Ed finds himself in the middle of nowhere, surrounded by forest and nature, ringing for attention at an electronic gate that leads farther into the overgrown forest. It's a long time since he left the hustle and bustle of the city, and the silence is suffocating. He tries to focus on the bell crickets, the only clear sound, but their grating screams do little to comfort him. He wonders what sort of a recluse would choose such a place to live. If he had millions of yen to fritter away, he would be in the hub of Tokyo, enjoying all that city life has to offer. Dining, dancing, and devilish pleasures. What can anyone gain from life out in the sticks, surrounded by greenery and desolate silence? Is it not lonely, or boring? For the hundredth time today, he wonders who exactly his prospective employer is.

After being buzzed through the tall iron gates via the intercom, he walks down the never-ending driveway. It's canopied by trees, their gnarled arms meeting above him like a private tunnel, eventually framing an enormous glass and wooden structure that stands on stilts above a basement garage. The roof is a classic Japanese style and extends out past the exterior walls, probably to avoid the building becoming a human oven, and to offer some shade and respite during the summer months. But today, it darkens the building ominously. The house feels wrong, an oddity amidst the otherwise natural landscape; its points and angles like shards of bone.

Ed approaches the looming structure with a sense of dread in the pit of his belly. In front of the garage, a man is washing an incredibly fancy black car. He looks to be in his early thirties, and is wearing a traditional chauffeur outfit, with a smart leather apron protecting him from the soap suds as he hoses down the vehicle.

"*Irasshaimase!*" The man welcomes Ed with a small wave and smile, gesturing for him to head up to the main house. Ed peers at the man curiously, and something about his kindly expression troubles Ed, though he can't quite put his finger on why.

He tips his head in thanks and wipes his clammy hands on his new, white, polyester trousers. They are part of a rented costume he got at his local party shop. They'd been flattened into a sticky, transparent plastic package labeled *Master Chef Adult Male.* He had the sense to leave the western-style chef's hat and giant inflatable spoon behind.

Ed jolts as a light suddenly flicks on at the front porch; a figure appears and opens the black-framed door. It's a Caucasian man, in his early fifties, perhaps. He is slim and slick in all black, his face entirely devoid of emotion, though the deep lines around his mouth and a craggy forehead give off a naturally stern expression.

"Oh, hello!" Ed calls out nervously in Japanese with a bow of his head, shuffling toward the figure. "Nice to meet you."

"You must be Cook-sama?" the man asks, his voice a deep and monotonous baritone, his Japanese heavily accented.

"Please, call me Ed," Ed says, instinctively switching to English and stepping closer to him, up onto the porch. The respectful use of surnames in Japanese culture is something Ed has never managed to wrap his head around, and hearing himself referred to frequently as "Cook" rather than "Ed" reminds him of being at school in London, on a sports field being chastised. Now, even Ed can see the ridiculous irony of being called Cook while costumed as a chef.

"Mr. Cook, come inside," the man says in English, gesturing at Ed to enter with a long, outstretched arm. "I am Rodrick Bauer, the housekeeper here," he adds. At this, Ed is able to detect his accented twinge as that of German, and up close he can see that Rodrick is in fact wearing a tailored black suit, a slight sheen to the fabric giving the impression of spilled oil. The polyester of Ed's costume makes a crinkling sound not dissimilar to paper, and he wipes his brow with the back of a sleeve. Spotting the tatami mat by the door, he removes his shoes; a rack of slippers indicates that house shoes are required. He slips his feet into the cushioned slippers as Rodrick waits in unimpressed silence beside him.

"Madame is expecting you and is waiting in the reading room. Please, follow me," Rodrick instructs him once Ed has righted himself, striding down an extremely wide hallway. The floors are made from long wooden boards, the grain gentle and coherent, as though the tree had been planted specifically to produce the most perfect planks for this home. The slippers squish against Ed's soles as he hurries to keep up with Rodrick.

Inside, the building is no less intimidating. The space is carefully curated, dotted with richly hued wooden furniture in modern designs, blends of angles and points. Ed thinks of his own abode, cluttered with Kaori's toys, and the cheap secondhand furniture in mismatched plastics and plywood squeezed into whatever space is available. He breathes out harshly, expelling his shame. Before the gambling, he used to treat Sayuri to random gifts and surprises, her favorite flowers or evenings out at restaurants. Their home was a happy sanctuary. Nowadays it is merely a reflection of his failures as a husband and a father.

Most of the walls they pass are made of carefully cut glass panels, the layout of the home appearing to be an almost-square hallway framing a beautiful Japanese garden, with rooms coming off from the hall that look out onto the dark surrounding woodland. An open doorway allows Ed a view through to the other side of the building, and he spots wooden decking laden with outdoor seating, bordered by jagged rocks. Ed passes several shoji doors, trying not to gape at the beautiful architecture of the home. He has to look acclimatized to this level of client luxury, after all.

As they walk past a garden fountain he spots through the glass pane, Ed stops in his tracks at the sound of a high-pitched, guttural scream. It comes from outside, on the opposite side to the zen garden. The forest. Ed turns, squinting into the woodland through a window, but he can't see past the initial dense packing of trunks and foliage.

"Is everything all right, Mr. Cook?" Rodrick turns to Ed, his face carefully neutral.

"Did you not hear that? The scream?" Ed asks, eyes still whipping back and forth in search of any suspicious movement from the other side of the glass panes. Nothing but trees, though the hairs on the back of his neck are standing up, as though his primal instincts are warning him of a danger he cannot see.

"A fox. Their shrillness echoes, due to the layout of the landscape. Probably in search of a mate. Rest assured, this entire estate is well protected and gated. There is nobody out there," Rodrick replies.

Ed is unsure whether this is meant to reassure him, because to his ears it sounds like a threat. He examines the housekeeper's features but still he finds him to be unbearably nonchalant, his eyes almost glazed over with boredom. Perhaps Ed has just spent too long being afraid of the Yakuza, and is reading between lines that don't exist.

"Silly me," he replies. "Must be interview nerves."

A short pause.

"Indeed," Rodrick says eventually, turning on his heel and continuing down the corridor.

Ed turns back just once, sure he'll find himself looking into the eyes of a mortally wounded person dragging their body out from the underbrush. But no. Nothing. No movement, no sound. Then, suddenly, the brush close to the house shakes quickly, a dark shadow darting through it. A fox after all. Ed shakes his head, attempting to gather his thoughts as he follows Rodrick to a set of double doors.

The housekeeper pauses at the washi paper doors, beautiful crane illustrations decorating them.

"Madame is just through here. Good luck, Mr. Cook."

"It's just Ed," he says as he slides both doors open.

A PARTY FOR MY PALATE

The doors open to reveal a large room: spacious, airy, and neutral-toned, with cozy woven mats and a jungle of houseplants shrouding the edges. A shoji screen splits the room into two; there is a smaller snug area hidden behind it. Wooden masks and ornaments hang from golden hooks and pegs, with other small relics indicative of extensive travel dotted around on wooden shelves between plant pots.

The strong smell of incense fills Ed's nostrils, and he follows the musky smoke around the room divider to find a strange, nest-like setup. Floor cushions form a little square; floating shelves above it are decorated with a vintage-looking shoji lamp and various small porcelain animals. The smog of the offending incense stick wafts out from between a little painted tiger and a clay zebra.

Ed blinks through the smoke, adjusting to the sudden change of scenery, and finds a small woman nestled amidst the blankets on the ground. It's as though she is a tiny creature who has retreated inside her burrow to hibernate. Within her arms, she cradles a small, fluffy white dog. It lunges toward Ed, but she holds it closely and scratches its head until it relaxes, body sagging but still eyeing Ed with mistrust. They say dogs can smell deception, and Ed looks away from it.

She is as fascinating as her environment, and he recognizes her instantly from the papers. She looks to be in her sixties, her thinning lips carefully colored a soft salmon pink, her eyes made up and her silver hair pinned back with a clip designed to look like a flamingo. This bird sits garishly atop her head in contrast to her simple, beige outfit, though even Ed can tell the fabrics are luxurious from the way they hang like drapes on her. Her neck is adorned with a gaudy choker, beads dangling like raindrops against her collarbone. Some look like teeth.

"Don't stare, petal, come in, come in," she says in English, her voice husky and deep. She waves Ed toward her with a flap of a hand, a cigarette clutched in her gnarled fingers. The incense must be to mask the smell of tobacco. Her nails are painted a deep red, and at first glance remind Ed of bloodied claws.

He hurries over to where she is sprawled. "Yamamoto-sama," he stutters, bowing from the waist. Sayuri will never believe him when he tells her about this!

"Pick your head up, for God's sake. You may call me Hazeline. Never Hazel, mind you," she says with a raise of her thin eyebrows. She speaks in a clipped British accent, crisp and southern.

"Yes, Yamamoto-sama. Ahem, Hazeline," he corrects.

She sticks her knotted hand out toward him and for a moment he stares at her talons, bewildered, wondering if he is supposed to kiss her rings.

Before he has the chance to humiliate himself, she grabs his hand and gives it a firm shake, then gestures at him to take a seat. He has begun to perch himself awkwardly on the corner of the floor cushion when the small white ball of fuzz leaps at him, teeth bared. Ed rears back quickly, exclaiming.

"Oh, Momo, hush yourself," Hazeline says lazily, scooping the tiny white dog up and holding it against her armpit.

Ed breathes out an uncomfortable laugh. "Momo. Japanese for peach?"

"Yes. Because he's absolutely *scrumptious*," she says, holding the dog up to her face and pushing her nose up against its own wet nose, rubbing them together in a bizarre dog-kiss. Ed tries not to grimace.

"So, evidently you know who I am, and you now know Momo," Hazeline says, watching Ed as he sits back down. "And you are?"

She speaks slowly, her breathing slightly heavy, as though she has just run up some stairs.

"I'm Ed Cook," he says, bowing his head again slightly.

She laughs, the sound an uncomfortable crack, like a whip. "Cook! Funny name for this job. And Ed. Good for a rhyme."

"Rhyme?"

She narrows her kohl-rimmed eyes, gazing up at the ceiling as though trying to remember some wording, before taking a long drag on her cigarette. As she blows out the smoke, she begins to recite, her voice a jaunty skip, the same way Ed slap-dashes English nursery rhymes for Kaori at bedtime.

"Ed, Ed, he'll kill you dead, he'll cut you up and mash your head. Ed, Ed, he'll boil your brains, he'll bleed you out and fry your veins . . ." She trails off with a wide grin, her yellowing teeth marked with a fleck of lipstick.

"I've never heard that before," he tells her.

"Of course not, petal. I just made it up." Another loud bark of laughter.

Ed isn't sure what to say so he laughs along nervously, placing his hands together in his lap. He peers at the stack of books beside her and notices that the majority of them are recipe books. At the top of the pile is a black notebook. She follows his line of sight and covers the notebook with her free hand, Momo still nestled in the crook of her other arm.

"My private recipes. Very personal," she tells him, her tone serious.

"I understand," he replies, looking away from the books. "Recipes can indeed be very personal. Would you . . . would you like to know about my cooking experience?" he asks.

She puts Momo down, and the dog sits beside her in the cushions. "Well, Ed, darling, to be honest I'm more of an experimentalist than a connoisseur. I just want someone willing to try some new and exciting things. Someone who can really throw a party for my palate," she explains, waving her arms wide and doing some jazz hands for emphasis. "I want to experience new things, to be enamored and stupefied by my dinner plates," she continues.

"I can definitely bring something new to the table," Ed assures her. If it is something different to what a trained chef can produce, then he is only too happy to provide her with what she wants.

"Are these your usual garments?" she asks him, eyeing the chef costume carefully, her eyes seeming to penetrate into his skin.

"Yes," he replies, forcing himself not to look away when answering. "I've brought some knives with me, too," he adds. Top chefs always use their own knives, so he pinched some from the knife rack at home—the good-quality Japanese ones they bought at a marketplace when they moved in together.

Hazeline narrows her eyes at his costume once more, then looks back up to his face, head tilted, as though trying to work out an intricate puzzle. "Interesting. Well, I would have to supply you with something more appropriate, of course," she says carefully.

"I'm happy to cook in anything."

"I know polyester when I see it, petal," she says. "It will soak up any oil and stain. I don't want you walking around with stains down your clothes."

"Oh. Well, yes, okay."

"And why are you looking for work with me?"

"I'm currently . . . out of employment," Ed tells her.

She eyes him, motioning a circle with her hand to indicate he should carry on.

"I lost my last job."

"Why?" she asks.

He shrugs. "Just restructures, I guess." He realizes his mistake immediately. No restaurant would restructure and remove a chef. He sucks in a sharp breath through his teeth, and watches her eyebrow raise the barest fraction, but to his great surprise, she continues.

"I've had Michelin-star chefs come in here begging for me to hire them, you know," she says breezily. "Why should I hire you, redundant Ed, over someone who can provide me with a current reference?"

Ed feels a fire in his belly as he realizes this opportunity—and the money he so desperately needs—may be slipping out of reach. If he can't impress her during this conversational portion of the interview, he will have to leave, and won't be paid for his time. He lifts his chin. "Because I will cook food that is like nothing you've ever had before. Because I'm unpretentious with my methods. Because I am discreet," he adds pointedly, now understanding the NDAs. The notorious Hazeline Yamamoto will not want people talking about her to the press.

"And just how much do you want this job?" she asks, taking another puff of her cigarette.

"I really, really want this," he tells her, driving all the sincerity into his words that he possesses.

"No, petal, let me rephrase. Do you *need* this job?"

He feels as though her eyes are looking into his soul, and for the briefest moment he is uncomfortable enough to hesitate. Then he remembers the real discomfort is from his bruised ribs, still recovering from his alleyway beating.

"I can tell you with all honesty that I fucking need this job," he replies. He takes a deep breath.

Hazeline purses her lips, looks away from him and begins petting Momo, who, with absolutely no dignity, rolls onto his back so that his little pink belly is exposed for scratches. Ed's chest tightens. She doesn't believe him. She's going to send him home without payment. She's not going to let him cook. Time for another gamble, and based on what she's asked him so far, he thinks he knows exactly what she wants to hear.

They say that the best lies are tinged with honesty. His CV is a work of fiction, with references and restaurants that do not exist. It is time to tell a truth. "My wife is unhappy with my current unemployment. I don't have a car, and I may be evicted from my apartment soon. My daughter is two, and I want to send her to college. I need this job."

Her eyes widen briefly. Whether it's with shock at his vulgarity or surprise at his honesty, he isn't sure.

"Well, Ed, I suppose we'll see how your trial goes. If you're happy to step up to the plate, excuse the pun." She chuckles at her own joke; a gravelly little sound.

"I would be honored," Ed says, feeling his shoulders relax a notch.

"If I'd known you were car-less, I could have sent Mr. Nakamura for you," she adds breezily.

"Your chauffeur? I saw him outside washing the car."

"Yes. He works as my driver, but really, he's more like family." She grins at him, and it feels like a predator smiling at its freshly captured prey. "I'm sure that, if your interview is successful, you and I will end up feeling like family, too."

Ed shivers, but hides it with a wide grimace of a smile.

ABSOLUTELY FAMISHED

Ed recognized Hazeline from the tabloids, of course. It would have been impossible not to—she once frequented the pages of the weekly magazines, and in those days you couldn't walk past a paper stand at the *konbini* without her gaze piercing you from a front cover. And, like most infamous women, her face was not plastered everywhere as a celebration, but because of scandal. Ed is aware the press all but eviscerated her reputation, and the remote home guarded by both landscape and iron fences suddenly makes a lot more sense.

Hazeline was *hafu*, her father a prominent Japanese businessman, her mother a British model. Raised at Japanese boarding schools, and having spent time in Britain growing up, she became somewhat of a low-level socialite in London, eventually marrying into the Yamamoto empire and being fully thrust into the spotlight. The media had a field day when Japan's finest eligible bachelor, billionaire Botan Yamamoto, married someone of mixed heritage. And what followed was the beating heart of what keeps journalism alive: tragedy. First, Hazeline's tragic infertility struggles, followed by Botan's death from a rare cancer that the family had kept secret.

Much to the distress of the Yamamotos, Botan left his entire estate and everything in his will to his beloved wife. This triggered a horrific media frenzy, painting Hazeline as a foreign gold-digger and an improper successor to their business, with Botan's parents even trying to sue her before they succumbed to old age. Hazeline then disappeared from the limelight, the press found their next scandal, and she lay near-forgotten on the pages of "where are they now?" website listicles. At the time, Ed felt sorry for the grieving widow who was seemingly being persecuted. Now, having met her, he can understand why the Yamamotos felt she was unsuitable to carry on their name. She is almost vulgar in her western-ness—her disregard for restraint and conformity evident even in the few minutes they have spent together.

"I'd like something with meat, veg, and a carbohydrate for lunch, please," she instructs as he follows her out of the reading room, Momo between them like security. "No dessert, but I'll have a glass of wine," she adds.

"Glass of wine, got it," he replies, fighting the urge to kick the dog and watch it skid across the wooden floorboards.

"So, Ed, tell me. How did you come to live in the land of the rising sun?" Hazeline asks.

"I was bored of life at home—" he begins.

"Home is where?" Hazeline interrupts.

"Just outside London," he replies. "I saved my money from working in restaurants," he explains, keeping things vague. Really, he saved his pennies from tossing burgers for people to grab through a small box window. "Came to Japan on a holiday. I just wanted to experience a different sort of life, I guess."

"Nowhere more different to the London suburbs than Tokyo," Hazeline agrees.

"I was doing the classic tourist loop. Tokyo, Osaka, Kyoto. I was on the train back to Tokyo when I met my wife, Sayuri. She'd been visiting her family in Osaka and was returning to Tokyo, where she worked. I fell in love, despite the language barrier." Ed thinks back to when he first locked eyes with her across the train aisle, enraptured by her beauty. A petite, doll-like frame contrasted by sharp, intelligent eyes. He tried to share his bento box with her and she giggled, blushing pink as he used his hands to gesture, unable to speak any Japanese. Horrified by his chopstick methods, she waved her hands and shook her head at him, still giggling. Eventually, she reached over, took the chopsticks from his hands and showed him how to hold them properly. He spent the rest of the journey pretending to forget so that she would reteach him, both of them wise to the game he was playing but going along with it to keep the connection they both felt building.

"I guess I somehow managed to woo her over time. We got married, and I've been here ever since," he finishes.

"A beautiful love story," Hazeline comments.

Ed pauses, hoping he hasn't upset her. "I was sorry to hear about your husband passing away," he says, head bowed.

She waves him off with a light flick of her hand, but he can see her eyes shining with held-back tears. "A long time ago. Gosh, nearly a decade." She pauses. "I know the media said that we weren't truly in love, that I was only with him for his fortune. But it was nonsense. I loved my dear Botan ever so much, and I miss him every day."

Ed purses his lips, unsure of how to respond. "And where did you meet?" he asks eventually.

Hazeline stops walking, as though halting to savor the memory in full. "It was an event. In all honesty, I can't remember what it was even for! Some sort of gala or something. I had been dragged there and knew nobody. I was supposed to be networking, or schmoozing, I suppose. Many of the guests knew my father, but nobody ever spoke to me at these things, you know. My mother had it even worse—she was almost ignored entirely."

"Why?" Ed asks, curiosity making him forget his place.

Hazeline raises her eyebrows. "Well, not only was she a white woman in a world of Japanese businessmen, but she was unqualified. A model. She may as well have been a beautiful statue. Whenever she spoke, it was as though she were an amusement, nothing taken seriously. Eventually, she learned to stop speaking, to merely stand by my father's side looking pretty while the men did business. Anyway, I was standing at the edge of the crowd, looking in and wishing I were anywhere else, when Botan emerged beside me and offered me a drink. I knew who he was, of course. Everyone in the Tokyo business world knew who he was. And he leaned toward me, and do you know what he said?"

"What?" Ed whispers.

"He said, 'I wish I didn't have to be here, too!'" Hazeline throws her head back and laughs. "It was as though he knew me inside and out instantly. We just . . . clicked." She smiles sadly, and begins walking once more. Ed knows, in his gut, that the media were wrong. That Hazeline loved Botan, and he loved her right back.

He is saved from the effort of changing the subject, as Hazeline throws a set of doors open to reveal the kitchen.

"Your new stomping ground," she says with a flourish.

Momo rushes in, galloping straight for a dog bowl that's sitting in the corner. He takes a twitching nose to the dusty brown dog biscuits, gives a small sniff of disgust, and turns away, disappointed by the offerings.

Hazeline sighs. "Momo, you can't have the good stuff every day! You have to be a proper dog and learn to eat your kibble! It's good for the teeth!" she chides. Momo blinks back at her dully. "He loves raw meat. Thinks he's a working spaniel or something," Hazeline says to Ed, who smiles politely.

The kitchen is styled as per the majority of the house. It's a gargantuan space in warm beige neutrals with wooden finishes, and an expensive island in the center that doubles as a wine fridge, emitting an eerie glow. At first glance, there are three fridges, three large freezers, and a top-of-the-line stove with so many oven sections and knobs that for a moment Ed is sure he has made a terrible mistake with his lies and is well and truly over his head. Everything else is hidden away from sight, with doors designed to mimic the wooden wall panels so as not to disturb the zen of the space with their practicality. Ed thinks of his own disordered kitchen, the rice cooker and microwave teetering together on top of the small fridge, a tower of necessary appliances with no space to breathe.

Hazeline drawls on about the extractor fan, her nails tapping on the countertops as she strides along, and Ed reminds himself that he only needs to get through the next day and a half before he can take home a fat paycheck to Sayuri. He imagines them chatting animatedly over dinner as he tells her about his time in *the* Hazeline Yamamoto's house. She won't believe it!

"I like my dinner served at seven on the dot," Hazeline informs him, pulling him from his daydream. She puts a strange emphasis on the *t* of "dot." "And I eat that at the dining table." She gestures at a low table, framed by floor cushions. "Whereas lunch can be between 12:30 and 1:30 and I will eat at the bar." She waves a hand at the wooden barstools lined up alongside the kitchen island. Ed nods and, satisfied, Hazeline opens one of the cupboards that are hidden by design in the wall. It is home to several pieces of expensive-looking equipment that Ed has never before seen in his life.

"This is the meat grinder. Very important," she tells him with a raise of her brows, and he nods along. "Air fryer, deep-fat fryer, processor, blender—in four different sizes—ice cream maker, cocktail maker—I enjoy a drink on a Friday night—bread machine, smoothie cups—I do like a spinach smoothie in the mornings, you know . . ." On and on she goes, pointing things out for Ed and moving at pace.

"You really like your food," Ed jokes, trying to build a rapport with her.

She pauses, peering at him from beneath her spindly, spider-like eyelashes. "I don't *like* food, Ed. I *love* food. I don't eat to survive, I eat to savor. It should always be worth it, every mouthful a justification for my body." Ed is bewildered by what he sees simmering beneath the surface of the look she gives him. He is sure it is anger.

"I—I'm sorry. I didn't mean to offend," he says, lowering his head in apology.

Hazeline narrows her eyes at him, and breathes out a long, pained sigh. Then she gestures for Ed to pull up a barstool and sit. He does so, feeling a lecture coming on.

"Do you know what it was like, growing up a half-white female in this country, Ed?" she asks.

Ed, embarrassed by his lack of consideration for his daughter's future, shakes his head dumbly, his mouth hanging open a little.

"It wasn't fun. Do you know what the nastiest breed of animal is?"

Ed racks his brains for an intelligent response. "Cats?" he hedges, side-eyeing Momo, who is sitting beside Hazeline watching him with dark, mistrustful eyes.

"Wrong!" Hazeline barks. "The cruelest creature is a teenage girl. I grew up a half-breed in this country. A mongrel. I had breasts that stuck out," she says, and Ed quickly averts his eyes and feels his cheeks pinken.

"I had hips that flared outwards. I had thighs that curved. I am five foot six—I may as well have been an Olympic basketballer! And do you know what the worst part about this society is?" she seethes.

Ed shakes his head silently, not willing to place a bet.

"The clothing stores," she hisses, "are by and large, one-size-fits-all. But it's not truly one-size-fits-all, because I am not pureblood

Japanese. I do not go straight up and down like their petite women do. I had a waist circumference much larger than the East Asian average. Do you know what it's like to grow up here considered a chubby girl? How hard it was?"

"No," Ed mumbles, ashamed of himself for ever making a comment.

"No, of course you don't. Well, let me tell you, *petal.* It wasn't fun. I was poked and prodded, called soft and pudgy. Boys would laugh at me, I was never a desirable date. School health checks meant weigh-ins, a chance for everyone to gawk at me in horror, girls giggling behind hands, whispering into each other's ears as though I didn't have the imagination to work out what they were saying about me. In the UK, I would have been considered small. Here, I was a freak. I couldn't fit into any clothes that the trendy stores offered. It didn't matter how pretty my face was, or how fluently I could speak the language. My body was not to their beauty standards, and I was picked on for being different. An oddity. So I stopped eating. I stopped eating, Ed, and for years, I was thin. Still tall, still my hips jutted out. But my breasts shrunk, and I could finally squeeze into their one-size-fits-all. Girls could try to pinch at my belly playfully, and they would come out empty-handed. I was thin, I was gorgeous, and I was fucking starving. For years, I was so skinny. I would parade around at parties chain-smoking, avoiding the canapés, relying on calories from champagne and highballs to keep me going. I attracted Botan. Hordes of women wanted his attention but somehow it was *me* he looked at with interest. An enigma, he called me. And after my darling husband died, do you know what I realized?" She has lowered her voice, and is leaning right into Ed's face, so close he can smell the stale cigarettes on her breath. He daren't move.

"I was absolutely *famished.*" She licks her lips and straightens herself, giving Ed a bit more breathing room.

She wags a finger, and gestures at him to stand and follow her once more. He tucks his stool back underneath the counter and wipes the sweat from his brow.

"That was when I decided, Ed, to enjoy every single morsel that crosses my lips. I'd deprived myself of the joy of eating for far too long. My husband is dead, I am largely alone, the media hates me. My friends are shallow and materialistic. The only enjoyment I have left comes from the food I consume. What use is dying skinny and hungry? When I join Lucifer I shall be plump and happy, and I can't bring myself to give a damn what anyone thinks about it," she says, flinging open another cupboard door and showcasing a spread of tinned goods.

Ed pats his own little stomach roll affectionately. "I agree. Food is to be enjoyed," he says.

"*Isn't* it?" Hazeline exclaims as though he has made a jaw-dropping revelation. "You know, the first thing a child learns to communicate is 'I'm hungry.' Their fat, wormy little fingers pointing at their maws. It is human nature to desire food, to ask to be fed. That is why you're here, Ed. I want to be fed. I want to be satiated. Tell me, do you read much?"

Ed hesitates. "No, I can't say I do," he admits.

"Well. Margaret Atwood once wrote, *last year I abstained, this year I devour without guilt.* That is my mantra for my remaining years. My manifestation, so to speak."

"I can help with that," Ed assures her. "You'll see. I can do the job. I will gratify you."

"I do hope so," Hazeline replies.

CANARD

Ed decides his tactic for the next thirty-six hours. He will cook simple meals he's confident with and cannot possibly make a mess of. But he will be brave and try to do something unexpected, adding a little twist that will appease Hazeline's eccentric style. Something to tick off her requirement for something unique, without being so wild as to ruin the meal. He'll play it safe, but the food won't be bad or bland enough for her to dismiss before he can complete the two-day trial.

"There is also an incinerator in the basement," she says, moving on to open one of the freezers.

"I'm sorry, did you say incinerator?" Ed asks, a chill running down his spine.

"Yes, Ed, do keep up."

"What would I need an incinerator for?" For some reason, the scream of the fox earlier haunts him as he asks the question.

She pauses, turning to look at him, one brow ever so slightly raised. "Well, you likely won't require its services today, but if you come to work here on a regular basis and cater for my larger soirées, there will be waste. It's the easiest way to dispose of it without overflowing our bins," she says simply, turning back to the freezer.

Part of Ed feels stupid for not thinking of this himself, as someone role-playing as a high-class chef. The other, much larger part, feels rage that while he is struggling to put food on the table for his own small family of three, this woman is wasting so much that she needs an industrial-grade machine to disintegrate it into ash. Does the thought cross her mind that people would scramble for her leftovers if given the opportunity? He can only imagine the quality of food being tossed aside as garbage. Expensive fatty fish, most likely, which would cost an arm and a leg back in the UK. While Hazeline's house may not be filled with decadent ornaments or designer displays, instead largely home to small sentimental trinkets from her travels and potted plants, Ed imagines her gathering her friends to soak in some of her wealth via luxurious morsels and mouthfuls—before sending them on their way home and burning the leftovers with no regard for their worth. Sea creatures dying in reeking rope nets to feed those who are too full or too fussy to consume them, the sacrificial lambs of a pretentious party.

She continues, oblivious to his discomfort. "And if you need anything else at all, do shout. I want to make this interview process as fair as possible, and each person who is cooking is welcome to whatever ingredients and equipment they need, though I'll be extra impressed if you can whip something up without having to purchase anything additional."

He forces a strained smile. "I'm sure I'll manage," he says, thinking of the crammed fridge she showed him barely a moment ago.

"Well, Ed, this morning has been busy, so I'd like to be seated for lunch at two today." She checks her thin, gold watch. "And remember my brief—be sure to include meat on the menu. For me, I feel a meal without meat is merely a side dish," she says, erupting into laughter at her own quip, her canines slick with saliva.

"Of course." Ed bows his head politely as she strolls out of the room, leaving him in the company of Rodrick, who has silently entered and appears to be restocking jars of grains in the pantry.

Ed collapses onto one of the barstools and begins to work out what he can cook.

"All right, Rod?" he calls out jovially, desperate to build some sort of rapport with the housekeeper. But the man remains stoic.

"Please, it's Rodrick, never Rod," he tells Ed as he begins to set up the island counter for lunch.

Hazeline. Never Hazel.

"Not Bauer-san?" Ed asks, half-joking.

"Either is fine," Rodrick replies, still not making eye contact with Ed, looking down from beneath his wiry bushy brows.

"How long have you worked for Hazeline? Have you lived here long?" Ed asks, intrigued by this man and how he came to be in this bizarre employment.

"I have worked for Hazeline for forty years."

Ed's foot slips off the stool rest as he jolts in shock. "*Forty years?* Why, surely you're not old enough to have been here that long?" He gawks.

"Flattered, I'm sure," Rodrick responds, his left eyebrow raising a fraction. "My family moved here from Germany when I was small. My father got a job transfer. I wanted some pocket money, and Hazeline's family hired me as a weekend cleaner when I was thirteen. I've been with her ever since. When Hazeline moved out of the family home and married Botan, I moved in with them as their live-in housekeeper. So, I have known Hazeline since she was in her early twenties."

"Wow! You must really like working for her," Ed says.

Rodrick pauses, seeming to stand a little taller. "Hazeline is a wonderful friend and employer. I'm proud to have become her most trusted confidant. She pays and treats me well. I've never felt any need to go elsewhere."

"And Botan? What was he like?" Ed asks, thinking of Hazeline's soft smile at his memory.

Rodrick pauses, frowns, then also softens. "Botan was a good man, and he was kind to Hazeline. It brought her great pain, watching him struggle with the cancer."

Then he turns his back to Ed, ending the conversation and fussing over the table setting while Ed tries to understand how anybody could be content working for the same person for so long. How could he not get bored or wonder about a life elsewhere, doing something different?

The countertop is simply arranged, with a placemat and cutlery laid out alongside chopsticks. Everything about the house is minimal and considered, as though true wealth means having nothing frivolous on display. Who needs *things,* when one can have power, or an overflowing bank account? Hazeline doesn't have to show off her wealth with fancy knickknacks and material objects; on the contrary, her wealth radiates around Ed through the lack of clutter. Rodrick turns his attention to the dining table, removing a small bonsai tree from the center to place on the countertop as a decorative feature.

"Snip, snip," he mutters to himself as he trims and prunes the tiny tree, spritzing it with a mister before stepping back to admire his arrangement.

"Hazeline sure likes her plants," Ed comments, thinking back to the reading room.

"Actually, she is nonchalant about them. It is I who get great joy from tending to the greenery," Rodrick says. "It brings a feeling of life and a freshness to the interior that I love." It surprises Ed that Hazeline's home is so filled with plants if they bring her housekeeper happiness rather than herself. Maybe Hazeline truly is a great employer and a thoughtful friend.

Ed glances at the clock. He has an hour and a half to put together a decent meal, and so far all he has done is watch an eccentric German housekeeper dance around the kitchen doing menial tasks when they both know he's actually there to assess Ed's performance and give feedback to Hazeline once Ed is out of earshot.

Ed wipes his forehead with the back of his sleeve, then rubs his hands on his trousers before prying the fridge doors open. They pop, a refreshing burst of cool air coating his sweaty pores.

I can do this, he tells himself firmly.

The meat drawer grates as he pulls it open. He gazes down at the packages of flesh, suffocating in their bloodied juices and cellophane wraps. They have all been delicately labeled with a black permanent marker. Rodrick's work, he assumes.

Beef (Sirloin), Pork (Ribs), Duck (Breast), Boar (Hind)—Ed works his way through the slabs of cold, wet meat in the compartment, trying to decide which will be the easiest to impress with. There is no option of chicken, he notes, though the second meat drawer is packed to the brim with seafood options—including *fugu,* or pufferfish, which he has never seen in person before but knows to be one of the most expensive delicacies for the bravest seafood fans. They say it takes a true master with a special license to be able to safely cook *fugu.* It's poison—more deadly than cyanide—and fatal if cooked incorrectly.

Ed trembles at the thought of being able to try something so exclusive, but isn't stupid enough to even attempt cooking it. He wonders if there is a way to check the recipe, out of pure curiosity, but doesn't want to risk looking on his phone while Rodrick is in the vicinity. No, he'll definitely be avoiding the *fugu.*

Eventually he sets aside the duck, assuming it to be similar to chicken in its cooking style and exotic enough to set him apart from anyone who would choose the beef steak or a grilled fish fillet. He doesn't want the predicament of combining something he has never even tried, such as boar, kangaroo, or rabbit, with complementary herbs and spices. The duck breast sits on a plate, a reflective sheen glistening on its plump, burgundy underbelly. The white fat sits tightly against it, a textured, honeycomb pattern contrasting with the sleek meat.

Ed remembers from Friday-night takeaways growing up that his mother always had duck with plum sauce from the local Chinese restaurant. He roots through the fruit bowl, but to his dismay, no plums. They're out of season. He turns his attention to the overflowing pantry, and finds an unopened jar of *ume* jam. He opens it, sniffs, and gives the jar a small shake. The orange contents wobble gently, shining and slimy under the bright kitchen lighting. A unique medley of European and Japanese cuisine. Perfect.

Another five minutes of hunting and Ed has an array of spice jars laid out for use, alongside some asparagus—which he has always considered a fancy broccoli—and potatoes. If he can cook the basics well, he can go on to embellish with pretentious garnishes. It's a shame Hazeline is half-British, as the meal would have a better chance of impressing a Japanese national. Ed wouldn't be surprised if this cultural medley of a meal was the sort of thing served up at Hazeline's fancy private schools, but it's the safest choice he has.

Ed finds, to his great surprise, that he takes to the kitchen environment quickly. Actions like sharpening his blade on the stone and salting the water as it boils come instinctively, almost from muscle memory. It's as though he's jumped back in time and is twenty-three years old again, running a dodgy knife down a cheap sharpening tool while the head chef bellows "Another burger, hold the pickle!" at him. Only, this time, he's in a mansion in East Asia working to the calming sound of wind chimes in the garden. *Not bad, Ed. Not bad at all.*

The duck breast is sizzling pleasantly in the pan when Hazeline saunters through the doors and comes over to the counter, peering with critical interest at the crackling slab of meat. She shuts her eyes and inhales deeply, her bosom rising dramatically.

"Ah, *canard,*" she announces breathily. "French, for duck," she explains, though Ed didn't ask.

He gives a curt nod, sprinkling salt liberally over the browning skin with his pinched thumb and pointer, for something to do.

"I gutted this one myself, you know," she goes on, leaning her back against the counter and turning to watch Ed.

He fumbles with the peeler, and it clatters to the ground.

She picks it up for him, rinsing it beneath the tap before returning it to his hand. "I think it's good practice to know what goes into putting the protein on the plate, don't you agree?" she asks.

"Yes, ma'am," Ed responds, running the peeler over a potato carefully. The rough skin spirals, falling onto the counter.

"And you, Ed. Have you ever plucked the feathers off a warbler, so to speak?"

"I admit, I have not," he replies demurely, wondering when on earth she thinks he would have done such an activity.

"Would you?"

He pauses peeling. "Now?"

She bursts into a shrill bleat of laughter. "No, not now, petal. *Hypothetically.*"

His heartbeat slows to an average pace again. "Oh. Yes, I suppose I would. If I had to survive."

"Yes, petal, we'd all snap the neck of a bird to survive. But what about for *pleasure*?"

"Kill . . . for pleasure?"

"No, no. Good God, we're not macabre here, Ed. We don't kill for pleasure. We *eat* for pleasure. And we kill to eat. You see?"

"Yes, I understand," he replies, a lie seeping through the gaps in his teeth. "But is every meal something you adore? Do you never simply eat for the sake of fuel?" he asks, hoping to find something relatable about the woman in front of him. He tries to picture Hazeline picking up a train station bento box after a long and tiring day, the sushi bites fueling her stamina to go on to late-night meetings. The vision won't come to him.

He suddenly wishes he hadn't asked, worried he's overstepped. It was inappropriate, disrespectful.

But she slowly turns to face him, and tells him, "There was a time when I learned to stop enjoying the comfort that mediocre food could bring and began to see it as an enemy. Thankfully, that time is long past."

Ed averts his gaze, unable to make eye contact with her. He is sure she is glaring at him.

"Every single bite has to count, Ed. It has to light a fire inside of me, make me wish for more. If I eat and do not close my eyes in sinful bliss, it has been a waste of calories and a pointless meal. I have decades of pleasured eating to be catching up on."

His hand snags on the blade of the peeler and he sucks in a hiss. A bubble of blood appears and begins to dribble from the cut. He turns the tap on, and as he goes to run his wounded finger beneath the water, Hazeline grabs at his wrist, her long fingers forming a tight claw. She brings his hand to her mouth and places a kiss on the cut, gently sucking.

Ed is immobile.

She drops his hand and licks the tinge of blood from her lips, her eyes closed just as they were when she smelled the duck crisping up in the pan.

"Careful now, Ed. We wouldn't want you losing any limbs over dinner," she warns with a wag of her finger, then she turns to leave the room.

VERY EUROPEAN

The clock hands hit their mark and Ed steps away from the counter. The steaming plate of food he has laid out looks wonderful to him, but he's well aware that for someone with as much experience of dining out as Hazeline has, it's average at best. Rodrick raises a single eyebrow at the offering before bending at the waist and expertly pouring a glug of *umeshu* wine.

"It is how she finishes every meal," he tells Ed, who nods, appreciative of any help he can get to make the meal go smoothly. Hazeline enters the room silently, Momo scurrying at her heels, and she watches Ed for a beat too long before her eyes flit down to the meal. She purses her lips, then checks the clock, and nods, almost to herself. Ed notes that prompt timing is clearly something she values. She makes no comment, but sits on the stool that Rodrick has pulled out for her, carefully arranging a cloth napkin in her lap.

The duck has crisped beautifully on one side, the fat hardened into a deep, rich maroon. Beneath it, a pinkish-brown pool of fat and juice slowly seeps out, caressing the fluffy roasted potatoes. Ed has stacked the asparagus into a strange, box-like sculpture, imitating the frivolous arrangements of television chefs in their final presentations. The air smells of meat, sweet but pungent.

"Enjoy," Ed tells her, desperate to fill the silence. He walks backward away from the kitchen area and is conscious of Rodrick leaning down toward her, conferring with her about something in a low hum, his baritone voice directed into her eardrum. She purses her lips with a slight frown, and for a moment says nothing.

"*Itadakimasu,*" she suddenly announces, humbly accepting the food Ed has offered, and begins cutting into her duck, her cutlery scraping the plate like nails on a chalkboard. Ed's ears redden. He turns on the tap to dull the screech of metal raking across porcelain and begins to wash up, unwilling to watch her expression as she takes her first few bites. The lack of conversation in the room is louder than the gates of hell.

When he turns, he sees that there is a scrap of wet meat on the ground, and Momo is sniffing at it tentatively. To his horror, the dog turns his back on the meat and begins scratching instead.

Ed's eyes dart to Rodrick, in search of some sort of comfort, but the housekeeper is watching Hazeline with interest. He turns back to the sink, puts his head in his hands for a moment, and envisions the dog choking on a piece of duck fat.

"Well," Hazeline says, breaking the bubble of silence and startling Ed at the sink. He turns to face her. "I must say, Ed, this is quite all right. Even if Momo said nono," she laughs.

His shoulders visibly loosen.

"He's terribly picky though, so don't take it too personally. Tell me, what did you use on the asparagus?"

"Uh, soy sauce," he replies. "Garlic, and a grating of ginger."

"Interesting. And this spice in the potatoes?"

He racks his brain for a beat, trying to remember what yellow powder he sprinkled over the potatoes experimentally in the pan before setting them to roast. "Turmeric?"

"Very . . . European," she says after a pause.

Ed glances quickly at Rodrick, unsure of whether this is praise or not. He also bites his tongue to prevent himself from asking why she chose "European" as a descriptor for soy sauce and turmeric. He realizes with great surprise that for someone willing to shell out so much money for a private chef, it's possible that Hazeline has very little culinary knowledge herself. Perhaps even less than him. She may like to eat, but she doesn't seem to have a palate for individual ingredients, or knowledge of how to actually cook. This is something that he can use to his advantage.

He bows his head at her and she pushes the plate away, half of it left forlornly behind as leftovers. Ed supposes he won't be feeding it to Momo.

"A coffee, please," she tells Ed.

"Of course. How do you take it?"

"We have a machine that does all the work for you. Usually Rodrick handles my liquids, but as you're already up there . . ."

She trails off and Ed notices that he is standing directly in front of a very expensive-looking coffee machine, one of the few appliances that went unmentioned during the kitchen tour. He places a porcelain mug beneath a spout and experimentally presses a button. To his great relief, it begins to sputter a steady stream of tawny liquid into the cup.

"I like a splash of milk and a sweetener and a half," Hazeline tells him from the island.

Atop the machine sits a jar holding what look like millions of tiny white tablets. Another label written in black marker, this time pronouncing them the sweetener tablets needed. They are minuscule. Smaller than his pinkie nail. Perhaps even smaller than his daughter's pinkie nail.

"Half a sweetener?" he asks, unsure if he misheard.

"Yes. Same as how people have a sugar and a half," she replies, but he can see her eyeing him for a reaction. Ed takes two of the pills from the jar and places them onto a cutting board. He sources the smallest, sharpest knife from the knife block and bends over the board, his back hunched and hand trembling a little with concentration. He places the knife horizontally across the pill, but it slips, skittering away from the blade, and he almost catches the tip of his thumb. He grabs it back quickly, a cat suddenly pawing at a laser beam, and tries again, hoping Hazeline didn't see the mishap. This time, he manages to place the knife more firmly, and puts his entire weight into it until he hears a faint crack and looks down to find the pill broken into two, a dusting of powdered crumbs beneath it.

The corners of Hazeline's lips have tilted upward a fraction. Ed carefully picks up the half-pill and drops it into the hot mug of coffee alongside its whole sister, then puts the other half back in the jar for next time.

He brings the coffee to her, and can't help himself as he tells her, "Sugar is probably easier."

She breaks into a full smile, all her teeth showing. "Petal, I'm watching my figure, don't you know? I can't be putting any old thing into my body at this age!"

Behind her shoulder, Rodrick stifles a small laugh, quickly covered by his hand.

She winks at Ed, and he assumes that after all she has told him, she's joking. Ed breathes out a small laugh alongside them both, the feeling that he has passed some strange test overcoming him.

MAKER OF THE MENU

When Hazeline leaves the kitchen to attend her afternoon meetings, Rodrick follows. Ed is sure they are speaking about him—about his first test. He regrets calling Rodrick "Rod" now. He takes the plate of leftovers and glances around to check he is alone before popping a potato into his mouth. It's cold now, the outer layer softened and no longer crispy, but the tang of the turmeric delights him. A completely random gamble which paid off. Maybe he's not done gambling after all. Next, he slices himself a piece of the duck, and finds it to be adequate, if a little bland, but well cooked. The dog is clearly fussier than his toddler—or perhaps just used to the finest dog food money can buy? The asparagus, Hazeline finished. Ed deems that, for a completely improvised first meal, he didn't do badly at all, and he may just make it through the rest of the day without too much embarrassment.

He notices Momo lingering at his feet and decides to have another go at making friends. He tosses the little creature a small spoonful of potato, which splatters onto the ground noiselessly. The dog sniffs, pauses to look at Ed quizzically, then decides that it's a better offering than the duck and hoovers up the beige fluff in a single motion, licking the grease from its black lips appreciatively. Perhaps he's a vegetarian.

Ed smiles and turns to continue washing up, handling each piece of tableware with great care. He can tell that the plate is hand-painted—a traditional Japanese design with careful calligraphic brushstrokes. He finds himself wondering, as he washes, what it must feel like to labor over a piece of artwork so carefully, only to have the rich and uncultured scrape spiced potatoes off its surface. He takes great care sponging it off, watching the suds pour away from the surface before placing it on the drying rack carefully. He wouldn't be surprised if this single plate cost more than his entire set of Daiso plates back home, and is not about to risk chipping it. He finds himself storing the idea of a painted plate in a crevice of his mind that is reserved for gifting; a part of his thoughts that has long been closed off due to debt. But maybe if he is able to get some consistent work, he'll be able to treat Sayuri to an anniversary plate. He could maybe find one somewhere in the markets that has cheaper offerings than the one he has just washed. But something that Sayuri can display on the wall, perhaps with her birth flower painted on it. She'd love that.

For the first time since arriving, Ed realizes that maybe he has an actual chance at getting this job. And maybe, just maybe, he actually wants it.

He glances at the clock as he dries his hands on a cloth and finds that it's already 3 P.M., and he has no idea what he will cook for dinner. Hazeline instructed a hearty lunch and a lighter dinner, letting him know that going to bed with a heavy belly is a pastime she loathes, so he decides to make the most of his solitude by searching online for light evening meals.

He somehow managed lunch through his basic knowledge, but it won't get him through dinner unless she's content with a sandwich.

At Ed's house, "light" isn't a word that is enthused over when it comes to food. Light is how Ed would describe the measly plastic-wrapped *onigiri* he brings home for supper, quickly purchased from 7-Eleven when he realizes he is home late from the pachinko parlor. What Ed's family rely on are the heavy, hearty meals that give them the energy to keep going through their daily woes, meals that are cheap to make but full of sustenance. Rich, golden *yakisoba,* often more noodles than meat. Yolky *omurice* filled to bursting with fried rice, the copious carbohydrates leaving his belly stretched. Or even *donburi,* thrown together using whatever leftovers they have at the end of the week, Ed's favorite being pork cutlet, the chewy fat sliding down to rest in his gut before bed.

Ed can't relate to the notion of going to bed unfilled, and wonders if Hazeline has ever been in a position where food is scarce, where every calorie counts for survival, and whether—if she had—she would still put such a strict emphasis on lighter meals before bed. He very much doubts it. In the end, he searches online for a fancy salad recipe, unsure of what else might constitute "light" but also pay off as a dinner and not a snack. He knows she wants something with meat, and he doesn't want to do something as unadventurous or common as miso soup.

In the end, Ed lands on a *kani* salad, but instead of doing the easy, ten-minute version that most websites tout, he will make the most of the ingredients proffered to him and prepare it with real crab, rather than the go-to replicas or crab sticks he might use at home. He has never tried to excavate the meat from a crab himself before, but he watches a video tutorial on mute and figures it can't be too hard. He is keen to impress that, despite being a westerner, he can cook Japanese cuisine, if that is what Hazeline wants. In fact, the more time he spends in the enormous, light-filled room surrounded by such easy splendor, the more he finds himself wondering if he maybe stands a chance of being offered the job for real. He may not be the best cook, but he is sure that he is willing to do just about anything to embed himself into this lifestyle, into this world of financial security. Maybe if he can make Hazeline see that, she'll take a punt on him.

An hour later, Ed feels that he has quite possibly launched himself too far out of his depth with the crab, but it's too late to make a new plan. Rodrick has returned to the kitchen to continue his charade of overseeing Ed work while pretending to do anything else. This time, he appears to be polishing some cutlery.

The crab Ed pulls from the seafood drawer is hard and damp, its two beady eyes dead and pink. He spends a suspicious amount of time poking around in the cutlery drawers searching for an object which looks like it might be useful for cracking the shell, something similar to what the guy on YouTube used, but is dumbfounded by the sheer quantity of contraptions and, in the end, Rodrick asks if he needs help with anything. Unwilling to show any potential flaws which can be fed back to Hazeline, and worried that he is staring a crab-cracker dead in the eye, he waves Rodrick away and lets him know that he is simply investigating the quality of their wares.

Unsure of what to do, Ed decides to simply rip the crustacean apart with his bare hands, popping the shell apart as little bits of wet flesh slid down his wrists. His hands shake slightly as he prizes it open, his nails bending uncomfortably.

"Are you using your hands, Mr. Cook?" Rodrick asks with a slight frown.

"Yes. Yes I am," Ed replies, trying to force himself to look casual. "I think it really helps me get a feel for the meat I'm working with, and I enjoy the hands-on feeling that comes with, er, this elusive and highly personal process," he adds, holding up a sad-looking claw.

"I see," Rodrick replies, allowing him to continue.

Ed wipes some sweat from his forehead and dives back in, trying to look enthusiastic and not as bewildered as he feels. He flinches as a bit of cracked shell somehow flicks up toward his face, and tries to pass it off as a twitch. Underneath the main shell he has just pulled away are gray bits of slime and muck, organs, and stringy tendons that look like something Momo should be fed. Dotted within the brownish mulch are little orange spheres: roe. The crab is female, her tangerine eggs mingled with the spilled innards.

Ed decides to scrap the main body, put off by the mucky-looking offering, and goes to rip the legs off instead. Usually he'd feel bad about the waste, but knowing there is an incinerator downstairs, he doubts Hazeline will notice or care. He's already boiled the crab, so the shell has softened, and with one good twist the limb rips off cleanly in his hand. With no seafood utensil to help, he mimics his coffee sweetener technique, taking a knife and placing it on the leg flat-side down, leaning his body weight onto the surface until the pressure cracks the leg open. To Ed's great delight, white fleshy meat spills from the sides of the broken leg. He uses the end of a teaspoon to help scrape the meat out into a bowl before turning to the claw. The video he watched said to pull the claw apart by hand first, and when he does so, he pulls out a long translucent plate of cartilage that emerges from the inner shell like a revolting yellow-tinged card being pulled from an envelope.

He repeats the process and finds even more meat within the claws, and though the countertop is a mess with stinking sea juice and brittle shell shrapnel, Ed finds himself glowing with satisfaction at the small feat. When was the last time he accomplished something so productive, and taught himself a new skill? He can't remember.

Time seems to slip away from him like coins in a pachinko machine, as he blends the dressing and tosses the vegetables together with flair. He is actually having fun! This is nothing like the days spent rotting away at the chain restaurants of Britain, throwing toppings onto fat, doughy pizzas and slicing mounds of pickles to be chucked onto a burger a week later. Here, it's Ed in charge of the kitchen, the maker of the menu, a god in his domain.

The time for dinner comes and Hazeline is punctual as before, taking her seat at the table before being presented with her salad. Fresh, peeled carrots stand out in orange spirals against the crisp, sliced cucumbers. Juicy slithers of mango are tucked in between the flaky crab meat, the entire bowl liberally drizzled with a creamy umami dressing, made just the way Sayuri taught him when they first began dating. He whisked Japanese mayonnaise made from golden egg yolks with salty soy sauce and rice wine vinegar for a tart, sharp kick. Then he added a dash of spicy sauce for a little heat, and sprinkled the dressing with panko breadcrumbs for a crunchy bite. Sayuri loves panko on her salads. Ed hopes that Hazeline will, too.

She peers at the salad for what feels like a long time. So long that Ed is sure the carrot strips will begin to sag under the weight of the dressing, losing their bite and becoming soggy and sad.

"*Kani* salad?" she asks, poking her plate. "But these aren't crab sticks?"

"Yes, I used fresh crab meat and a light panko crumb," Ed replies.

"Well, you followed my brief of a light supper," she acknowledges. "*Itadakimasu!*" she says, scooping a great wad of the salad between her chopsticks and shoveling it into her mouth. She nods, slowly at first, then a bit quicker. "Yes, the panko is nice," she mumbles through her mouthful, and once again, Ed's shoulders drop slightly in relief. "The crab is a nice effort, and I like the dressing you've made. I will enjoy eating this tonight for my supper," she tells him, pausing to take a swig of her plum wine.

Ed takes this as his dismissal and steps away from her, retreating toward the kitchen area again.

REFRESHED AND REJUVENATED

Once the dishes have been cleaned and Ed has restored the kitchen to its original state, he wonders what to do with himself, feeling lost in the abyss of space the house offers him. He can hear Rodrick mumbling to himself in the corridor, and eventually pours himself a glass of water and settles in front of one of the large glass panes that look out onto the garden area, which opens out onto the untamed wildness of the forest beyond. The foliage is dazzling—reds and yellows mixing to birth warm golden hues, the ground beneath the trees sprinkled with lost leaves. Ed slides the glass doors open and steps out onto the wooden *engawa* that terraces the building, and finds the air is mild and fresh, drawing away the scent of salted crab which clings to his nostrils.

He closes his eyes, listens to the rustling of the leaves, and imagines a world where this is his home, where Sayuri is preparing green tea behind him, her arm wrapping around his waist as she passes him the cup and they both watch Kaori playing with the koi fish that twirl in the pond. A fantasy, but one he is happy to get lost in as he watches the magnificent koi lazily swishing their way through the water from his perch. They look as though someone has let droplets of watery tangelo and crimson ink fall onto them, the spots bleeding out slightly into the pearlescent white scales.

The pond itself is a work of art, with moss-speckled rocks and pebbles covering the sandy floor, some of the bigger boulders jutting out above the water's surface. Around the edge is a carefully curated selection of shrubs and foliage, reeds and deep purple leaves broken up only by some decoratively placed lanterns.

"Relaxing, isn't it?"

Ed almost drops his water in surprise, but it's only Rodrick, standing behind him with his hands clasped behind his back.

"Yes, it's very beautiful. My wife would love it. Do you have a wife, Rodrick?" Ed asks, still watching the fish.

"No. I'm . . . devoted entirely to Mrs. Yamamoto," he says eventually.

Ed turns to face him. "But she would allow you to marry, surely?"

"Of course. She denies me nothing. I just don't have the inclination to meet anybody," Rodrick replies.

Ed wonders if he is a robot, or an alien of some sort.

"We must keep the insect screens down to keep the mosquitoes away," Rodrick warns, turning away from him abruptly and pulling a mesh screen down that Ed hadn't noticed, to replace the door panes. "They love Mrs. Yamamoto's blood, absolutely feast on her," Rodrick continues with a shake of his head, now standing beside Ed and sharing the view. "Terrible little bloodsuckers."

"My wife is similar," Ed says. "Always gets bitten after dusk. Must be their lovely skin."

"You said you heard a scream earlier," Rodrick says, changing the subject again. "If not a fox, it may have been a cicada, one of the last left lingering. The season finished recently, but in the summer they can be quite deafening, the shrill bleating so loud it occasionally wakes me at dawn."

Ed nods. The cicadas are loud in Tokyo, too.

"Speaking of waking, Mrs. Yamamoto has requested that I show you to your chambers for the night. You are to help yourself to any food or drink in the kitchen to sustain yourself, and there is a tub in your room. So please, follow me." Rodrick beckons, releasing the insect shutter.

Ed follows him, carefully sliding the door panes shut behind them, leaving the oasis of the forest in its close.

"Your room is on the second floor," Rodrick explains as he makes his way up the stairs, holding on to the railings for support. At the top, he takes a left, and while Ed is desperately curious to see the entire home, he follows him. At the end of the hallway Rodrick opens a door to reveal a magnificent guest room. In the center, a low bed has been prepared for Ed to sleep on, with a plush white cover and cushions that look as soft and plump as cotton balls. His overnight bag has been collected from the *genkan* where Ed left it on arrival alongside his shoes, and placed carefully in the corner of the room. Behind the bed is an opulent room divider screen, with a stunning traditional artwork of samurai charging through the air sweeping across its panels.

Ed peers behind the screen and finds a small, tiled area with a freestanding round soaking tub waiting for him, the cover partially unrolled with spirals of steam escaping from the edges. Rodrick must have run the hot water and prepared it for Ed already.

"Thank you," Ed says to Rodrick with a nod of his head, keen to look nonchalant. Inside, he is dying with excitement to soak the day away and rest without the nagging of a concerned wife or cries of a tired toddler interrupting him.

"Anything you need, don't be afraid to ask," Rodrick says, retreating slowly toward the door. "Oh, and Mr. Cook?"

"Yes?" Ed stops gaping and turns to Rodrick.

"Mrs. Yamamoto has requested that you do not prepare a meal

for breakfast. She has decided to give you alternate instructions for the final portion of the interview."

Ed frowns, confused, but nods as Rodrick leaves, closing the door gently behind him. Once alone, Ed allows himself to marvel at every crevice of the room—all his for the entire night! The dark wooden beams and flooring make it look luxurious despite the lack of personal items, and circular beams of mood lighting surrounding the bathtub make it look even more heavenly than it already does. There is even a small balcony terrace, from which all Ed can see are treetops and mountains.

Ed finds himself feeling grimy, and doesn't want to put his soiled, sweaty body into the bed, so he decides to make use of the bath that Rodrick has run for him. He unrolls the cover fully and steps into the deep barrel, finding, to his utter delight, that some salts have been sprinkled into the water. They give off a spa-like aroma, and the grit of them on his feet as he steps in soon evaporates against Ed's tired skin, the heat of the bath enveloping him like a caress. *I could get used to this,* Ed thinks as he sinks in entirely, closing his eyes and laying his head back on the wooden rim. All he's missing is a cold beer, or he would be in complete heaven.

The rituals of bathing had shocked Ed when he first came to Japan. The groups of men, strangers, sitting companionably—naked as the day they were born—in giant pools of hot water felt repulsive and overly familiar to Ed. He had never seen a family member nude, let alone other random men. But Sayuri assured him it was common for the Japanese to enjoy a hot bath in the onsens, with many parents taking their children. There are even mixed onsens, where men and women bathe together, completely nude and uninhibited. Ed has never gone to a mixed bathhouse, but he has come to enjoy the odd soak after a long week, his eyes closed as he focuses entirely on himself. His favorite is when he is in the position to book a private onsen for himself and Sayuri, where they can slip into the tub together and talk the evening away. They haven't done this since Kaori was born, but it is one of his fondest memories of getting to know her. Secrets shared over the steam, the gentle ripples, and the sound of the water lapping against the sides as they edged closer together, heads close, voices low.

As he lies in the heat of the tub, he begins to wonder whether this crazy interview has any legs. He came with the intention of getting through it for the two-day salary, then leaving it all behind. But what if, by some miracle, he were actually to be offered the job? Would this be what his life would become? Popping into this mansion to feed Hazeline before retreating to this bedroom, and falling asleep to the sounds of the forest? Having access to his own private tub to help him and Sayuri rekindle their relationship? He finds himself with a burning desire to make this life his, to catch what is being dangled so close to his reach. He's unsure whether the change of plan for breakfast is a good thing or not. Perhaps he is being challenged, because he has not impressed her enough with the evening salad. But whatever the morning brings, Ed knows one thing for sure: he will give the final task his all, and he will become Hazeline Yamamoto's private chef.

In the morning Ed wakes feeling refreshed and rejuvenated. His skin is smooth and soft after his salted soak, and he can't remember the last time he slept on sheets so silken. He almost molded into the mattress, with the temperature perfectly mild and no whirring clunks of old air-cons or weepy nightmare-woken toddlers disturbing his dreams. He blinks, rubbing the grit from his eyes, and opens the balcony doors, standing topless as he looks over the landscape and feeling like a king. They say money can't buy happiness, but it can certainly buy a good night's sleep.

Ed dresses in his scratchy chef costume and pads down the hallway. The stench of crab still clings to the fabric, and there's an ugly brown stain on his cuff—a sloppy splash of soy sauce. The house is eerily quiet, and he takes the opportunity to soak in his surroundings as he ventures back toward the kitchen. The light fittings are mostly set into the ceiling, but when they aren't, the bulbs hang within ornate glass pendants that reflect beautiful patterns onto the walls where the sun hits. The floors are all polished—a deep hazelnut tone of wood—the irregular knots and gnarls in the grain identifying them as authentic, rather than the symmetrical imitation vinyl in Ed's own home. Any windowsills are decorated by plants, most of them housed in antique *mizubachi* made from glazed terra-cotta and decorated with whimsical dragon and botanical illustrations. There are also *kintsugi* vases, repaired using golden liquid seals. The results are imperfect vases cracked with shining webs, the wreckage part of the beauty. Ed thinks of his own cheap dishware at home, often broken during clumsy dinner dashes around Kaori, the pieces swept hastily into the bin before anyone can cut themselves on the shards and edges. He fingers the gold rim on a bowl, almost lovingly, wondering if he could ever accrue such wealth that he could afford to break an expensive piece of ceramic, only to have it made even more costly, more beautiful, by a golden repair.

He sighs, shakes the fantasy away, and makes his way down the stairs. He can hear Rodrick humming to himself again, the sound coming from a door he has not yet been through. He doesn't want to be seen snooping, so he continues past and heads to the kitchen as he knows the way. Momo scuttles past him, giving a low growl as he passes. Ed ignores the fluffy little dog.

Once in the safety of the kitchen, he decides to help himself to some coffee. The machine spits out the most delightful scent of caffeine, the liquid molten and chocolatey as it trickles steadily out of the machine and into his *yunomi.* He drinks it black, and closes his eyes at the flavorful first sip.

"Those are my favorite beans."

He jolts at the sound of Hazeline's voice. He didn't hear her approach. This morning, she's dressed in black satin trousers with a simple white T-shirt tucked into the waistband, and her house slippers finish the casual outfit. It is, however, elevated by the layers of jewels and pearls she has strung around her neck and wrists. She sees him looking at them.

"I found as a teenager that the more jewels I wore, the less people noticed my shape," she says.

"It's the best coffee I've had in a long time," Ed says, not wanting to discuss Hazeline's teenage insecurities again, unable to imagine her in any form other than the fragile, birdlike creature that stands before him.

"I get it imported from Italy," she tells him. "The blend is strong, but the taste is smooth and reminds me of caramel."

"I've only got instant at home," Ed says. "So this tastes like luxury!"

She smiles at him. "Caffeine is what fuels my soul, so it feels like a worthy investment to get the beans I so adore."

"Would you like a cup, Yamamoto-san?" Ed suddenly asks, feeling embarrassed it took him so long to make the offer.

"Yes, I would. You know how I like it," she says. He nods and rushes over to the machine. While the beans grind and the coffee pours, he fishes out the broken tablet of sweetener he halved the night before, popping it into her cup along with a whole one. In his peripheral vision, he sees her nod in approval at his memory. Another test passed. Hopefully she hasn't noticed his grubby cuff.

When it's ready, he places the coffee before her with two hands, bowing slightly. "What would you like me to do this morning,

Yamamoto-san?" he asks, unsure whether he should be preparing anything in place of breakfast.

"Ah, yes, your final test!" Hazeline smiles, her eyes sparkling with childlike excitement. "Rodrick is setting up now, and all should be ready soon."

Ed simply nods, and the two sit in silence, Hazeline at the table gazing out of the window toward the pond and Ed standing awkwardly by the sink, sipping his drink and rolling the mug between his palms for something to do. A sudden garbled shriek tears through the room, gone almost in a blink. It was a shrill bleat, but Hazeline does not react, does not even move her gaze from the garden pond.

"Did you hear that?" Ed asks her, turning toward the hallway where the sound came from. "What was that?" he asks, taking a step toward the door. The scream yesterday may well have been a fox, or a cicada, but this one was different. He knows he heard something, and he knows it came from inside the house.

"That, my dear, is your next test," she replies. This time, when she smiles, she looks like a cat that has just caught its prey.

JUST A STUPID CHICKEN

"Please, Ed, follow me." Hazeline beckons Ed out of the kitchen and toward the mysterious room he heard Rodrick bustling around in earlier.

"Come, come!" she says, excitement in her voice as she shuffles forward, coffee cup in hand. She pauses outside the door, and opens it to reveal a small bathing room. It's tiled with dark slabs, wooden bathmats and bamboo accessories, creating a very zen atmosphere. What isn't zen is the chicken hanging upside down above the tub in a metal cone contraption.

Ed takes a half-step backward before steeling himself.

The cone is narrow-side down, attached by an arm to a hook on the wall beside the tub. For a bizarre moment, Ed finds himself thinking that it looks like a tall wineglass. Apart from the bird—whose feet and tail feathers are sticking out of the top, its head and neck dangling from the bottom opening of the cone. For an upside-down chicken, it's remarkably calm, occasionally making gargled clucks but not putting up much of a fight by way of movement.

"Well, Ed, this is the final test." Hazeline beams at him as though she is offering him a silver platter of diamonds.

"We would like to see you quickly and humanely kill this chicken," Rodrick explains, though the hatchet lying on the bamboo bath tray has already given Ed a hint that this is where this absurd setup is heading.

"You want me to . . ." He trails off lamely, blinking at the sad little bird, at the indignity of it being killed while dangling upside down above an expensive stone tub. "All for an interview?" he finishes, still hopeful that he's misunderstood, or that it's some sort of joke.

"It's humane, of course, Ed. We don't want the poor thing to *suffer.* We aren't sadists!" Hazeline says sharply. "This is the most humane way to do it. All of the farmers say so. And it's not for entertainment or fun, or even just for your interview. It's for dinner."

"Could you not just . . . buy some chicken meat from the store?" Ed asks, his voice small, silently wondering how many farmers Hazeline has conferred with about her poultry-slaying habits.

"Well, yes, but then there wouldn't be a test for you, would there? This is a test of character," she replies, tapping her foot on the floor, her arms crossed.

"I thought the test was going to be cooking a Japanese-style breakfast," Ed tries again.

"Well, I changed my mind. I want chicken. I want *this* chicken," she says, gesturing again at the cone.

Ed swallows, his mind racing to assess his options. The issue is, there aren't any. He wants this job. He needs the money. He has no viable alternatives. And . . . well, it's just a chicken, isn't it? He can do it quickly, hopefully make it painless. If he doesn't kill it, Rodrick will only go and do it anyway, and Ed will lose the job opportunity.

And really, isn't this better, in a way? He will be able to bring this bird to the end of its life quickly and painlessly. Really, isn't it merciful, if anything? The alternative could be much worse. It could have been raised for slaughter, in a cramped room with other molting hens, before being killed by some inexperienced teen working for minimum wage in a slaughterhouse. Really, he's doing the right thing, isn't he?

The room feels still and the air is wet and heavy.

Jesus Christ, Ed thinks to himself as he steps toward the hatchet, its blade glinting in invitation. *God forgive me, but I need the fucking money.*

He picks it up, and it's heavy in his hand. Rodrick stands there, his lids heavy, as though watching a very unentertaining lecture occur. Hazeline is behind Ed, and he can feel her stare drilling into his back as he takes one step closer to the chicken.

He looks at the sad, pathetic animal as it sways, its clawed feet twitching slightly.

He hesitates, his hands clammy, and Hazeline senses his unease.

"Do you remember what I said before, Ed, about what a child's first movements are?" she asks him.

He nods dumbly, unable to swallow the lump in his throat in order to reply.

She gestures, bringing her pointer and middle finger to her thumb and patting her lips. "Remember, Ed, to eat is nothing but human nature. It's not a choice, it's an impulse. A necessity. To consume is to live. To feel that gnawing hunger means that we are alive, that we are in need of being filled. This chicken is sustenance for us today, nothing more, nothing less. It has lived its life and now it's time for it to sacrifice itself to give us the nourishment we need. It's just the way of the animal kingdom, the natural food chain. It's how we were intended to live. Do you think the cavemen hesitated to kill their lunch?"

I doubt that cavemen had the option of buying a prechopped chicken breast for a few hundred yen at the shop, Ed thinks. But he just shakes his head and raises the cleaver. He has to do this. He needs the money. And besides, it's just a stupid chicken.

He hears Hazeline take a short intake of breath. He holds the cone in one shaking hand, aims the cleaver for the gullet, and swings.

"How did it go?" Sayuri asks, Kaori in her arms as she juggles child and remote control, eventually putting on some garish cartoon on the television and dropping Kaori in front of it, the child immediately entranced, her little guppy mouth hanging open and her eyes wide.

"I'm not sure. I have to wait to hear back, but I got the money from the interview," Ed tells her, holding the envelope up with pride. He killed a fucking chicken for this money, after all.

"One envelope of petty cash does not a career make," Sayuri says, and in an instant Ed is consumed with rage and an overwhelming desire to rip her pretty head off her body. She has no idea what he did to try to secure this job for them. What he had to do to that bird in the bathroom. In the blink of an eye, the thought is gone, and he breathes out slowly. She's tired. She was probably up all night with Kaori, who hasn't been sleeping well, and he wasn't around to help or chip in. He's been failing to do his fair share with their daughter since she was born, but for some reason he can't bring himself to do better.

He sighs. "I know. But it's better than nothing. And I think she was happy with my performance." He thinks of the swinging hatchet, Hazeline's small smirk afterward, as though she had been proved right about something. As though *he* had proved her right.

Sayuri harrumphs, and he marvels at how unattractive it is to him. When did he start seeing his wife in this manner? Was it when

Kaori was born and they had less time to relax together, or when he realized his gambling had tethered them to the life of debt that he is trying to hide from her? Perhaps he hates her because it's easier than hating himself.

"I cooked duck," he tells her. "I think it came out okay. She didn't spit it out, anyway." A half joke.

Sayuri says nothing, her back to Ed as she picks Kaori's toys off the floor while the little girl is distracted by animated cats. Ed notices her hands have aged, fine lines appearing and the skin raw and red from constantly working, cleaning, washing. The rest of the time she is caring for Kaori, doing the best she can with her meager café salary to raise their child safely.

"And I made your famous salad. With real crab!" Ed tries again, suddenly overcome with compassion for his tired wife. "She liked the panko," he adds.

When it becomes clear that she is not up for a conversation, he turns toward his desk.

"Ed," she calls after him. He turns, hopeful for her to apologize, to have some faith in his attempts. Instead, she says, "Leave the envelope on the table. I need to pay Kaori's daycare lady. We're behind." Her voice is clipped, and he drops the envelope on the table before heading to his laptop. He's already snuck half of the contents out to pay Ikagi, anyway.

Sayuri picks it up and silently goes to the kitchen, leaving Ed at his desk and Kaori gawking at the television.

Ed boots up his old laptop and it whirrs with the sound of awakening, then he reaches underneath the desk to the second drawer where he has hidden a bottle of cheap sake. He takes a long, slow sip, wincing slightly as it burns its way down his throat, allowing a moment before the warmth hits. He doesn't know why he bothers to hide the bottle. Sayuri knows he occasionally drinks, can smell it on his breath when he crawls into bed beside her, when her hand smacks his creeping paws away from her soft, sloping body. He takes another swig, his mood quickly worsening.

When the computer has breathed its first breath, Ed clicks onto the shining notification on the email app, and his stomach does a flip.

From: chefwanted@jobad.jr
To: edward.cook@mailer.jr
Subject: RE: Private Chef Application

Mr. Cook,
I am writing on behalf of Hazeline Yamamoto following a successful trial period to offer you the role of Private Chef if you should so want it. Madame was impressed by your initiative and thinks that your attitude and experience lend themselves well to this particular position. If you would like to confirm via email, I can send the contracts over and we can commence working together.

A reminder that the benefits of working for Mrs. Yamamoto include room and board Mondays through Fridays as desired, though she is aware you have a family and may wish to commute instead. She understands you do not own a car, and is happy to send a driver or expense your trains as required.

She would like to extend an invitation to celebrate your new position with dinner at Untamed Teppanyaki. Let us know when suits you and we can arrange the details.

Many thanks.
Rodrick Bauer

Ed opens the drawer and takes another, longer drag of sake, and this time there's no wince.

UNTAMED TEPPANYAKI

Ed has heard of Untamed Teppanyaki, of course, from his time in hospitality recruitment. But he never placed any employees within its esteemed walls, and the entire place is shrouded in mystery. It's a very small restaurant, intimate, with only enough seats for four diners at a time, and it's almost impossible to get a reservation for. It's tucked away down an alleyway in central Tokyo, with no signage, and you have to go up a few flights of stairs before reaching the unassuming yet infamous red door.

Untamed Teppanyaki is an exotic meat restaurant, specializing in rare cuts of meat cooked in the traditional teppanyaki format—on the grill in front of diners. Ed can't believe he has a reservation.

"What should I wear?" he asks Sayuri, who is almost as excited as he is, despite not having her own invitation and staying at home with Kaori. Ed tries not to let the fact that she's so happy to see him out of the house bother him. He's sure that now he has a new, high-paying, reliable job, her mood will begin to lift considerably. It might just take a short while for them to get out of their rut.

"Well, it's a nice place. But I think for somewhere so intimate, a jacket may be too much." She chews her lip as she considers. "I think just a nice shirt and your fancy trousers will be just right," she decides, placing a hand on his shoulder.

Ed pulls them out of his wardrobe. The shirt needs ironing; it hasn't been worn since his salaryman days and has become sad and crumpled. It's a reminder of his previous, more conventionally successful life. And now it is coming full circle, taking him out to dinner to start a new life of success. Or so Ed hopes.

"I still can't believe you're working for *Hazeline Yamamoto,*" Sayuri says, whispering her name as though she's a ghost who might appear as if summoned. "You have to tell me absolutely everything about her and this fancy dinner. How fascinating!"

"Don't forget the NDA. You can't go around telling people that I work for her," Ed warns. "I could lose my job!"

"No, no, of course I won't. Our secret." She smiles at him.

Ed smiles back. She said *our.* They're back to being a team again.

"Ed! Ed, oh come look! Quick!" Sayuri rushes to the doorway, Kaori in her arms, her eyes wide with excitement. Ed hurries to finish buttoning up his shirt and follows Sayuri to the front of the house, where through the window he sees a large, black limousine. "Ed, is this for you?" Sayuri gasps. Kaori slams her chubby palms against the glass in excitement.

The man Ed saw in the driveway at Hazeline's home emerges, standing outside the car with his hands clasped at the front. Nakamura, Hazeline called him.

"I . . . I suppose so." Ed swallows, immediately second-guessing his attire.

"And to think, all of this has come from a random ad in a newspaper."

Ed frowns briefly; her tone seemed almost sarcastic.

"You look great," Sayuri tells him, her voice back to normal, immediately reassuring him and patting down his shirt. "Well, hurry! You don't want to keep her waiting," she says, placing Kaori down on a cushion and flapping at Ed with her hands. He barely has a chance to feel flustered as he is essentially thrown out of his house by his tiny yet absurdly strong wife.

The driver tilts his head at Ed as he approaches, opening the back door for him. "*Konbanwa,* Cook-san," Nakamura greets him politely, though he avoids eye contact with Ed as he gets in the car. Inside, Hazeline is draped across a few seats as though lounging on a chaise, and she is wearing a smart black dress that covers her shoulders and chest, up to her neck. She's also toned down her jewelry, opting for a single statement piece. It hangs on a discreet gold chain, and to Ed's revulsion, resembles a human canine tooth.

"Ed, I'm delighted you have accepted our offer. I simply cannot wait for us to start a long working relationship together," she drawls. Ed is surprised to find Rodrick is joining them. The housekeeper greets him with the tiniest tilt of the mouth—the closest he's come to a smile since Ed met him.

"Oh, no, the thanks is all mine. And for this dinner as well. Thank you so much for the invitation," he says.

"It's a fun little restaurant, I've not been in a while," she replies flippantly, as though referring to a Hard Rock Cafe.

Rodrick sits silently beside them, gazing out of the window as the colors and lights of Tokyo trickle past them. Ed takes a moment to drink in his surroundings. The interior leather is a soft, clean burgundy, and the driver is hidden behind a dark glass pane. Classical music tinkles through the speakers at an inoffensive volume, and beside Hazeline is a small crevice in the car interior which seems to house champagne and flutes.

Hazeline catches Ed's eye.

"A drink?" she proffers.

"Oh, no, I was just looking, really," he replies hastily, embarrassed to have been caught out.

"Nonsense. This is a celebration of your hiring, after all," Hazeline says, already yanking the bottle out and expertly twisting the neck. She gives another hearty wrench and the bottle pops neatly, a tiny wisp of condensation trickling from the crack between the bottle and cork. Ed is impressed.

"Please, allow me." He reaches over for the bottle and flutes and begins to carefully pour out the champagne. It's a silken light gold, the bubbles dancing excitedly. He passes the first glass to Hazeline, who takes it happily.

"Rodrick?" He offers a glass, but Rodrick merely gives a brief shake of his head.

"Rodrick doesn't drink," Hazeline explains.

"Oh, I see," Ed says, turning pink. "Apologies."

"More for me," Hazeline replies, reaching out to take the second glass from Ed. "*Kanpai!*" she toasts, holding them both out for Ed to clink against.

He obliges and takes the first sip from his own glass. It's sweet and sharp, dry and crisp. It's the most delicious champagne he has ever tasted, including his own wedding champagne.

"Not the best," Hazeline comments, her nose in the air. "Though what do you expect for a short car ride."

"Is the car yours?" Ed asks Hazeline.

"Yes, though I only use it for business trips or when I have to come into the city. I don't really have the need for a car like this, I so rarely leave my little sanctuary." She smiles, and Ed tries not to react to her use of the word "little." He takes another long sip of his drink, thinking of his awful commutes into work, crammed onto a bus so full of bodies that there was no need to hold on to the railings—because even when the bus juddered, there was no space for any of the bodies to fall. They held each other up like matches crammed into a box without room to rattle.

"And Mr. Nakamura drives all of your vehicles for you?" Ed asks.

"Yes, he does. Botan used to quite enjoy driving, I think he found it liberating, but I find it distastefully busy and stressful. When he died, I found Mr. Nakamura and employed him to be my driver," she explains.

"Ah, I see. How did you find him? Are there directories for specialist drivers?"

There is a short pause, an awkward silence. He watches as Hazeline darts a quick, warning glance at Rodrick.

"Something like that," she says dismissively. "Really, we stumbled across him at just the right time. But it's a story for another day." She smiles.

Ed feels that he has hit an awkward topic, and desperate not to relive the rant about her teenage body dysmorphia, he instead silently sips champagne and watches the streets he thought he knew so well fly past him. He doesn't know if it's the champagne, or the view from the limousine, but it all looks a bit hazier and dreamlike tonight.

NO PERFUME

As the car pulls up the alleyway outside the restaurant, Ed feels a thrill of excitement run down his spine. He is about to eat at Untamed Teppanyaki! Who would have thought?

He has another reason for his good mood—he has paid the first installment of his debt, and bought himself a substantial amount of time for the rest of the repayments after explaining he now has a job and, hopefully, regular income. While not renowned for their patience, the Yakuza also aren't known for wanting to draw attention to themselves, particularly in relation to gambling, and hinting that his new employer is a woman from high society with a huge amount of power means that Ikagi will take a step back. Killing off the private chef of someone of Hazeline's standing would leave room for unnecessary investigations. Ed is feeling on top of the world.

They scale the narrow, winding staircase past several floors of tiny *izakaya* bars, cigarette smoke wafting from the door cracks. When they reach the top, he holds the infamous red door open for Hazeline to step inside first, then Rodrick with her bag. There is still no restaurant name signposted anywhere, but above the door a sign reads: *No perfume, no smoking.* The scent of perfume is said to distract from the taste of the food; the sign warning them in its own way that they are about to enjoy a truly exemplary dining experience.

"*Irasshaimase!*" A server beams at them, holding a small silver tray of sake. Hazeline takes a glass, followed by Ed. Rodrick declines again, and is promptly offered some sparkling water instead.

The space is indeed small, and they are seated in a little line, right in front of a gleaming silver grill. The surface is flat and mirrored, and behind it is the chef, who has already prepared most of the meal so he can now simply grill the food and present it to them with some flair. Although seated at a wooden counter, they are close enough to the grill that the heat is radiating up to them, causing Ed to break out in a sweat.

"To drink?" the server asks them with a small bow.

"A draft beer," Ed replies on instinct. There is a short pause, and Hazeline smiles at him.

"Charming," she purrs. Somehow, it sounds like an insult. "I'll take a glass of the Yama Sauvignon," she adds.

Ed immediately feels stupid. "Can't beat just a good old beer though, right?" He forces a laugh and grins at Rodrick, who looks at him blankly, and then pointedly glances toward his own glass of water. Ed's false laughter fades out into the hissing of oil on the grill.

"Very British," Hazeline agrees, and Ed can't tell if his face is hot from the embarrassment or the grill.

They are presented with menus, a single sheet of silky *gampi* paper, hand-painted calligraphy forming the menu of the day. Ed begins to salivate as his eyes trail down the options—some sounding delicious, some bizarre. Buttered lobster, Kobe Wagyu beef mix, pickled crocodile, fried crickets, python carpaccio, glazed pork belly, grilled snapper, kangaroo skewers, and alpaca steak. Ed blinks, unsure of what to choose.

"Let us all share some beef to start?" Hazeline offers, and Ed nods, grateful to be relieved of a decision. She nods to the chef, who immediately begins to fry some garlic slices, his tongs slipping and dancing in the oil as he flips the tiny slivers of garlic one by one, so quickly that Ed can only gape at his accuracy.

"I'm going to go for the python, I think," Hazeline says. "I've not tried it before, though Rodrick has and said it was exquisite."

Beside Ed, Rodrick nods silently, and Ed can't help but think he can't imagine Rodrick speaking praise for anything, least of all raw snake meat.

"I'll join you," Rodrick replies, and Hazeline beams.

"Ed?"

He chews his lip, conscious they are all waiting on his decision. The python clearly is the fan favorite, but he's worried he won't like it. He can't go wrong with lobster, albeit it's a boring choice amidst the weird and wonderful menu items. But he doesn't want to risk ordering something he dislikes; he wants this entire dining experience to be savored and enjoyed. He knows it's very unlikely he will ever get to eat here again, after all.

"I can't choose between the lobster and the python," he says.

"Well, just order both!" Hazeline laughs, as though splashing out that sort of money to save the deliberation is normal.

"No, no! Really, I couldn't possibly," Ed says, immediately horrified.

"Well then, why don't you get the lobster and we can both share a bite of our python?" she offers. "I'll never finish a full portion on my own anyway. They're very generous here."

"Okay. Okay, I accept your kind offer," Ed says, still uncomfortable and wishing he had just chosen the lobster from the beginning.

"Excellent choice!" Hazeline remarks, telling the server their orders. Ed realizes that their beef starter is almost ready, the cubed hunks of meat delicately marbled with veins of fat. The chef is flipping them rapidly on the grill to give each side the perfect amount of searing, eventually using a spatula to transfer the eight perfect cubes of browned beef over to a plate which has been prepared with wasabi, salt, pepper, and the fried garlic.

The plate is placed in front of Ed, as he is seated in the middle, and Hazeline and Rodrick both lean toward it in tandem, eyes closed as they inhale the beautiful scent. In that moment, Ed realizes that while he couldn't recognize a friendship between Hazeline and Rodrick before, perhaps it's their clear love of food that connects them.

"*Itadakimasu,*" Hazeline cheers.

"*Itadakimasu,*" Ed and Rodrick echo, their eyes not leaving the plate.

"Here, Ed, you must pile it all on together to enjoy it to its fullest," Hazeline recommends, using her chopsticks to create a tower of garlic and wasabi on top of a beef chunk before dabbing the entire thing in the salt and popping it into her mouth whole.

"Divine," she sighs after a moment of chewing.

Beside Ed, Rodrick is making an odd groaning sound. Ed hastily builds his own mouthful, and the explosion of juicy flavor when he takes the first bite is tremendous. The meat seems to melt away in his mouth, giving way to the mellow, herby wasabi and the savory kick of garlic.

Ed groans, and Hazeline laughs. The trio don't speak as they polish off the plate in slow silence, every bite relished as Ed makes sure to close his eyes to take in the taste as best he can.

By the time the plate is cleared away, Ed is positive that nothing can beat the mixed beef starter. But he still has the lobster to look forward to.

The lobster has already been cut in half when it appears before them, delivered by a sous chef. The chef liberally coats the two halves in flour before placing them down onto the grill. To Ed's great horror, he watches as the legs begin to thrash, spasming and reaching out toward him as if begging for help.

"It must be terribly fresh!" Hazeline claps with delight. "What a treat, Ed! I'm almost jealous!"

Ed nods mutely, watching as the legs begin to slow their wild jerking to a sad, desperate final few twitches, as though literally dancing the line between life and death. The chef throws on a tab of butter and it instantly begins to melt, pouring over the sides of the lobster before settling beneath it in a pool of fat, the rich smell mingling with the shellfish scent and making Ed salivate despite himself. The imitation of life as he watches his meal being cooked makes him feel a bit sick. He knows the lobster is dead, that it's just reflexes in the nerves that are causing the twitching, but for some reason it makes him think about what it would be like if he were stripped naked and placed onto boiling oil on a grill himself. He rubs his arms and looks away from his meal, wishing he'd ordered a salad.

Beside the main chef, the sous chef is preparing the python. Ed has never seen snake meat before and is underwhelmed to find that it looks exactly as he imagined it would—a large, pale tube, not dissimilar to a giant sausage. It's incredibly unappetizing, and he feels relieved to have ordered the lobster after all. The sous chef is using a glinting sharp blade to slice the thinnest leaves of meat away from it, arranging them on top of some peppery salad leaves and mixing an unknown dipping sauce to accompany it. Impeccably timed, the plates are presented to the three of them in sync.

"Gorgeous," Hazeline remarks, after enjoying the first bite of her meal. "Here, Ed, try a bit," she says, offering her plate to him. He hesitates, but only for the briefest of moments, unable to refuse her. There's only so many faux pas he's willing to make this evening, so he takes his chopsticks and helps himself to a disc of the anemic meat. It's pale, like a slice of human skin, almost. Strange white lines are visible—he's not sure whether it's fat or tendons—not unlike the marbling on beef. Hazeline is watching him eagerly, waiting for his reaction.

"Go on, expand your palate, Ed! Welcome to the world of luxury," Hazeline encourages.

Trying not to think too much about the venomous snake that bore the meat, Ed shovels it into his mouth. He finds it chewy, almost like calamari, and a little bit tasteless, like a richer version of chicken. He's surprised to find that not only does he like it, but it's actually very inoffensive and unexciting, as far as flavors go. It must be the sort of thing you order just because it's difficult to come across, unconventional, something to brag about.

"It's good," he tells Hazeline after swallowing.

"Well done for trying," she says, as though proud of him.

Embarrassed again, but unsure why, Ed looks down at the lobster meat adorning his plate, the golden chunks glistening with butter, coral hues like paint splatter. It has been served on the empty shell, a corpse husk splayed out beneath the innards. Ed stares at the legs, wondering if they will suddenly jolt to life again, but of course they don't. He wishes he could ask for a doggy bag, take it home to Sayuri who will surely enjoy it more than he will in his current mindset, but he would never be so rude as to break Japanese dining etiquette like that. He breathes in, picks up his chopsticks and takes a mouthful, scooping the meat from its rigid skin-suit.

Ed is horrified. It is delicious.

A GLUTTONOUS FOOD HAZE

At the end of the meal Hazeline offers to drive Ed home, but he politely turns down her invitation. He is so bloated and full, the walk will do him some good, he assures her.

She nods, sends him off on his way, and assures him she is looking forward to working with him again soon. He stands on the pavement and watches as she clambers into her elegant limousine, and once she and Rodrick have driven away into the distance, he feels himself relax. He doesn't know when he became so tense over the course of the night, but it feels good to loosen his shoulders. He rubs a hand over his satiated belly, smooth and round and filled with an excess of the most expensive food he has ever eaten. He feels greedy, slow and sluggish as he wanders down the bustling streets toward his home. Groups of drunken salarymen jostle past him, tourists stop abruptly in the middle of the street to take photographs of nothing in particular, and Ed strolls thoughtlessly between them all, in a gluttonous food haze.

"Cook-san?" he hears, a bellow over the crowds. "Cook-san!" This time more delighted, and he looks to find a couple of his old colleagues pushing their way toward him.

"Ito-san! Yamada-san!" Ed greets them, slapping his old co-workers on the back.

"It's been a while," Yamada tells him. "How have you been?"

"Have you found a new job?" Ed asks Ito, ignoring Yamada's question. He is a little drunk from the beers, and feels unjustly bitter that Yamada was one of the few on the team who managed to somehow keep his role. Ito, on the other hand, is one of the men who drank themselves into a stupor with Ed after the dreaded HR meeting.

"I have, it's just working in a bank, but better than nothing," Ito says with a shrug. "And you?"

"I'm working as a chef, as of very recently," Ed says, relieved that he isn't admitting he's still unemployed.

"How cool!" Yamada whoops.

Ed stands a little taller and smiles. "And how is the company doing?" he asks Yamada.

The man shrugs, tilts his head. "Same old. Not the same without you guys." He smiles politely.

"We were just heading to play pachinko if you fancy it?" Ito says, nodding toward the bright lights of the parlor.

Ed was so swept away in his post-meal daydreams that he hadn't even noticed the parlor.

He pauses, momentarily torn. The garish lights and signs outside are flashing, huge posters featuring cartoon characters promising big money plastered over the windows. *Enter and play!* reads the speech bubble coming from the mouth of an adorable cartoon mouse in a waistcoat. The door swings open as an old woman exits the building and there is a sudden burst of deafening noise, loud and brittle, a mix of the small metal balls inside the pachinko machines rattling against each other and the audio of joyful screaming that the parlors play to mimic people winning to keep the punters playing. Ed knows the sound is only a fraction of the racket inside.

He could make a good night even better with a quick game and a little win. He opens his mouth to reply to his friends. Then he thinks of Sayuri waiting for him at home, wanting to hear about his big night out. He thinks of Kaori, of her diminished college savings. He thinks of his head clanging afterward, unable to clear itself of the noise of the parlor, the sound of the metal balls clattering in his skull as he fails to fall asleep.

But what if he wins?

With extreme effort aided only by his lethargy and the light pain of a rarely stretched belly, he shakes his head. "I'm gonna call it a night, guys. I had a big dinner and am ready to lie down!" He pats his stomach dramatically.

"Where did you go?" Yamada asks.

"Untamed Teppanyaki," Ed says, puffing his chest out slightly.

"*Majide*! No way! How was it?" Yamada asks.

Ed glows slightly. "Delicious."

"How did you even get a table?" Ito asks, his eyes wide.

"I went with my employer," he tells them, relishing the envy in their eyes.

"No way! I didn't know being a chef paid that well!" Yamada gawks. "Cook-san, you must be an excellent chef!"

Ed smiles.

"What did you eat? I hear they serve lemur," Yamada says, his voice dropping a little.

"Well, *I* heard they have the spines from pygmy hedgehogs, illegally gathered," Ito says.

Ed laughs. "I'm afraid to say both of you are wrong. But I did try python, which was on the more exotic end of the menu," he says, raising his brows.

"Python? Cool! How was it?" Ito asks.

Ed thinks of the limp, washed-out scrap of flesh, stamped into a perfect disc. It was bland, the dipping sauce its savior. "It was the best thing I've ever eaten," Ed lies with a grin.

Both men make noises of envy and excitement, much to Ed's satisfaction.

"Well, yes, we imagine you must indeed be well fed. You go home and enjoy the rest of your evening," Ito tells him earnestly.

"Thank you. See you both soon," Ed replies, tipping his head.

"Yes, yes!"

His friends hurry away, and as Ed watches them walk into the pachinko parlor, he finds that not only does he feel good about his decision to go home, he feels smug. As though he is better than them, somehow. Upgraded past the level of life that they're both still riding.

The rest of the journey home, he feels a little lighter, a small skip in his step. When he is a few streets away from his house, he pops into a little market stall that sells trinkets and knickknacks.

He picks up a small stuffed dog for Kaori, and a beaded necklace for Sayuri. He doesn't flinch as he pays, doesn't begin racking up totals in his head and calculating how many games he will have to play to win back the amount. He takes the bag, wishes the shop girl a good evening, and returns home to his family, gifts in hand.

The door creaks quietly as he opens it, and Ed is delighted to find Sayuri awake, reading in an armchair.

"How was it?" she asks in an excited whisper, standing to meet him. Kaori was long ago put to bed. Sayuri flushes. "I couldn't sleep, I wanted to hear all about it."

"It was brilliant. The best lobster I've ever had," Ed admits.

"Beats our rice and tuna supper." Sayuri smiles, pulling him over to the table where she makes him describe all the dishes in excruciating detail. He's not sure why, but he omits telling her that he tried the python. She sighs, her chin cupped in both hands. "It must have been amazing to eat such luxurious dishes, and all on your employer's budget!"

Ed feels a stab of sorrow that his wife and child weren't able to share the experience with him, that he will never be able to offer them the sort of fine dining that Hazeline is clearly accustomed to. But he is able to offer them small, cheap tidbits of love; especially now Ikagi and his henchmen have backed off him for a while.

"I got you something. It's not a butter-soaked piece of lobster, unfortunately, but it's just something to apologize for how . . . strained things have been recently. I really do think this job is going to be a great thing," he tells her, pulling the beaded jewelry out for his wife.

"Oh, Ed!" she exclaims, bringing it to her neck. "I can't remember the last time you gifted me something." She smiles stiffly, fastening the necklace quickly.

He wants to smile back, but finds he can't, the shame of what a poor husband he has recently been to her consuming him. When they first met, he would turn up with random bouquets of flowers for her, or little anime keyrings from her favorite shows which she'd happily clip onto her bags.

"I know. I'm sorry. Things have been tight, but I'm going to knock the socks off Yamamoto and make her realize she can't live a day without something cooked by yours truly!"

Sayuri claps her hands quietly in delight.

"Oh, and I got something for Kaori, too. Though we will have to wait until morning to give it to her," he says, pulling the dog toy out to show Sayuri.

"She'll like that a lot. Let's put it beside her in the cot, so when she wakes she finds it," she tells him, taking the dog from him and heading toward Kaori's tiny bed.

Left alone, Ed looks around his humble home, and allows himself to daydream about how life might be different if he can guarantee regular work with Hazeline. His wife is so excited to just *hear* about his dinner, imagine if one day he could take her out to try it herself, perhaps for an anniversary. It's the first time in a long time he's sat with Sayuri and chatted happily, and he realizes with some guilt that their conversations over the past few months have been curt, snappy, and exhausted. Is it that she's delighted by the idea of her husband spending time amidst the rich? Or is it something deeper? Is she perhaps living a fantasy life through him?

Ed has never thought of his wife as a materialistic person. She was raised humbly and never frittered away cash, only buying what she needed and never seeming to want for excess. But tonight he has seen a different side to her. A side which salivated as he described his hand-grilled Kobe beef. A side whose eyes shone as he described the luxurious car journey. A side who wistfully sighed as he told her about the upscale menus and stellar service. And Ed wonders if perhaps he and his wife are more alike than he has realized.

CHILDHOOD SWEETHEARTS

An antsy week passes before Ed hears from Hazeline about work. She requests that he come to the house for another evening to undertake a "lesson" with a "dear friend," and then in the morning he's to present a brunch for her and another guest. Ed is particularly worried about the elusive lesson, thinking back to the chicken-slaughtering incident. But he has been awaiting this call for the entire week, wondering if he dreamed the job up and it really was too good to be true. Plus, as always, he needs the money.

He stands down the street from his house, waiting to be picked up by Nakamura at the arranged collection spot. He is checking for a fancy-looking car when he feels the hard point of a blade digging into his back through his jacket. He instantly stills, his breath caught at the base of his throat. He feels the presence of someone behind him, smells spice and tobacco and too much cologne as they lean forward toward his ear.

"Turn around and follow me. Be quiet and calm. Ikagi-anikibun sent me." Ed swallows, slowly pivoting to find himself facing a Yakuza member, his eyes dark and lifeless. He is in a western-style suit, the edge of a tattoo snaking out at the collar, and he has a small knife scar by his downturned lips. In his hands is a small blade. Ed bows his head, following the man farther down the road, glancing behind him skittishly. They walk in strained silence until they reach a quiet backstreet, the man turning to face Ed and opening his jacket to flash his main weapon—a butcher knife—as a reminder that Ed is to cooperate or face the repercussions. Ed clenches his fist, thinking of the threat to cut his finger off, the inviting grin that had accompanied the wave of the tanto knife in the alleyway scorched into his memory.

"I've paid Ikagi his first installment. I was on time!" Ed begins, raising both hands in surrender.

The Yakuza spits on the ground lazily, leaning back against a building. "He heard you got a pretty good gig cooking for some society bigshot," the man says.

Ed says nothing, but his mouth hangs open.

"I'll take that as a yes. So the situation has changed," the man tells him, smirking slightly. "Ikagi wants his money sooner. He was being generous with the timings before, see? But now you're in a sweet situation, it's time to get real. He wants the next two installments by the end of the week. Now you've got this job, that shouldn't be a problem, should it? You were on your way to work just now, were you not? Waiting for someone, it looked like. A chauffeur, I suppose?" The man's lip curls up in enjoyment as Ed blinks rapidly. They've been watching him.

"The end of the week? That's a lot of money!" Ed splutters.

The man shrugs. "You owe a lot of money. This is, really, not a lot at all when you look at the big picture." He makes a box with his fingers as though looking through a camera lens, shuts one eye and tilts his head, watching Ed through his hands. Then he pushes off from the wall and begins to walk away.

"I'll see you in a few days to collect what is owed. If I can't find you, perhaps your pretty little wife will be able to help me track you down." Then he smiles, his thin, downturned mustache twitching as he does so. The threat is well understood.

"I'll have the money," Ed grinds out.

"Good. Don't forget now." The man waggles his finger at Ed patronizingly before lurching forward and kicking Ed hard in the shins. He goes down fast, legs buckling beneath him with a cry. By the time he has dusted himself off and righted himself, he is alone on the street.

He crouches down, allowing himself a moment to collect himself, and is still squatting when he hears a voice.

"Cook-san?"

He looks up and finds the driver, Nakamura, jogging toward him in concern. "Are you all right, sir?"

"Yes, yes, sorry. I just tripped," he mumbles. Nakamura puts his arm on Ed's back and helps him walk to the car, which he's parked at the end of the alleyway, the hazard lights blinking.

"You're lucky I saw you! I was just coming up to our meeting point when I saw a man in a suit leaving this alleyway. I looked down and saw you crumpled up down there," he says, helping Ed into the back of the car.

Ed grunts, embarrassed, and rubs his shin.

Nakamura gets into the driver's seat and lowers the window dividing the front from the rest of the car. "So what really happened back there?" he asks. "That guy looked like Yakuza. You don't want to be getting mixed up with them," he warns.

"Too late," Ed mumbles.

He sees Nakamura look at him with shock in the rearview mirror.

Ed sighs. "I owe a bit of money. I'm paying it off, it'll all be fine soon. That's why I took this job, I need the money. Please, don't tell Hazeline," he adds.

Nakamura mimes zipping his lips. "Your secret is safe with me, sir. Although . . ." He trails off, looks away from the mirror and back to the road.

"Although?"

Nakamura seems to battle internally with himself before opening his mouth again. "Just, make sure you know what you're getting into with Hazeline, too." He flushes red.

"Rodrick seems to think Hazeline is an amazing employer," Ed says, confused.

"She is," Nakamura replies quickly. "But, you know, no job is perfect."

"Struggling through a dinner beats getting my hands sliced off by the Yakuza," Ed mutters. "And how about you? How did you get a job with Hazeline?" Ed thinks back to the strange look shared between Hazeline and Rodrick when he asked the same question just a week ago.

Nakamura shows no sign of discomfort; he is happy for the subject change. "You know her husband, Botan? How he died?"

Ed frowns. "He was sick, right?" In truth, he doesn't know much. It was in the papers that he had cancer and nobody but the immediate family had known, but no other information was ever made public. He was quite old, and the death was far from unusual.

"Yes, so it was quite a rare disease. It's called ACC cancer," Nakamura explains.

"Right," Ed says, unsure how this relates to Nakamura being a driver.

"So obviously, the Yamamoto family have all this money from the land they own around Tokyo. You know, I heard they make billions a year from ground rent alone! They even own some of the land Tokyo Station is built on," Nakamura says with excitement.

"Okay?"

"So anyway, obviously Botan Yamamoto was getting the best medical care anyone could ask for. Whatever he wanted, any chance of it helping, Hazeline was willing to climb mountains to get it for him. They had a private medical suite built for him at home, full-time care and nurses, specialists flown in, the whole works. And I mean, he made it to seventy before he died, so it must have done some good, right?"

"Sure," Ed says.

"And when he died, Hazeline still had all this stuff. All these medical personnel on her payroll, the in-house setup for an ACC patient, all the drugs. And she approached the local hospital, explained that while she was mourning her husband, he wouldn't want all of it to go to waste. She wanted to know of any other ACC patients. And they told her about Suki, my wife."

"Your wife?" Ed gasps. "But she must be so young to be so sick!"

"Yes." Nakamura grimaces. "We are childhood sweethearts, she is only thirty-two. But she was diagnosed with ACC very young, and we didn't know what to do. It was, by far, the hardest time of my life. All our money went to subsidizing her care, but the debt was building up, and the treatment results were up and down. So when Hazeline offered to house us, to give us all this additional medical help and access to international specialists, all in exchange for a full-time driver . . . Well, needless to say, it felt like heaven was answering my prayers," he said.

Ed is suddenly reminded of the feeling he had when he found the job ad on his desk, the promise of two million yen for the interview alone.

"And that's how you became her driver? She just . . . approached you through the hospital?"

"Yep. Been working for her a few years now."

"Why wouldn't she have just told me that when I asked?"

Nakamura shrugs. "She's very humble. Doesn't brag much. She probably didn't want you to take pity on me. But honestly, I am just grateful."

"And all you have to do is drive?" Ed asks, unsure if he's misunderstanding, if there are lines he is being too naïve to read between.

"Yes sir, I drive her anywhere she needs to go, whenever she needs. I pick people up and drop them off as instructed. I keep the cars clean and safe. I signed the NDA, I am discreet, I don't tell anyone who I am driving or where, and in exchange I live in an annex of her home with Suki, who is largely bedridden but getting all this incredible healthcare. I truly think she may even be getting better!"

Ed smiles at Nakamura, but spends the rest of the journey in silence, something feeling off.

Once back within the glass walls of Hazeline's fortress, Ed feels as though his encounter in the alleyway was a million years ago, the scuffs on his knees the only proof it really happened. He has been asked by Rodrick to stay out of the kitchen while it's being prepared for the mysterious class, so he is waiting up in the guest room, pacing back and forth in front of the balcony. Then, as he looks toward the forest treeline, he stops. He sees movement, and when he squints he realizes that there is a small building he hasn't noticed before. Nakamura is entering it, and with him is a uniformed nurse. They are speaking closely, Nakamura nodding along to what she is saying, and she is holding a clipboard. It must be the annex where he lives with his sick wife. Ed sits and watches for a while longer, but nothing else happens. In the back of his mind, the Yakuza are still lingering, alongside their threats. He doesn't have time to worry about Nakamura's wife; his own wife is in danger and he has to resolve it.

Eventually, he summons the courage to leave the room, stopping outside of Hazeline's bedroom door and giving a tentative knock. He knows she's in there, because he heard her humming, but interrupting her feels unbearably intrusive. "Yamamoto-san? It's Ed. I'm so sorry to disturb you but I need to speak with you regarding something," he calls out. He stands for what feels like forever, waiting for any sound or response, his heart hammering. Eventually, he thinks perhaps she isn't even in the room anymore, and he is turning to leave when her door suddenly slides open and Hazeline peers at him with interest, one brow cocked.

The room behind her features a large, low bed. Above it is a huge framed portrait of Hazeline and Botan, both serious in expression, his hands placed over hers as they look directly into the camera.

"I was reading," she tells him, nodding to a book lying on a large accent chair.

"I'm so sorry to disturb you," Ed says, lowering his head. "It's just, I needed to ask a favor." He thinks of Nakamura, and decides that in the grand scheme of employee favors, his is small fry compared to keeping Suki alive. Although, in a way, this favor will help to keep Sayuri alive, too.

"A favor?" Hazeline echoes, her lips curving up into a smile. "How intriguing! I wonder whatever I can do for you, having barely just met you." She tilts her head like an owl and Ed shifts in discomfort. She is making a barbed point, and they both know it. He can read between the lines. No favor comes free, and he will owe her.

He clears his throat. "I was hoping you may be able to offer me an advance on my wages."

"Oh?" she says, her smile widening.

"I, er . . . I'm having some boiler problems and have booked to get it fixed on Friday. But I could really do with having the money early to help pay for it."

"What's wrong with your boiler?" Hazeline asks him, and he feels as though they are in a strange dance.

"An issue with the . . . pipes?"

She stills, as though she can sense he is lying, then she glances down at his scuffed knees and shrugs herself back to life. "Sure. I'll make sure Rodrick pays you tomorrow before you leave, in cash," she says, and Ed exhales in relief. "If you really blow my socks off, you might even get a little bonus!" She smiles.

"Oh! Thank you. Thank you so much!" he babbles.

"No problem, Ed, petal. We care for our own here, you'll soon learn. Now, you should head downstairs. I think your little lesson will be ready to begin in the kitchen."

"Thank you, Yamamoto-san, thank you so much! I will not forget this kindness," Ed tells her, bowing several times and clasping his hands together as Hazeline shoos him away with a flap of her hand and closes her bedroom door.

It's only once Ed is walking to the kitchen that he realizes he now owes debts to two very powerful people.

SMELLS LIKE HOME

Ed is surprised to enter the kitchen to find Rodrick laughing joyfully alongside another man, who has his back turned to Ed but is dressed in a chef's uniform. A proper Japanese chef's outfit, not a western-style costume from a fancy dress store. When Ed enters, the laughter immediately dies down, and when the chef turns to face him, Ed's mouth drops open in amazement. "Chef Chungpu!" he gasps, face-to-face with the Chinese celebrity chef who is the frequent guest of several daytime TV shows.

"Nice to meet you. I'm Chef Chungpu, though I gather you already know that. I will be your teacher today," he introduces himself in Japanese. He grins at Ed, who notices one of his canine teeth sticks out at a funny angle. He's never noticed it onscreen.

Ed quickly recovers from his shock, bowing his head deeply in return. Wait until Sayuri hears about *this*! She has definitely watched one of his cooking series before! "Such an honor to meet you, Chungpu sensei."

Rodrick clearly knows the star well, because he smiles at him warmly, asking him if he needs anything.

"No, no, I am fine. We will be finished in a couple of hours,"

Chungpu assures Rodrick, placing a familiar hand on the housekeeper's broad shoulder.

Spread along the counter is a plethora of ingredients, many of them already chopped and ready to go. Thankfully, there is no live animal kicking from a metal contraption for Ed to murder.

Rodrick turns to Ed. "Madame loves lamb shank. It's her favorite meal, and it has great sentimentality for her. She grew up eating it on Sundays with her parents, and she is very particular and nostalgic about how it is cooked. It may not be the fanciest way, but this is *exactly* how her mother cooked it. Chef Chungpu was her go-to for enjoying lamb shank until he moved to work in France."

Ed blinks at Chungpu, filled with a newfound respect for this man, who left such a cushy job working for Hazeline in search of a new, presumably more economically prosperous, adventure.

"She has flown him in specifically to teach you exactly how to make her family lamb shank, and you will only have this opportunity once, so please ensure you soak it all in and make the most of the teachings," Rodrick finishes.

"I will, thank you," Ed assures him, feeling slightly nervous about the challenge, but excited to get a private lesson from such a prestigious chef.

Rodrick exits the kitchen, sliding the door shut behind him, leaving Ed and Chungpu alone.

"Wow. France, huh?" Ed whistles low.

Chungpu smiles. "Yes. Very different, but a culinary delight. Though the sushi is terrible!" He chuckles.

"How long did you cook for Yamamoto-san?" Ed asks.

"On and off for many years. She discovered me, some might say, when I was working in a tiny *izakaya* that specialized in noodles. She told me she could see my potential, that she liked my flair, and took me in. It took many attempts to perfect her mother's lamb shank recipe, but I got it down to a fine art, and ever since then she's been putty in my hands. I'll make sure you know how to create it in just the same way." He winks at Ed, nudging him conspiratorially in the ribs. Chef Chungpu has nudged Ed! He can't believe this is his life.

"I suppose, thanks to Hazeline, the lamb shank became my signature dish of sorts. She told me nobody made it better except for, of course, her late mother."

Ed nods, understanding the challenge and the sentimental importance of this dish. He has to get it right.

"The most important part, of course, is the meat," Chungpu begins, gesturing to a slab of lamb on the counter. "It all starts with the perfect cut, the right amount of fat, the ideal weight and texture. You can't . . . how do Americans say it . . ." He pauses for a moment, frowning at the ceiling. "Ah! Polish a shit!" he exclaims with a smile, the phrase coming back to him.

Ed laughs. He likes Chef Chungpu, and for the first time he feels at total ease in this house. Chungpu is exactly as he comes across on television—charming, affable, and very entertaining.

"Tell me, Ed, have you cooked much? What's your experience look like?" Chungpu asks, suddenly serious, arms folded.

"I admit, not much. Especially compared to you!" Ed says.

"Well, we all start somewhere. Hazeline must have sensed the same hunger for success in you that she did in me," Chungpu says.

Hunger for success . . . Ed has never thought about it like that.

"I just hope you know what you're getting into," Chungpu adds, his tone suddenly serious, his eyes tinged with concern.

"Oh, I'll be fine!" Ed laughs nervously, struck by how much Chungpu's warning sounds like Nakamura's earlier.

"Right. Let's get stuck in, then. The meat is from just above the knee joint, so there are many of these sinewy fibers, you see." Chungpu gestures at the streaks of white running through the red flesh, the translucent webbing that seems to stretch over parts. "It may not be as fancy as a rack of lamb, but it is the most flavorful when cooked slowly and carefully. You cook it with love until it falls apart, juicy and tender," he continues. "You know Agawa-san?" he asks, looking at Ed expectantly.

Ed shakes his head dumbly.

"Best butcher this side of Tokyo. Nobody can beat Agawa-san's cuts. You go, you say Chungpu sent you for Yamamoto lamb shank, they will give you the perfect cut," Chungpu instructs, wagging his finger at Ed, who dutifully notes the name.

"You need very little cooking. You let the meal cook itself, you let the lamb come to flourish on its own," Chungpu says sternly, covering the meat with olive oil and seasoning. "It must marinate, soak up the flavors of everything, and just sit and grow into itself," he explains, showing Ed how to rub the seasoning in to ensure an even coating.

Ed has a go himself, his hands quickly slippery and shiny from the oil as he massages it into the meat, grains of salt clinging to the wrinkles in his hand.

While the lamb browns in the oven, Chungpu teaches Ed how to make the sauce. A mixture of colorful, carefully diced vegetables, flour, seasonings, and red wine. "It must be *this* red wine. Yamamoto-san has many bottles in the cellar, she has it imported from Britain. It is the exact wine her mother used." Chungpu holds the bottle up and Ed tries to commit the label to memory. "Shit for drinking, good for lamb shank," Chungpu warns with a shake of his finger.

Ed wonders if he was to use a different wine, whether Hazeline would truly notice. But if she cares enough to import it from her mother's birthplace, he will make the effort to use it.

Once the sauce is finished, they pour it over the meat and Ed hastily scribbles the timings and the temperatures for each stage in his little chef's notebook.

"Now, we wait, and magic will happen." Chungpu smiles. Nothing about the recipe is difficult, but it's clear that Hazeline is very specific about the quantities. It requires a pinch more salt than Ed would normally use, and some of the spices are a little unexpected, but nothing is too complex or painstaking. It's not too challenging for Ed, and he feels reassured that he should be able to replicate this dish perfectly if ever asked.

He begins to wipe down the countertops, working easily in tandem with Chungpu, who clearly knows the space like the back of his hand. Ed sweeps some fallen onion-skin flakes on the floor into a dustpan and goes to the bin. When he opens the lid, he pauses. At the top of the almost-full can are what look like teeth. He frowns, and leans down closer to the bin to try to get a better look. Strange creamy shards, and a couple that appear whole. They look human, blunt and wide, lightly stained with brown in areas. It's almost as though someone has put a handful of human teeth into a mortar and pestle and ground them into splinters.

"Everything all right?"

Ed jumps, Chungpu behind him, frowning.

"There's something in the bin. It looks like teeth," Ed admits, laughing to show he knows it sounds ridiculous.

Chungpu peers in. "Ah, dried fish bones." He smiles.

Ed immediately feels idiotic and empties his dustpan.

After they've cleaned all the dishes and countertops, the two sit at the window seats companionably with cups of matcha tea.

"Where in France do you work now?" Ed asks, taking a small sip.

"I have my own restaurant I was invited to open by an investor," Chungpu says proudly. "East Asian and French fusion dishes. If you're ever in Paris, you must visit. It is called Petite Etoile Agneau," he adds.

"I'm not sure I'll remember that name," Ed admits, unsure how to spell it to make a note.

"It means 'Little Lamb Star.'" Chungpu smiles. "It is what Hazeline called me, and stuck! I would never be where I am today if it weren't for her. I'd probably still be tossing a wok in the noodle joint."

"I'm guessing there's a lot of lamb on the menu?" Ed asks.

"Some. The lamb dishes are our specialty," Chungpu says with a smile.

"And you like Paris? You don't miss home?" Ed asks, pleased to have someone in this house with normal social cues to speak to.

Chungpu shrugs. "I left China when I was very young. I miss Japan, of course. But I visit when I can, and I am still enjoying the beauty and novelty of Paris. But it is very dirty, and the people are very loud and abrasive compared to here," he admits.

Ed thinks of the small, rough estate outside London where he grew up, and of the kids who would shove and shout in the streets and try to intimidate anyone who walked past them into buying them beers and cigarettes. "Yes, Europeans can be very different," he says. "I haven't been to Paris, but I imagine it's nicer than where I come from."

"You have not been to Paris, yet you came all the way to Tokyo?" Chungpu says, surprised. "What made you travel such a distance?"

Ed chews on his lip, considering the question. Finally, he admits, "I think I was just searching for something more. I needed to know there was a world that I wasn't a part of, but that I could assimilate into."

"Ah." Chungpu nods knowingly. "You did not fit in at home?"

Ed shrugs. "I suppose I didn't, not really. I didn't feel like it was where I belonged."

"And you feel like you belong in Tokyo?" Chungpu asks.

Ed thinks of his untidy home, of the pachinko parlors, of the cramped bus journeys to work. Then he thinks of the last time he was here, soaking in a salt-filled tub, looking out into the surrounding woodland. "I think I feel like I belong here, at Yamamoto-san's," he says.

"Ah, yes. It's easy to feel at home in such beauty," Chungpu agrees, looking out toward the pond.

"What's it like, being famous?" Ed asks after a small pause.

Chungpu throws his head back and laughs. "Everyone wants to know that," he says. "But the truth is, it's nothing like what they say."

"Annoying and suffocating? Claustrophobic and boundaryless?" Ed guesses.

"No, quite the opposite. It's really quite something, to think that I will always be recognized, remembered, perhaps even cherished," Chungpu admits, his voice quiet.

They are startled by a shrill beep. The timer is going off for the lamb, and Ed realizes that his tea has long gone cold. They have been conversing for much longer than he thought.

They return to the oven and lift the tinfoil, releasing a steam which smells meaty and hearty. They take the lamb out and put it on the hob. "We let it rest while we make the rice," Chungpu says. The pair set to work, quickly throwing together some steamed rice, and then Chungpu carefully transfers some of the lamb and juices onto the rice bed. He taps the lamb on one side and the meat falls apart, sliding off the bone like a silk robe falling off a woman's body; tantalizing and seductive. Ed wets his lips.

The kitchen doors slide open and there is Hazeline, a huge smile on her face.

"Oh! It smells like home!" she exclaims joyously, rushing across the oversized kitchen to the humble dish.

LAMB SHANK

The evening is still. Ed, Hazeline, Chungpu, and Rodrick all enjoy the lamb shank dinner together, the four of them sitting around the table like a haphazard family unit. Hazeline gushes over the recipe, delighted at every bite, and her plate is scraped clean by the end. "Just like Mummy used to make," she sighs.

Afterward they bid goodbye to Chungpu, and Ed finds he is sad to see him leave. As soon as he is gone, the atmosphere regains its odd, unsettling nature, with Rodrick silent and unemotional while Hazeline disappears into the depths of the house. Ed attempts conversation with Rodrick to see if there is any chance of replicating the easy-going rapport he had with Chungpu, but after fifteen minutes of stilted conversation in which the housekeeper replies mostly monosyllabically while spritzing his bonsai tree, Ed gives up and takes himself to the garden for a stroll.

He hasn't walked around the garden properly yet, only admired it from the decking, so the first thing he does is go right over to the pond and squat down, peering at all the koi. They assume he's brought food, and swarm around him, their little mouths opening and closing in silent o's. "Sorry, guys," Ed says, standing. "No grub for you. Don't think you'd be into lamb shank."

He continues around the garden, passing benches, flower beds, rounded shrubs, and stone lanterns. The narrow paths are shingled, with wooden stepping planks, and they all seem to curve and flow into each other carefully. Before long, he finds himself heading down a small path which takes him to the edge of the home, looking out into the dense woodland. To his right is that outbuilding, the one he spotted from his room earlier today. Curious, he goes toward it, realizing that on its other side is a small, private driveway. There's a van parked there, and the logo on the side reads *PRIVATE MEDICARE*.

Ed approaches the front door and finds that it's been left wide open. He hesitates for a moment, but his curiosity wins and he steps into the small building. The air has a strange smell, a mix of bleach and air freshener. He takes a few steps in and notices a gentle and consistent beeping sound. He edges toward the room the noise is coming from and peers inside. There is a beautiful young woman lying in a bed. She has her eyes closed, and looks frail, her skin almost translucent. She's hooked up to several machines and has a mask over her face. It's a heart monitor that is beeping, letting everyone close enough to hear it know she is resting and well. She is safe here. The room is stark and strangely technical against the natural forestry—a classic hospital room setup—but someone has done their best to decorate it for Suki, and Ed sees that Nakamura has framed their wedding portrait and hung it in front of the bed for her to look at when awake. Beside her is a vase filled with fresh flowers, and a small portable radio.

Suddenly, Ed feels horrible watching this stranger sleep, and turns to leave. It's when he does this that he notices a cupboard door with a large sign on it which reads, *Keep Out! Authorized Personnel Only.*

He looks around, chewing on his top lip. He hovers a hand over the door handle.

"What are you doing?"

Ed leaps out of his skin, and rubs the back of his neck, embarrassed to have been caught snooping. It's Nakamura.

"I—I'm sorry! I was taking a walk around the garden when I heard the beeping of the heart monitor. I only wanted to see what it was, I'm so sorry," he explains, his hand snapped back to his side and away from the door.

Nakamura is standing still, but eventually he nods slowly. "Well, yes. This is our home, and that is my wife, Suki. But really, Ed-san, you shouldn't be hanging around here. Not only because it's my private home, but there are spaces here that Hazeline deems to be off-limits, such as the door you were about to open," he says pointedly.

Ed flushes crimson.

"Curiosity is not a virtue here, Ed." Nakamura marches forward, flings the door open, and reveals rows and rows of expensive medical equipment, medicine bottles, and surgical tools.

Ed looks at his feet shamefully.

"Is this what you wanted to see? Cancer medication? Medical supplies?" Nakamura shakes his head sadly, then shuts the door. "Hazeline won't be very happy if she catches you snooping around," he says. "You really don't want to get on her bad side, or discover something you're not ready to understand."

"I'm very sorry," Ed says, bowing in apology while walking backward, toward the front door and garden. He doesn't look back, and hurries back to the main house before Hazeline catches him and calls off their arrangement.

It's 2 A.M. when Ed is awoken by a sound, startled out of his dreamless sleep. He sits up in bed, confused, and squints toward the window. Now, straining to hear something, he can hear nothing at all, and the unnatural quietness makes him feel uneasy. At his own home, there's always background noise, regardless of the hour. Cars driving past, neighbors creaking above, plumbing groaning, even Sayuri's deep breaths of sleep have become part of Ed's comforting nighttime symphony. But here, there is nothing. As though the house is in some sort of vortex. He finds he needs the bathroom and stands, quickly draping a robe around himself. He slides the bedroom door open and quietly pads out onto the landing, trying to remember which way the washroom is. Thankfully he soon finds it and relieves himself quietly. But as he returns to his room, he hears a sound. It's strange, animalistic and low, guttural and grunting. He pauses, his eyes darting in the darkness. There it is again! He's definitely not imagining it, and this time it sounds like a husky, strange bark. It's coming from behind the door beside the bathroom. Rodrick's room. Ed moves as though in slow motion, a strange creeping crawl toward the door, which he can see is open just a sliver. He doesn't even dare breathe, his heartbeat pounding in his eardrums.

He tilts himself forward so that he's almost pressed against the door, his eye squinting to focus in the darkness of the room. That's when he sees them: two shapes, moving in sync, the sounds coming again. With great horror, he realizes what he's looking at, and manages to swallow the sound of his gasp as he reels backward, away from the door. With wide eyes he silently scrabbles back to his bedroom, crawls under the sheets and tries to make sense of what he has witnessed: Hazeline and Rodrick, naked, hunched over like gargoyles in the bed together, devouring the leftover lamb shanks, shoveling flesh and gristle and bone past their greasy lips with sticky, bloody hands and sharp teeth.

MAIN

A TUMULTUOUS PLACE

Morning breaks, the hazy orange light dripping into the bedroom in silken streams as Ed blearily replays the night before in his mind. It was a bizarre and animalistic scene, something so intimate and carnal but also rabid and foul. He lay awake afterward, listening to the silence of the house cloaking him in his room until sleep took him, and revisiting the memory in his nightmares made the bottom of his guts roil with discomfort until he woke drenched in sweat. The dream was hazy on waking, but he recalled Hazeline and Rodrick leering at him with pitch-black eyes, dragging him over to join their naked feast, and then his teeth had begun to crumble in his mouth, filling his gullet until he was choking on the dental splinters.

He does not want to go downstairs and serve breakfast to these people. He wants to go home to his wife, cuddle his baby, and never eat lamb shank again. It takes him quite some time to muster the bravado needed to leave his room, but he makes it to the kitchen where, to his great dismay, Rodrick is preparing the table.

"Good morning," the housekeeper says, without looking up. As resigned as always, clean and tidy, with soap-smelling hands. This version of Rodrick is worlds away from the creature Ed witnessed last night shoveling scraps of meat into his mouth, eyes rolled back in bliss, jaw hung half-open.

"Uh, yes, good morning, Bauer-san," Ed replies quickly, blinking like a rabbit in headlights and looking anywhere to avoid making eye contact with Rodrick, flashbacks of the housekeeper's tall, lanky frame hunched over the tray of meat making Ed feel distinctly unwell.

"Did you sleep well?" Rodrick asks, his voice an uninterested drawl.

"Yes," Ed squeaks, turning away and putting the kettle on, his heart beating quickly. "Did . . . did you?"

"It was fine," Rodrick replies. Monotone. No sly sarcasm hidden in the tone, no twinkle of a secret in his eye. Ed frowns to himself. In the light of day, here in the kitchen, what he saw last night doesn't just seem out of character—it seems almost impossible. Perhaps it was all just a dream? Though it felt so real—the low-pitched grunt, the bathroom trip, the bedroom scene . . .

The kettle has started to scream when Hazeline joins them, in a new neutral outfit, soft melts of fabric draping over her in warm beige.

"Good morning, gentlemen," she sings. "Rodrick, I'd like a coffee, please. Ed, my friend will be arriving here at ten and we would like brunch served at 10:45 A.M., please," she instructs. Rodrick silently makes her coffee, and no knowing looks or secret eye contact pass between them as Ed was prepared for. No, it must have been a dream, a nightmarish imaginary scene birthed from the stress of his debts. He takes out a carton of eggs, deciding to make *omurice* for brunch, and a vision hits him: Hazeline and Rodrick, raw egg yolk dripping from their maws, the clear, gloopy parts webbing between fingers as they lick and lap at them, naked, spines protruding as they hunch over together.

"Ed, are you well? You look terrible," Hazeline says candidly, pulling him back to reality. He blinks the vision away and finds his boss peering at him, a concerned frown on her face. "Will you be all right to cook this brunch?" she asks.

"Yes. Yes, sorry. I just didn't sleep too well," he stutters.

"I thought you said you slept fine?" Rodrick interrupts from the other side of the kitchen where he's cutting Hazeline's sweetener with the precision of a samurai.

Ed flares with irritation. Rodrick, who so rarely bothers to speak, is pointing out Ed's conflicting statements now, at a time when he's clearly flustered, a film of sweat clinging to his forehead despite the mild temperature.

"I had nightmares, if you must know," he snaps. Rodrick has the decency to look embarrassed and takes to spritzing his bastard bonsai tree again while the coffee machine gurgles into action.

"The inner mind can be a tumultuous place," Hazeline remarks. "We sometimes do not even realize things are bothering us at all until we close our eyes and visit dreamland. Then our inner conscience springs all manner of shame and guilt on us, like a showreel of all our failures as human beings. Pay no mind to it, Ed, petal. It's just a dream, and you're in the land of the living now."

He looks at her, and she's smiling gently at him. Suddenly, the idea of this elegant, vastly wealthy woman being in a curled squat, naked, with her housekeeper, huffing slimy meat with her bare hands in the middle of the night, seems so utterly preposterous that Ed lets out a chuckle. How stupid he was! How could he have ever thought that wild dream to have been real? He had been half-asleep, disoriented, and could have been pissing into a cereal bowl for all he knew. No, there was no way that what he thought he saw last night was real.

. . .

Hazeline's friend turns out to be an old pal from her boarding school days, a woman called Octavia Harris-Ward, whose upturned nose matches her name perfectly. From the moment Ed hears her snooty, shrill voice echoing from the entryway as she oohs and aahs over Hazeline, he knows she is not a woman whose company he will enjoy.

Hazeline brings Octavia through to the kitchen to introduce her to Ed. She's teetering in silly high heels and is wearing a short, tailored black dress. Diamonds sparkle in her ears and Ed reckons just one of those rocks would pay his rent for a year.

"Your own personal chef? How Kardashian of you," Octavia laughs delightedly.

"I don't watch reality TV. Do I take this as a compliment?" Hazeline asks.

"Oh, gosh, no, nor do I. So lowbrow, isn't it?" Octavia quickly says in a hurried bleat, which immediately gives away the fact that she is, most likely, the Kardashian family's number one fan.

She then sticks out her gnarled, veiny hand to Ed before hesitating, pulling it back, and looking to Hazeline. "Do I shake hands, or bow?"

"Mr. Cook hails from London. He will be happy to do either," Hazeline says, making Ed feel like a pedigree dog able to spin on command.

"Oh. Lovely! Did you fly out specifically for this job?" Octavia asks him, her voice effecting a grating vocal fry that could be from class or age. Ed saves her the difficulty of the choice of greeting by bowing his head a fraction, which he notes she does not return.

"No, I already lived in Tokyo. My wife is Japanese," Ed explains, his voice flat.

"Married! No dipping your ink into this squid then, Hazeline, he'll be missed by someone!" Octavia shrieks, laughing loudly.

Hazeline smiles tightly. "I wouldn't ever do such a thing. Ed is a wonderful employee and only ever totally professional."

Ed flushes scarlet, shifting uncomfortably and turning his back on them to face the hob, where he shifts some pan handles and waits for them to leave. Finally, they do, Octavia's voice still echoing around the room. "God, I am absolutely starving, my jetlag has just ravished me! I hope that mail-order groom can cook."

Ed wants to smash her skull in with a frying pan. It's one thing to disrespect him, a fraudulent chef, but another entirely to disrespect his marriage. Despite the secrets he's hidden to protect his wife, his marriage is the only real thing in his life. His tether. His chopping has become more violent as he hacks wildly at an onion when he feels Rodrick's presence looming behind him.

"She is tactless. Don't let her get under your skin," the housekeeper says, voice low.

"She's rude," Ed hisses.

"She is. But she is a business friend of Hazeline and she will be gone as quickly as she arrived. She comes and goes hastily usually and, if I'm honest, I think Madame sees her out of duty rather than true friendship at this stage."

"Because they've known each other so long?" Ed asks.

"Yes, mostly. A friendship of so long means they are entangled by shared secrets, shared tastes, some of which I imagine Hazeline would rather did not become public with the Japanese media," Rodrick says in a hushed tone.

Ah. Societal scandal. Blackmail. Now it makes sense. "I understand," Ed growls. "But if she speaks of my wife again in front of me, I shall have to say something, employee or not."

"Sometimes we have to put up with the vermin our loved ones pity and bring into the house," Rodrick murmurs, before leaving Ed to finish his cooking alone.

. . .

Ten forty-five comes around and Ed delivers a platter of crisp, fresh fruits, gooey, savory *omurice,* and sweet, fluffy soufflé pancakes. A simple, quick brunch menu full of flavor.

"Beautiful, Ed, thank you," Hazeline says, sitting down at the table and eyeing the fruit platter.

Octavia, Ed notices, says nothing. He doesn't mind. He doesn't care for her comments and she is not the woman he needs to please with this meal. He excuses himself, retreating from the table and cleaning what can be tidied away quietly, so as not to disturb their conversation.

"Quite a simple spread," he hears Octavia remark.

"Not everything has to be a big show," Hazeline retorts.

"God, of course, no. Not at all. Simple is often best," Octavia trills, slipping fruit into her mouth.

Ed rolls his eyes when she's not looking.

"I have a potential new bit of business for you," Octavia says, her voice lowering slightly. Ed keeps his eyes on the chopping board, which he sweeps distractedly, his ears pricked.

"Oh?" Hazeline drawls, popping a berry into her mouth.

"American," Octavia adds, her eyebrows raised in emphasis. "Ripe and ready."

"We don't usually mess around with internationals. Importing is a messy business and there's plenty of produce available on my own soil. Not to mention, I've not had any good cargo from you in a while. I thought you were out of the game," Hazeline replies cattily.

"My tastes change with the seasons, darling, and you know I love a challenge. Besides, I never turn down a good business deal!"

"Give me some figures," Hazeline says.

Octavia glances indiscreetly at Ed. "Are you sure now is the time?"

"Anything you say to me can be said in front of my staff."

"My, my. Surprising as always. You must have them trained well!" Octavia smiles.

Ed feels increasingly uncomfortable and confused about where this conversation is going, or why Hazeline seems to think that he's happy or loyal enough to hear the intricacies of her business deals.

"Okay. Well. Just the usual, when it comes to the Americans. A-grade cattle, a prime cut but in need of a little fattening. It would be a very quick turnaround—the seller is working to a deadline. Big and expensive operation coming up, they need to sell before that. Presumably to afford it. You know American healthcare: a tragic business."

"Yes, barbaric," Hazeline agrees.

"In any case, the seller thinks that without this operation, his partner won't survive. So he needs a quick sale. Very desperate, and will probably accept a lowball offer," Octavia says, her voice dropping lower still. Ed takes a step closer, desperate to keep on hearing.

"The farmer is willing to trade the calf for the money to keep his cow. Sad," Hazeline sighs. "I suppose there could be room for another." She shakes her head sadly, takes a deep drag of her cigarette. "The poor are so desperate." She picks at a piece of apple and tosses it to the floor. Momo rushes over and greedily gobbles it up, tail wagging happily.

"Desperation is what keeps us fed, watered, and wealthy," Octavia reminds her.

Hazeline leans back in her chair and drops a star-shaped fruit into her mouth, chewing carefully.

"You know I don't like to dally with the Yanks," she warns.

"I know, I know. I just figured this was a good opportunity, that you'd rather see the cards laid out than not know of them at all," Octavia says. "Also, it's rare to get one ready to go. It'll save you the time and money of rearing."

"Hmmm. Yes. Well, it has been a while, I admit. Okay. Okay, but you know the rules. You're the middle woman with the money, I don't want any links to me here. Cash only. You disappear today. I don't want to see you again for a while. Send the arrival date to my PO box under the name we used last time, and I'll be sure to send my driver to collect on the day from Haneda airport."

"Of course. Glad to be doing business with you again." Octavia grins, lifting her glass to cheers Hazeline.

The cryptic way they are speaking reminds Ed of the Yakuza, and it is not the first time he's felt unsafe in the Yamamoto fortress.

He can barely wait to see Octavia take her leave, and decides that he has absolutely no desire to know more details about what they were speaking of. He feels irritated that Hazeline found it appropriate to talk business in front of him, especially when it sounds illegal. Is it another test of his loyalty? The less he knows, the better. He is ready to wash his hands of the entire day.

DINNER IS READY

After leaving Hazeline's home, Ed struggles to shake his discomfort at her conversation with Octavia. It clings to him like an itchy sweatshirt, and without understanding the full context of what he heard, it's an itch that Ed is unable to scratch. Their dealings sounded dodgy, illegal, and possibly dark. And what does he really know about Hazeline Yamamoto, anyway? What does *anyone* really know about her? Since the drama surrounding her marriage, she's kept well out of the spotlight. And before then, she was only known for what she wore and where she partied, what celebrity circles she was in. Aside from her late husband, Rodrick is perhaps the closest person to her, and does he even get the real Hazeline?

Ed opens his phone and types her name into the search bar. He's hit by hundreds of images of Hazeline in her younger years, looking glamorous and oh so thin, many of them on the arm of Botan, who was handsome and confident-looking with salt-and-pepper hair. Then, a sentence catches his eye. It is a comment on a Reddit forum dedicated to Japanese socialites. He clicks through.

I went to school with Hazeline, back in the UK. At Saint Helena's. She was only around for a year before she returned to Japan, but she was a bit of an oddball. Obviously had an ED of some sort, and said that in Japan, nobody eats like we do in England. She didn't have too many friends, she seemed sort of lonely. She could have fit in with the popular crowd if she'd wanted to, because she was thin and rich even by boarding school standards, but she was really quiet and reserved. Maybe that was from growing up in Japan, I don't know. She only really came out of her shell when she got to talk about doing something nobody else did, like when her mum somehow got her a ticket to the Grammys. That was the first time I saw her come out of her shell a bit, telling us all what it was like and describing all the singers for us. I think she liked that it was something we all had to take her word on, because she was the only person to have been there. It was weird seeing her in the papers later as an adult, looking so confident and grown-up.

Ed tries to imagine Hazeline as an awkward, skinny teenager, too shy to speak to others but desperate to be part of the most exclusive of elite society, even then. He feels a little sorry for her, and also worried about the struggles Kaori might have growing up mixed-race in a country that only sees Japanese, or Not. Will she feel tall, or broad, or wide? He's relieved that at least she has inherited Sayuri's thick, dark hair, which will help her fit in with her friends at school, and not his own mousy blond waves. He never wants her to feel like an outcast for being different, the way Hazeline seems to.

Ed chews his lip and puts his phone away. He only has more worries now than he did before, this time about his own daughter and what experiences might wait for her in high school. He feels his body begin to search for something to take his mind off the few days he's had, something to distract him. To make him feel in-the-moment. He takes out his phone again, but this time, fingers moving on autopilot, he reinstalls a sports betting site he deleted a few weeks ago. He has a little cash at the moment, after all. He's forgotten that, just a few weeks ago, he felt actual relief at having no money in his bank account. Having nothing to gamble away, nothing tying him to his addiction, outweighed the stress of having to hide from Sayuri that he had frittered everything away. He tries not to think too deeply about what he's doing; he'll just put a couple of hundred yen down, nothing big, just a little treat to himself for continuing to play the role of chef, for paying off his first payment with the Yakuza on time. It's about taking part, not the win. After all, it's only a couple of hundred. Even if he loses, it's not really losing, is it? It's more like . . . paying to play an online game.

But as soon as he submits his bet payment, he feels . . . empty. There's no rush of excitement or anticipation like he used to get; instead, just shame and guilt for going back to something that has ruined his life so badly. Why is he unable to quit? To keep his paychecks safely stored away in his bank account?

He ends up putting two thousand yen on a horse race. The horse he needs to win is called Kuro Kaminari, or Black Thunder, and if it wins Ed will take home ten thousand yen. Enough for a fancy meal at home with Sayuri, and some pretty flowers to surprise her with. If he loses? Well, it's just the cost of the train commute to Hazeline's, which he isn't paying because Nakamura picks him up. This is how he justifies it in his head, trying to shake the guilt away.

It doesn't work. He spends the rest of the journey thinking of all the ways he could have cheered himself up and distracted himself from Hazeline's world that don't involve money, or gambling. He could have taken Kaori to the playground. He could have made love to Sayuri. He could have cooked dinner for the family, surprised his hard-working wife with a night off. He could have gone to a karaoke bar, sunk a few beers and sung away his troubles. Instead he's pissed away money on a horse with a clichéd name. He feels more miserable than ever as Nakamura drives him home, knee subconsciously jiggling in anticipation of the race results.

. . .

"How was your night? Did you sleep well?" his wife asks as he walks in the door. She kisses him on the cheek and mutes the television, which is playing a drama series she likes to watch when she has half an hour to relax. In the corner, Kaori is playing with the stuffed dog Ed bought her, a piece of rope tied around its neck as a makeshift lead, which she is using to yank the toy around behind her. Ed thinks it looks like a noose. He scoops Kaori up in his arms and she squeals in delight, gripping on to his shoulders, still clutching the floppy little dog.

"How is my favorite girl?" he asks, nuzzling into her with his nose. "And how is Little Inu?" he asks the dog, looking at its small button eyes. Kaori laughs happily, then thrashes to be put back down. He wonders if he has done something wrong, upset her in some way. But no, she's a toddler, she's always wriggling to get away from Sayuri, too. He's not a bad father. *He is not a bad father.*

"I didn't sleep so well this time," Ed admits, turning to his wife, who is still waiting for his reply. "I had a really weird dream. It made me feel . . . well, I don't know. It kept me up for a while," he admits.

"A nightmare?" Sayuri asks. "What about?"

Ed considers telling her he doesn't remember, because saying it out loud it will sound so silly. But they have enough secrets between them, including the looming horse race this evening, so he decides to share. "Well, Hazeline and Rodrick—you know, the weird, silent housekeeper? They were in her bed eating the leftovers from the lamb shank I cooked, with their hands. And they were doing it"—he lowers his voice—"*naked,* and making these weird animal noises."

To his surprise, Sayuri bursts out into peals of laughter. "How bizarre! Did you eat something strange before bed?"

Ed immediately feels stupid, and brings a hand to his face, trying to force a smile for her. "No. I know it sounds weird, and kind of funny if you don't know them, but it was creepy and it felt *real.*"

"Well, Ed, I think if your biggest nightmare relating to Hazeline is that she eats your food naked in bed with her hands, you're probably doing a good job," Sayuri tells him, wiping a tear from the corner of her eye.

"Yes, I suppose you're right," he says slowly, and though he still feels unsettled by the dream, seeing his wife cry with laughter makes him rethink it as a ridiculously dramatic hallucination, rather than a dark and sinister nightmare.

"I was about to start preparing dinner," Sayuri says, shutting the TV off. "Will you keep the baby occupied?"

"I can cook dinner tonight if you like," Ed offers, thinking back to his mental list of distractions on the train. Who knows? Maybe the cooking-dinner distraction will even lead to the making-love distraction.

"No, no, you've cooked enough the last couple of days, I imagine. And I'm tired. Kaori has been very bolshie the last twenty-four hours, and I could use a little grown-up alone time," she says.

Perhaps not.

Ed nods, scooping Kaori up and tossing her merrily onto the sofa. "Playtime!" he bellows, tickling her stomach wildly. She shrieks and kicks and Sayuri smiles before leaving to go to the kitchen, where Ed can hear cupboards opening and closing as she searches for ingredients.

"Something simple tonight—just some grilled fish and vegetables, perhaps?" she calls out.

"Sounds delicious!" Ed replies, and he feels like for the first time in ages he is falling into a comfortable, easy routine with his wife. By the time dinner is almost ready, Kaori has taken out more teddies to join Little Inu and has lined them all up, talking in gibberish to herself. Ed goes to turn the TV on to watch the races, but realizes that Sayuri will hear it. He should be playing with Kaori, perhaps doing silly voices for some of the teddies, not watching the horse racing. So instead he keeps refreshing his phone, waiting for the live updates impatiently. It isn't a lot of money up for grabs; he doesn't know why he cares so much. He just does.

Finally, the results refresh and the race has been run. Kuro Kaminari has placed fourth. The winning horse is Sakura Senshi, Cherry Blossom Warrior. Dammit! Ed puts his phone down and stews on the sofa, his brain consumed with the loss, and the anger he feels at himself for betting again—for losing two thousand yen that could have been spent on literally anything instead of putting it in the pockets of the big gambling corporations. With one click of a button he sent his money into thin air, never to be seen again. And why? To distract him from a stupid dream and an off-putting conversation he'd overheard his boss having? What he truly wants is Hazeline's financial lifestyle, and it doesn't take a genius to know that Hazeline Yamamoto has not got where she is today by seeing her money disappear on risky bets and useless purchases. Everything she spends her money on is probably some sort of investment.

Ed feels stupid and tired. He wants to make that money back tenfold, and for once he has the clarity of mind to know that the easiest and quickest way to do so is by cooking up food for a ridiculous woman living in a mansion, not by putting his wallet in the center of a game being played by other men.

He turns the TV on, and quickly flicks the channel from the horse racing to a cooking show.

During dinner, Sayuri picks up on his mood. She has always been able to do this, as though she has a telescope that gives her a view right into the crevices of his brain, the fat folds and swirls. "What's wrong?" she asks.

Ed stiffens briefly, unable to tell her he's gambled again. Instead, he asks, "Do you ever worry about Kaori growing up mixed-race here? That kids will tease her when she's older, or she'll feel as though she doesn't belong?"

Sayuri puts her chopsticks down and purses her lips, carefully thinking before answering, as always. Eventually, she gives him a small smile. "I think she will be even more beautiful for her differences. She will not be mixed, she will be *both.* Both Japanese and British. Kids can be mean for many reasons; they find excuses to tease others. If the worst thing we have to worry about is Kaori being teased for being so special, then I think she'll be just fine."

Ed pauses, amazed by his wife's ability to give him a whole new viewpoint in such a short amount of time.

"You don't think she'll have struggles? Or be seen as *gaijin*?"

She shrugs, a small, graceful tug of the shoulders. "She's born and raised here, will be fluent in the language. If they see her as *gaijin,* that reflects more on them than on her. Besides, times are changing, Ed. Things are getting more liberal here with every generation. I think she will be just as loved and welcomed by everyone she meets as she deserves to be. It's not bad to be different, and Japanese people are curious about that now. Excited, even. When was the last time you felt discriminated against?"

Ed stops to think. "It's been a long time," he admits.

"See! Changing times. People are more open now about race and sexuality. There are newer, different things to worry about in your daughter's future."

"Like what?"

"Social media," Sayuri says seriously.

Ed smiles.

HUNGRY FOR LITTLE KIDS

Ed looks out over the balcony onto Hazeline's garden, where an army of workers are currently erecting a large tepee, several firepits, and stringing fairy lights around. Behind them, the foliage is a melding of ocher and rust. Hazeline has asked Ed to cater a wilderness charity event this weekend, which seems to involve a lot of children coming to stay at her house to camp and learn survival skills. This will be the easiest couple of days' work ever, with Ed effectively chaperoning some bonfire barbecuing and perhaps throwing some snacks their way if they get hungry. He isn't sure just how much they'll be learning about real-world survival on the edge of some woodland with fairy lights illuminating their way, but he is intrigued to see how involved Hazeline will be in all of it—whether it is a checklist chore to humble-brag about at dinner parties or whether she is actually invested in the kids.

When he goes downstairs, there is a lively energy and the house is in full swing. Momo is skittish in apprehension of the day ahead, occasionally giving small whines, and Hazeline is outside barking out orders with gusto.

"No, I need more rugs in the tepee please, this isn't Glastonbury, for God's sake! No, no, don't put the firepit there, do you want these children to lose a limb?"

"She's in her element, isn't she?" Nakamura says. Ed didn't hear him come into the kitchen, and the two men watch Hazeline wrangling the staff outside together for a moment, Momo perched on the decking to watch from a safe distance. "Does she do this often?" Ed asks. "Host children and turn her garden into a glamping site, I mean?"

"The kids do come here for camping every now and again. Often they go to the lakes instead, or the sites at the base of Fujisan for fishing opportunities. They do that much more regularly, but I think Hazeline likes to be involved every now and again, to catch up with them and see how they're getting on."

"Can't quite imagine her slumming it in a tent," Ed chuckles, remembering his early camping trips with Sayuri, both of them struggling to light the fire then giving up and going to a local café instead.

"No, well, that's why she likes it when they come here. This way she can retire to her bedroom while they hunker down in their sleeping bags," Nakamura chuckles.

"What are the kids like? What sort of a charity is this?" Ed asks, comparing it to the Duke of Edinburgh Award back home in his head. All he really remembers from that is trekking around some National Trust woodland sporting a large rucksack on his back and trying to work out how to use a compass and map, before giving up, cheating, and asking a local dog-walker for directions instead.

Nakamura makes a strange sound—a sort of sucking in on his teeth. "The kids are fine. I think they come from quite tough backgrounds, but I don't really know. I try not to ask too much or mingle with them, you know? Just pick them up, drop them off, do my job. I have to focus on Suki." He glances in the direction of his annex, where his wife is fighting for her life. There's a beat of silence, and Nakamura shuffles. "You know, it's not too late to back out," he whispers to Ed.

Ed turns. "Back out?"

Nakamura coughs awkwardly. "I just mean, before you're too . . . entangled. Emotionally, or otherwise."

"I don't really get what you mean," Ed says.

"Just, getting close to the kids and then learning more about them. It can be hard."

"Oh. Oh, right. No, I'll be fine," Ed assures him, though he's not really sure what Nakamura means. Ed wonders if perhaps because Nakamura is childless, he finds it difficult to be around them? Perhaps he's being reminded of what he and Suki cannot have together. "I mean, I won't get attached, you don't need to worry about me. I have enough trouble fathering one child," he admits.

"Trouble?" Nakamura asks.

Ed sighs, runs a hand through his hair and tries not to notice how thin it feels between his fingers. "I just always feel like I'm doing things the wrong way—or, I don't know, ruining her spirit somehow. I don't have any friends with kids here, and so I just constantly feel like everything I do is wrong."

"Does your wife help?"

"I'm embarrassed to admit to her how hard I find it all. It doesn't seem to come naturally. Even holding Kaori, I sometimes feel awkward. I get afraid that she'll die in the night, that I've laid her down wrong or something. She's not even a baby anymore, but the thought still comes. Less regularly now, at least. And if it isn't that, it's thinking of the future, of all the money I need to save to provide for her properly. I don't think it should be that way, should it?"

Nakamura smiles sadly. "I wouldn't know."

"I'm sorry."

"Don't be. I'm lucky to have Suki, and when she gets better, we can think of building our family. For now, she is more than enough."

Ed wonders if he should have waited a little longer with Sayuri before having Kaori, but he's not sure any amount of time would have prepared him for parenthood.

"So, what are you cooking?" Nakamura asks, slapping him on the back and breaking the tension.

Nakamura leaves that afternoon in a car Ed hasn't seen before—a large, child-friendly number with plenty of seats. When he returns, the kids explode out of it, joyful and excited, all of them wearing shorts, caps, and knitted jumpers, rucksacks and tents hauled between them. Ed is surprised at the variety; they appear to be of all different ages, ranging from very small to almost adult. There are also fewer than he thought there would be, based on all the commotion with the tepee and the firepits—there are only five.

Rodrick is leading them to the garden like a very stern Pied Piper, while Nakamura makes sure the car is emptied of all belongings. Ed hurries to get some water jugs filled, and brings them out for the children with some cups as they take in their surroundings. He is surprised to see Hazeline chatting with an older child, her hand on his arm in a rare gesture of affection.

"I don't want my tent too close to the trees in case of bears!" a little girl says, her eyes wide as she scans the treeline.

"Don't worry, Hiroshi will keep us safe," another small girl says, holding up a well-loved stuffed lion.

"Bears don't come this close to houses," the oldest boy says from where he is standing with Hazeline. He is as tall as Ed, and wiry and strong.

"Unless they're hungry for little kids!" a teenage boy says, holding up his arms and pulling a snarling face at the girls, who shriek delightedly.

Ed coughs, and they turn to look at him in unison. "I'm Ed, I'll be your chef," he says to them, bowing and offering the water.

"Speak to them in English, Ed, petal. It's good for them to learn, and they've been studying hard," Hazeline tells him.

"Ah. Okay. Well, nice to meet you," he says, switching to English.

"Nice to meet you," the oldest boy offers. "I'm Daiki."

The rest of the group follows suit. After Daiki is the younger teenage boy, Koji. There is a girl about Koji's age, Asuka. The two little girls are Hana, with the stuffed lion, and Aiko, who is too shy to introduce herself, so Hana does so on her behalf.

Ed smiles at Aiko in what he hopes is an encouraging way. "How old are you, Aiko?"

She still doesn't speak, but holds up seven fingers.

"Wow! Such a grown-up. Well, I hope you feel brave enough to say hello soon!"

She flushes and hides behind Asuka.

"Right!" Hazeline claps her hands. "It's getting dark now, so let's hop to it and get these tents up! Here, I'll help the girls," she says, already hustling over to Hana and Aiko's tent and pulling out some poles.

Ed takes this as his dismissal and retreats to the kitchen, where he watches in amazement as Hazeline erects the tent alongside the two girls, laughing and showing them the ropes as she goes. The three teenagers all have their own tents and manage just fine on their own, working quickly and efficiently. They are clearly not camping novices. Soon, he can only see Hazeline, who appears to be inspecting all their setups and warning them to keep the nets zipped shut to keep bugs out. Eventually, she marches back up to the house and busies herself picking up a bag of secret supplies, Rodrick in tow.

"Where are you off to? What would you like me to do regarding supper?" Ed asks her.

"We're going into the woods to teach them about plants and animals," Hazeline explains, tucking her feet into some boots and wedging a cap onto her head. "As for dinner, there's pheasant breasts and some whole fish ready in the fridge. We will only be a couple of hours. When we get back, I'd love you to show the kids how to cook over the campfire. Maybe make some of those repulsive s'more things that Americans love. They'll be excited to try something like that."

Ed can't believe how much he is being paid to hold some fish on sticks over a bonfire, but he smiles and waves Hazeline and Rodrick off, before returning to the kitchen to prepare the meat and sort out some rice and side salads. He is so busy working that he almost doesn't hear the scream coming from the woods.

YAMA UBA

Ed runs out into the forest without thinking, tripping over roots and uneven turf as he goes. His heart seems to be beating in his ears, but all he can think about is the little children, and what might have happened to one of them. He should have brought bear spray.

To his great relief, he finds the gaggle not very deep beyond the treeline, and the source of the scream is, unsurprisingly, the tiny Aiko. The kids are all standing together, Hazeline crouched beside a sobbing Aiko. The cause of the distress is clear. At the head of the throng stands Rodrick, and he is wielding some sort of homemade trap made from branches and twine. Inside it is a copper pheasant, feathers ruffled and eyes wide in fright. It seems disoriented and is smacking its head stupidly against the sides of the cage.

"What's going on?" Ed pants, out of breath.

"Ed, petal, really, there's no need for all this drama. You can go back to the house, no white knight needed. Aiko is just upset about the bird."

"What . . . what are you going to do to it?" Ed asks, wary. The chicken in the cone is all too vivid in his memory.

"We're teaching the kids how to make traps out of sticks and twine," Rodrick explains. "This one was made and placed out here yesterday by myself. It appears to work."

The pheasant squawks hysterically.

"It's cool!" Koji says, wielding a handful of branches.

"I want them to let the birdie go!" Aiko sobs, huge gulps of air sucked in between each word. Beside her, Hana is weeping quietly.

"But how do you think you'll survive in the wild if you let loose every cute meal you come across?" Hazeline asks.

"I don't care! I'll starve! I'm not eating that chick!" Aiko argues, crossing her arms and stomping her foot.

"I don't want to eat that either," Asuka says, her nose scrunched up. "It looks dirty, and I don't want to watch you kill it."

"You clean them before you eat them! And you'll appreciate your meals more if you understand what happens to get it to your plate," Hazeline tells them.

Ed opens his mouth to speak, then thinks better of it, and shuts it again.

"I am not eating that birdie," Aiko repeats sternly.

Rodrick is still holding the bird in the trap, waiting for further instruction from Hazeline, who is eyeing all of the children carefully.

Daiko shifts awkwardly, Asuka clinging on to his arm as though wanting him to speak up for the group.

Eventually, Hazeline lets out a long and dramatic sigh. "Oh, fine. Let the creature go, Rodrick. We'll have to fill your bellies with disgusting American s'mores, instead!"

The children all whoop joyfully, and even Koji gives a small smile of relief.

"But we're still learning how to make the traps, right?" he asks with a frown, holding up his collection of branches.

"Yes, we'll still make the traps. We just won't eat from them. Not today, anyway," Hazeline says, wiping Aiko's sodden cheeks with her sleeve.

The little girl sniffs. "Thank you, Yama Uba," she mumbles.

"Yes, thank you!" Hana joins in, rushing to hug Hazeline.

Before Ed can ask who Yama Uba is, Rodrick releases the trap's hatch and the bird darts out, scurrying into the brush as quick as a flash. The girls shriek in shock and the boys all cheer as it disappears into the foliage, eager to live another day.

As Ed wanders back to the house, he can't tell if Hazeline would really have killed and served the pheasant up to them for dinner. If they hadn't kicked up such a stink, he thinks that just maybe she would have. He thinks of the pheasant breasts waiting to be barbecued and decides to tell them it's pigeon if asked.

Evening falls, and the group is huddled around the firepit, sticks of gooey marshmallow held in the flames. The barbecue went without a hiccup, though Ed noticed that despite telling them the meat was pigeon, they nearly all opted for the fish instead. All except Hazeline, who took the breast as though making a point, ripping into it with her teeth daintily.

"Stories, please, Yama Uba!" cries Hana now, her face lit by the bonfire.

"Oh, yes, scary ones!" Koji grins, nudging Daiki.

"Yama Uba?" Ed asks.

"Ooh, who is going to educate our British chef on the folklore of Yama Uba?" Hazeline asks, holding her hands up to the sky eerily.

The children suddenly shrink back, shy. Daiki turns to Ed. "I will explain," he offers.

"See if you can do it all in English," Hazeline encourages.

Daiki nods, open to the challenge. Ed has learned he is eighteen, the oldest of the group, and he is the best at English by far.

"Yama Uba is from Japanese fairy tales. There are different stories, some scary, some kind, but we like this one," he starts, looking around at everyone who has hushed to listen. "Yama Uba lives deep in the woodlands, and is said to be very beautiful."

Ed notices Hazeline smile smugly at this.

"They say she can repel hunters' bullets with her bare hands," Daiki says, splaying his fingers out in front of Ed's face, "and that she nurses missing children who are lost in the woods. She is like a forest spirit, or mother of the mountains, and is said to bring good fortune to people who pass her. That is why we call Hazeline Yama Uba," he finishes.

Ed smiles at him. "That is very clever, and all makes sense. Hazeline, perhaps you really are Yama Uba. It all seems to fit! You live in the forest, apparently nurse children, and certainly brought me good fortune."

"Not if you believe the other Yama Uba story," giggles Asuka.

"The other story?" Ed asks.

"Some people say Yama Uba looks beautiful, but is really a monster who eats the missing children!" Asuka shrieks.

Ed smiles and looks to Hazeline, who he notices has stilled, her smile slightly fixed on her face. "All right, all right," she says, rubbing her knees. "Let's tell another story then. Who has a good one?"

Silence befalls the campfire.

"Tell us one of yours, Yama Uba," Koji pleads. "Yours are always the scariest!"

Hazeline smiles at the ground, apparently embarrassed. Ed collects the roasting sticks and fusses around clearing the salad bowls, resisting the urge to sit down and listen alongside the kids.

"Okay, okay, I have a good one. All this talk of Yama Uba has reminded me of it," Hazeline says. "But it's the scariest type of scary story . . . because it's true," she continues, her voice low.

The kids all lean in, eyes wide and shining in the flames. Hana clutches the toy lion, giggling behind its mane.

"Not *too* scary?" Aiko asks.

"No, don't worry, it's a story about a long, long time ago. Way before you, or even your great-grandparents, were born. Not anything to worry about today," Hazeline says.

Aiko nods and wraps her arms around her knees.

"Many eons ago, there lived a tribe called the Aztec. They existed because five young gods had sacrificed themselves so that the Aztec people could live. These gods were called the Five Suns, and the Aztec people were eternally grateful for the gift of life they had been given. They felt they had to return the favor and repay the gods for their kind sacrifice. They were sure that if they gave back enough, they would continue to be blessed and nourished," Hazeline says.

"But what is the value of a life?" asks Asuka. "Surely they can't pay back something so great?"

"Aha!" Hazeline nods. "Clever girl, Asuka. Well, you're right. The only fair trade is a life for a life. But these were *gods,* not mere people. The life of one person wasn't enough to balance the scales. So, they decided to hold rituals and banquets, where they would perform human sacrifices to thank the gods over and over again."

"Who did they kill?" Koji asks, eyes wide. "Their own people?"

"Well, it depends," Hazeline says. "Often, they would use slaves, or prisoners of war. Sometimes someone would offer themselves up honorably. And the noble men, who had the most money of them all? Well, they would purchase humans to sacrifice, an act of charity for their people. The more high-ranked the warrior or victim, the more of a prized sacrifice they would make, because the Aztecs believed that they held a strong life force. But what a waste of flesh to sacrifice them and leave the bodies to rot. So, after they slaughtered them, they would go on to devour them, consuming their life force and strength. This made those noble Aztecs even *more* noble, because they believed that they were becoming what they had consumed. And the more noble and powerful they became, the closer to the gods they were. You see, what had started as a way of thanking the gods quickly turned to greed. In the end, more than being thankful for the life they had been given, they wanted to be gods themselves. And so it was that the Aztecs would hunt down victims, bring them to their banquets, and gobble them all up in the hopes of becoming living gods!"

"Eww!" Hana says, scrunching up her nose.

"I bet you'd taste disgusting," Asuka giggles, prodding Koji in the ribs.

"No way!"

"I think he'd be delicious, personally." Hazeline smiles.

"I think that story is silly. Eating someone doesn't make you more powerful," Hana sniffs.

"How do you know? You've never eaten anybody!" Koji heckles.

"And they never would turn into gods, either," Hana adds. "No matter how many people or warriors they ate!"

"Well, maybe they did, in a way. After all, they chose who would die. That's a decision usually only gods get to make. And then they consumed them, which is something nobody else would get to do. They may not have been born gods, but they certainly were living like them, playing without any rules," Hazeline says.

The group hushes in thought.

Ed turns to leave, and finds he has goosebumps on the back of his neck.

BIRD, BEAK, BONES, AND ALL

A couple of weeks have passed since the camping weekend, and Ed has managed to get another payment to the Yakuza on time. Now, he's at the meat market, deciding what to center the next meal around. It's eerily quiet, other than the sound of the meat cleaver occasionally slamming onto the chopping board; customers are silently assessing their options and examining the shiny, vacuum-packed meat parcels with critical eyes. It's almost blindingly white, the bulbs cool-hued to make the red of the meat slabs pop, the refrigerated units emit a low buzzing sound, and there's a fresh chill in the air.

Hazeline has informed Ed that they have a "very special guest" to cater for and that they are coming into "party season," and so if all continues well, he'll have a lot more work coming his way. He understands what she means: perform this dance with flair, and you can host all the future tangos. He aced the charity event catering, but there is a big difference between hosting a barbecue for a bunch of kids and serving up something sumptuous for an illustrious guest of Hazeline's.

He strolls up and down the aisles, taking in his options with the rare opportunity of no budget restrictions. Hazeline has provided him with her metallic and onyx credit card, and he is able to purchase anything he desires at all. He won't take the piss, of course. She may go through the receipts, demand evidence of the purchases made. He's not idiot enough to shit where he sleeps. But still, the weight of the credit card in his back pocket is surprisingly comforting for an item so small.

So many options, so few ideas. Thin strips of Wagyu beef perfect for *shabu-shabu,* red and mottled with threads of creamy fat. Large pork joints, shaved and rounded, sitting proudly in their little white polystyrene trays. Pale, pasty chickens, their chubby little legs tied with strings that cut into the fat, the pinkish skin tinged yellow and stippled with lumpy rivets that were once hidden by feathers. Ed just can't decide.

Nothing feels special enough, exotic enough, for what Hazeline will want served. He needs to impress her without over-challenging himself. He has to remain realistic about his skills. One of the market vendors sees him dithering and beckons him over. He's young, almost a boy, with the wiry arms of corded muscle built by hefting boxes of carcasses around, and hanging three-foot rear legs onto ceiling hooks before repetitively slicing away at the meat.

"Can I help you find anything today?" he asks, his face shining and eager to please.

"I'm not too sure what I'm looking for, to be honest," Ed says. "I need some meat to cook for my boss, but she enjoys unique meals and I'd like to try to put together something a little special for her." His eyes skim the rose-hued aisle, the smell of coppery meat pungent. "Something not too tricky to cook."

"Ah!" exclaims the man. "I think I have just the thing. Please, wait a moment. It arrived just this morning, fresh from Nishiki Market!"

He hurries away, disappearing into a back room. Nishiki Market is one of the most famous and frequently visited food markets in

Japan, located in the center of Kyoto and rammed with tourists eager to visit the abundance of restaurants and street food stalls on offer. It's renowned for its high-quality and specialist food items, and Ed's interest is certainly piqued as he waits to see what the man can offer him.

The vendor returns with a tray of shell-pink meat. Ed can't quite make out what it is at first.

"*Suzume!*" The man beams proudly, bringing the tray under Ed's nose so he can see properly. Sparrows. A dozen fat little plucked birds, still whole, their tiny beaks intact. Ed's nose scrunches up in disgust. They look like they may have just been born, fallen from their nest and scooped up into this tray, broken-necked.

"Delicacy in Fushimi, cook like *yakitori!*" the man says in broken English, despite being spoken to by Ed in Japanese, giving the tray a shake for emphasis. The little bird corpses jiggle with the movement and Ed steps back.

"Like *yakitori?*" he repeats. Skewered chicken. This implies that the meal will be quick and easy to cook, even for Ed.

"Yes. Cook whole—too small to pull bones. Little fat, very tasty," the man says.

"Cook it whole? Even the head?" Ed checks.

"*Hai!*" The man nods eagerly. "Whole like a fish. *Kushiyaki* style."

Ed can simply grill or fry them whole, then serve them straight on the skewer. The ease is greatly appealing, and while the idea of eating one of these birds—beak, bones, and all—is repulsive to him, he has a feeling that Hazeline will adore the macabre show of it.

"Okay. Okay, I'll take the lot," he agrees. The man's eyes light up and Ed can't believe the total on the till once racked up. For a tiny bird offering substantially less meat than a chicken, and so much more off-putting to look at, it is costly!

The man sees Ed's surprise at the cost. "Import, fresh, from Kyoto," he explains.

"I understand. No problem," Ed says, flashing Hazeline's card. He enjoys the feeling of paying without having to second-guess his decision. No buyer's regret when it's Hazeline's money, even if he is spending an insane amount on the ugliest meal ever.

He is just at the exit to the meat market when he hears an almighty roar and a clatter. He turns alongside the rest of the shoppers to see what's going on, and sees a staggering old drunkard shouting abuse at the man who just sold him the sparrows. The man has glazed eyes, and wisps of white hair atop a haggard, wrinkled face.

"I'm sorry, sir, but you must leave now. I've told you, we cannot serve you here," the vendor says.

"Filthy!" the drunkard slurs. "You fucking filthy *burakumin!*"

There is a gasp from someone in the crowd and Ed steps forward, quickly placing himself between the drunk and the butcher.

"That's enough," he says in Japanese. "The man said leave."

"Shut up, you fucking *gaijin!*" the drunk shouts at Ed, his breath reeking of beer, but Ed's been called a foreigner enough times out here in Japan—even denied apartment rentals due to his race—that the insult slides right off him. By now they've caused quite a stir, and the drunk is hooked by both arms and hauled away by a group of meat market vendors, all the while kicking and shouting and cursing.

Ed is shocked, and is left standing with the man who sold him the sparrows. Japan is such a safe and quiet country, it is very rare to see any sort of outburst like this, and he can tell that everybody is rattled.

The man gives Ed a small smile. "I'm sorry he called you an outsider. And I'm sorry I spoke to you in English. Your Japanese is clearly very good," he says in his native tongue, head hanging low.

Ed shrugs. "It's okay. I'm used to it. Though I bet you're not used to being called a *burakumin,*" he adds.

The man gives a small snort of laughter. "It's the first time," he admits with a wry smile.

When Ed decided to marry Sayuri, he spent a huge amount of time researching Japanese history. He wanted to understand her culture, her country and its past. He particularly enjoyed learning and reading about the Edo period of Japan, and remembered this when he heard the drunkard yelling at the butcher. In the Edo period, the term *burakumin* was used for those who worked with dead bodies. This could be the obvious—executioners and morticians—but also spread to encompass butchers, tanners, and slaughterhouse workers. They were considered the lowest of the low by societal standards, stigmatized and ostracized. They were thought of as dirty, and faced terrible discrimination, treated as though they were barely even human. The term is long outdated, and before today Ed has never heard anybody use it outside of a historical context, but he feels bad for the butcher anyway. After all, he might be the one who slices the flesh, but at the end of the day it's Ed who will take it home and cook it.

DISSECTION PROJECT

Nakamura is in the parking lot of the meat market, and when he sees Ed he rushes over to help him with his bags. "Did you see the drunk guy? They carried him out right past the car!" the driver says.

"Sure did. Glad he's gone. Hey, do you know much about the guest we're serving tonight?" Ed asks, keen to make some easy conversation and put Nakamura's past warnings behind them. Perhaps Nakamura just doesn't think Ed is good enough to be a chef for Hazeline—and he wouldn't be wrong!

He could swear that he sees Nakamura bristle at the question, but pushes the thought aside. Maybe he just felt a sudden chill.

"She's American. I picked her up from the airport yesterday," Nakamura tells Ed, his tone slightly clipped. Ed immediately recalls the strange conversation between Octavia and Hazeline a few weeks back. The one about cattle.

"American?"

"Yes, from Mississippi."

"And she's a friend of Hazeline's?"

There's a slight pause before Nakamura responds. "Not really.

Hazeline gets a lot of guests coming and going. Some of them do short stints of work for her, or intern, or are part of her international charity work," he says vaguely. "Anyway," he goes to change the subject, "what will you be cooking?"

"Sparrow *yakitori,*" Ed says.

"*Majide!* A Kyoto specialty!" Nakamura nods enthusiastically. All tension is eradicated in this moment, food bringing the two men together.

"You've tried it?"

"Yes, my family are originally from Kyoto. We moved to Tokyo for the better hospitals when Suki was first diagnosed, but *suzume no yakitori* is something we would often enjoy at the markets and food stalls." He smiles fondly.

"And it tastes good? I've never cooked it before," Ed admits. He refrains from mentioning how off-putting the visual of the meal is; he knows better than to be the ignorant, judgmental white man, particularly when the conversation is centered around someone's regional dish. The longer he spends living abroad, the more he feels that he has no leg to stand on when it comes to judging the culinary choices of other cultures—particularly when all the British have to offer for unique experiences are congealed, slimy orange beans and deep-fried Mars bars.

"Yes, mostly it is served with a sweet soy sauce, but it's good without. Gamey, like deer or boar," Nakamura says.

"Well, I'm excited to give it a go," Ed says, and to his surprise he is being truthful. Living in Japan has certainly increased his boldness, and he's glad for it.

"And for you, what are the English specialties? Fish and chips?" Nakamura chortles.

Ed grins, and decides not to try to explain the concept of baked beans. "The fish here is ten times better than the fish in England."

Nakamura smiles. "I hear your sushi is terrible."

Ed thinks back to the tiny, bland sushi rolls at Tesco, filled with minuscule avocado cubes and accompanied by fake wasabi paste. "It is! Hmm . . . I suppose roasted meat with all the trimmings is traditional for Britain on a Sunday," he muses. "Or . . . steak pies?"

Nakamura looks at Ed cluelessly.

Ed sighs. "To be honest, the food in Britain isn't great. People don't have the most exciting or adventurous palates. They boil their veggies and love to eat chicken. It's pretty bland and beige. I guess that's why cooking in Japan is so much more fun."

Nakamura nods. "It's the best cuisine in the world."

"Even your egg sandwiches at the convenience store are a treat," Ed says, thinking of the way that Japanese mayonnaise is made with only egg yolks—it's so rich and creamy and thick compared to the watered-down, white, British variety.

"Ahh, *tamago sando,* delicious," Nakamura agrees.

They spend the rest of the car journey enjoying each other's company, enthusiastically sharing recipes and favorite meals. Ed's relieved to have put all the tension behind them.

When he arrives back at the house, there is a terrible racket coming from beyond the garden.

"Is that a chainsaw?" he asks, frowning. "Is a gardener in today?"

Nakamura stills for a moment. "Yes, perhaps. I'll go check it out, but Hazeline does often get people to come to trim the bushes and keep things looking tidy. You head inside, Ed."

In the house, Ed can hear Hazeline's excited chatter echoing down the hall. He lugs the bags of groceries through to the kitchen, where he finds her speaking quickly to a small, wiry girl with lank blond hair and a large nose. Hazeline is flushed, blotchy with apparent excitement, and abruptly stops speaking as Ed enters.

"Ed! Oh, Ed, come meet Ellie. She's traveled all the way from the

States," she says, raising both eyebrows as though this fact is hugely impressive.

"Hello, Ellie," Ed says, reaching a hand out, surprised. He expected someone similar to that awful Octavia again. "Nice to meet you."

She reaches out to shake his hand, her small, close-together hamster eyes boring into him.

"Ellie is here for some work experience with me, organized by her parents. And Ed is my incredible in-house cook. He can provide anything you need during your stay, can't you, Ed?"

Ed hadn't realized his job would involve meeting the demands of random American teenagers, but he quickly agrees.

"And Ellie certainly needs some filling up, doesn't she? Look at her, the poor, pathetic waif!" Hazeline barks a loud laugh and Ed shoots an apologetic look at the girl.

"Oh, don't feel *sorry* for her, Ed. It's not like she's being dubbed *debu* like I was at her age." Hazeline waves a hand in dismissal.

Debu is a profanity that translates to "fatty." Ed looks awkwardly at the ground, while Ellie blinks with a small frown, clearly unaware of what the word means.

"I will cook whatever you'd like," he assures the girl, and she smiles thinly at him.

"You got any Lucky Charms cereal?" she asks, looking around the kitchen as though expecting a box to magically materialize in front of her.

Hazeline shrieks dramatically. "*Ugh!* Absolute processed *poison,* that stuff. Honestly, petal, the Japanese do it so much better. Everything is fresh and natural, deliciously put together. None of that sugary junk you Americans seem to love so much."

The girl rolls her eyes sullenly. "So what's for the special dinner then?" she challenges Ed, who is quickly deciding that he doesn't like this new houseguest at all and can almost guarantee that she won't be impressed by a small dead bird presented to her on a skewer.

"A Kyoto specialty. I won't give it away," he says.

"Ooooh!" Hazeline seems delighted. "Kyoto specialty . . . it could be . . . *Nishiki soba*? Or *yuba*? Oh, oh, what about *hamo*? Conger eel, is that what it is, Ed?" She's hopping up and down with excitement, eyes bright.

"Eel? Ew!" Ellie grunts.

Feeling slightly frazzled, Ed simply taps the side of his nose. "You'll have to wait and see!"

"Oh, you terrible boy!" Hazeline swats at his arm affectionately before linking her arm through Ellie's and dragging her out of the kitchen. "Come, Ellie, let's leave Ed to his magic. I'll show you the bathing rooms. We have an outdoor onsen tub, you know. Water direct from the mountain springs!"

And with that, Ed is left with a bag full of dead sparrows and a decent amount of time to cook them in.

He lays the fat little chicks out on a baking tray, inspecting them all carefully. They are curled up into themselves, their tiny claws hooked, their puckered flesh red-raw with black coloring around the wings, eyes, and beak. They're minuscule, almost the length of Ed's thumb, and he prods at one curiously. The gizzard must be the size of a fingernail! His curiosity is too great; he wants to pull this little thing apart, inspect how much meat is on its bones, and decides to sacrifice just one. Otherwise, he won't know how long to cook them for, and he can't afford to dry them out—or give his boss food poisoning.

He begins to carefully carve away at it, using a tiny serrated knife. The man at the market was right—there is very little fat, and very little meat. In fact, the bones are so thin and flimsy that he finds himself cracking several by accident between his fingers, despite being careful and light-handed. He understands how they can be cooked whole; these bones will just slide right down the throat like the dainty toothpicks on a perfectly grilled fish.

He hears footsteps approaching and finds Hazeline and Ellie returning. "Just popping in for some coffee," Hazeline explains, heading over to the machine. She turns to Ellie. "Usually Rodrick can make coffee, but today he's helping my driver, Nakamura, with some things around the annex. Which, by the way, is off limits," she says meaningfully. "As part of our working agreement, Nakamura and his wife live in the annex, so consider it a different property entirely from this one."

Ed is about to ask Hazeline about the grating sound of something being sawed apart when she notices his dissection project.

"Oh my! What are those? Quails?" she asks, hunching over to get a better look.

"Sparrows," Ed says. "From Nishiki Market."

"That is so gross," Ellie says, scrunching her face up and sticking out her tongue in a silent gag.

"No, it's a regional dish and is very similar to the chicken your country so loves to cake in batter and deep-fry. Mind your manners," Hazeline says sharply, making Ed instantly soften toward his boss.

"And look, look here, Ed." Hazeline is hunched right over the tray now, poking at the bird Ed has half ripped apart. She seems to be picking at something within its flubbery, uncooked flesh, and is peering so closely that Ed's sure she must be able to hear the wet squelch each time her finger twitches. Finally, she very slowly straightens up, holding between thumb and forefinger the tiniest little bone. He has to squint to even see it—a tiny hair-strand of calcium.

"The furcula!" she says triumphantly.

"Aka the world's tiniest wishbone," Ed comments.

Ellie has turned her back to them both, and is looking out at the zen garden toward the jarring whirr of whatever the gardeners are using, her eyes glazed over in disinterest.

"Come, let's make a wish," Hazeline says, and Ed obediently steps forward, taking hold of one side of the minuscule bone with the lightest of touches.

"On three," Hazeline says, closing her eyes.

Ed follows suit. What should he wish for? He's not superstitious, but it's always nice to make a wish. He could wish for all his debts to be cleared. He could wish for eternal happiness for his family. He could wish for great successes for Kaori. So many things that he wishes for subconsciously every day.

"Two . . ." Hazeline counts down.

I wish for Hazeline's life.

"One!"

They both pull at the bone, splintering it in half.

"Come on then, let's see who has the longest." Hazeline grins mischievously. They put their bones side by side to compare. Even Ellie leans in to scrutinize the result.

"They're both the same. Equal. What does that mean?" Ed asks.

"It means we'll both have our wishes come true," Hazeline answers.

I THINK I'M A VEGETARIAN

Ed has watched Ellie twirl the skewered sparrow around on her plate several times now. She's making no move to eat it, instead picking halfheartedly at the side salads. He's hit by a sudden flashback of his first time meeting Sayuri's parents. They put on a grand spread for him, and the whole affair was a disaster. Sayuri was acting as translator, but her English was terrible, so they were using their phones to translate every other word. The meal was a traditional Japanese feast, with what felt like dozens of little dipping dishes and side plates, and Ed hadn't a clue what to eat when or how or why. He ended up having to apologize to Sayuri's father after sticking his chopsticks into the rice and leaving them there, which is considered terribly disrespectful in Japan. He stammered his apologies and waved his hands about a lot, flustered and sweating. Eventually, Sayuri smoothed out the misunderstanding in hushed tones with her father, and he returned to the table with a stiff smile plastered on his face. As soon as they left, Ed and Sayuri burst into laughter together, much to his relief.

"Don't waste your food," Hazeline snaps at Ellie, who is still shifting the skewer around absentmindedly. "Ed worked very hard to cook you a delicious meal, and Lord knows you could do with some fattening up."

The afternoon spent with Ellie has clearly done Hazeline no favors, because her mood has worsened considerably since Ed last saw her for the wishbone saga.

"I can't eat this. There's still a beak! I can see its eyeballs." Ellie grimaces.

"You can't see its eyeballs when it's rolling around in your mouth being chewed into mulch," Hazeline retorts.

"We don't eat stuff like this in America," Ellie whines.

Ed bites his tongue to stop himself telling her that perhaps she should go back to where she came from if Japan is so terrible and his cooking is so disgusting.

Hazeline huffs out a long, weary breath. "Ellie, *petal.*" She spits out the term of endearment. "You aren't *in* America, are you? And you know why that is, don't you? Because your parents are sick to fucking death of you, and needed some extra cash so your mum can get decent medical care because that beast of a president insists on charging his citizens to keep them alive. Do you understand?"

Ellie's eyes become watery, and Ed feels a stab of pity for the girl.

"So you'd better buck up and stop being so difficult, or I'll ship you back and your mother can drop back down to the bottom of the hospital waitlist."

Ed's mouth drops open in shock at her words, the cruelty so cutting.

Ellie looks down at her plate sadly. "I think I'm a vegetarian in Japan," she mumbles.

Hazeline slams her fist down on the table, causing both Ellie and Ed to jump.

Rodrick charges in. "Hazeline? Madame? Is everything okay?" His eyes quickly sweep the scene; Ed holds his hands up in innocence and Rodrick focuses on Ellie, narrowing his eyes into a glare.

"No, actually. Rodrick, take Ellie to her quarters. She's not feeling very well. Perhaps if she skips dinner, she'll feel better and have a return of appetite in the morning for breakfast."

Rodrick tips his head and Ellie huffs as she stands and stomps from the room.

Hazeline massages her temples, pulling her eyes as she does so with an exaggerated groan. "Times like this, Ed, I'm almost glad we weren't able to have children. They all turn into teenagers at some point."

Ed's not sure how to respond, so instead he begins to clear the plates.

Hazeline slaps his hand quickly. "Wait! Don't waste it."

Ed looks to her questioningly and she looks back down at the uneaten food meaningfully. "Eat."

"Me? Are you sure? I can just put it in a storage—"

"I said, *eat.*" She cuts him off.

Ed swallows thickly, stops clearing the table, and sits down slowly opposite Hazeline.

He picks up Ellie's discarded meat skewer and refuses to look at the bird skull he's about to deposit into his mouth. He tells himself it's just chicken, just regular chunks of chicken breast, and brings it to his mouth.

During his years in Japan, Ed has eaten many famous, cheap street food delicacies. *Takoyaki,* the golden batter opening to reveal tiny little suckered octopus tentacles. *Natto*—slimy fermented soybeans which instantly made him gag, to the great amusement of Sayuri, who had tricked him into believing it was a delicious Japanese favorite. (It's not.) He even once tried *shirako,* dared by his colleagues on a night out after too many draft beers, the bowl of fish prostate reminiscent of fat white maggots. But none of these things had a full face and skeleton. So he looks away and shovels the bird into his mouth and begins to chew.

The skull crunches so lightly between his teeth that he'd almost have missed it; the skin is delightfully crispy, like deep-fried chicken skin; and the soy sauce gives a sweet yet salty tang to the meat.

"Tastes like liver," he says, going in for a second bite.

"It does a bit, yes," Hazeline says, openly more relaxed now that Ellie has left the room and Ed has done as she demanded, restoring all order to the house.

"It's good," Ed says.

"Well, you enjoy Ellie's loss. Spoiled brat. Most children her age and of her class would die for such a meal, and she takes one look and turns her nose up at it! How can someone with so few options be so picky?"

"I can make her something else," Ed offers.

"No. Absolutely not. Children should learn to eat what they are given and enjoy it. They expect the world, want all the riches, but don't want to work for any of it. How can you possibly know what foods you love if you don't even bother to try them?" she says, exasperated.

"Many kids are picky eaters," Ed says, thinking back to his childhood meals made up of mostly beige ingredients and little else.

"Yes, but this girl comes from *poverty.* A level of poverty that Britain with its welfare system cannot fully comprehend. She should be grateful for what she's given. Back in my day, she'd have been raised on mulch and goop. Yet she's being handed a regional specialty, cooked to perfection by a private chef." Ed warms at the compliment as she continues. "Yet she deems herself too good for it. And why? Because it has a *beak*? Is she aware that the fast-food burgers she probably tosses down her gullet come from cows, complete with full faces? That when they pulverize it into patties it's with their organs and eyes? Or all pink slime? That because she doesn't have to look at its face while she devours it, that it's suddenly okay?"

Hazeline pauses her rant, and takes a deep slug of her *umeshu.* "I'm tired, Ed. And frankly, in a foul mood. For an intern, she's terribly difficult. This is why I should stick to my rule and work with my charity children only. They're much more polite and grateful for all I do. I'm going to slink away for the night. I'll see you in the morning," she says, picking up the bottle of wine alongside her glass to take away with her.

Ed finishes the entire plate. The room is silent except for the crunching of tiny bones.

POP POP POP

Ed hasn't seen or heard Hazeline since she took herself to bed early. He isn't in the mood for an early night, and instead makes himself at home in front of the television in his room, watching a cooking show. The contestants are scrabbling manically to put together the perfect ramen for the judge, and Ed finds himself calculating the odds of each person's chances of winning. One puts the noodles on far too early—she'll be out first, he bets. Then another forgets to put in vinegar somehow. *Amateur!* Ed thinks. He finds himself enjoying it, seeing the imaginary bets he's placed come to life during the elimination round.

Eventually, he begins to crave a small snack, and as he watches a chef slather a stick of butter over corn on the cob, he decides to go back to the kitchen and make himself some buttered popcorn. He knows there are kernels—he saw them in a neatly labeled jar in the pantry earlier. It's nearly twelve, so he considers it a midnight feast after the tiring day he's had catering for Hazeline and Ellie.

He puts on his robe and pads down the stairs. The house is dark, and quiet. He wonders if Rodrick is still up and about, but it looks like he went to bed early as well, likely making the most of his boss not needing him to perform duties on her request. He's probably watching the telly, same as Ed was a moment ago. What would a man like Rodrick watch in his downtime? Definitely not reality TV or game shows. Perhaps upmarket anime, or animal documentaries? Perhaps he's not watching TV at all. Maybe he's joined Hazeline in her bedroom for a night of passion . . . or lamb shank. Ed doubts he'll ever find out for sure.

He finds the popcorn kernels and throws them into a pan with a generous slab of salted butter, then puts the lid on and stands, waiting, listening to the *pop, pop, POP* of them as they burst open in the heat and turn carnation yellow with the coating. He closes his eyes, inhaling the rich, warm smell, and when he's sure that the popcorn is ready, he transfers it to a bowl to carry up to his room.

He'd better wash the pot though, he thinks, and he takes it over to the sink. As he's rinsing it, he hears a strange beeping sound. He frowns and turns the tap off. There it is again! A very high-pitched, quiet beep, like an alarm or a smoke detector. In fact, he knows exactly what the sound is, because his fridge at home makes it if it's been accidentally left open. He frowns, heads over to the fridges and checks them all, one by one. They all seem fine, but the beeping continues.

He's straining to listen when he hears someone approaching, and he stands up straight. It's Ellie, yawning and in her pajamas. She frowns when she sees him. "What are you doing?"

"Can you hear that?" Ed asks her.

"Hear what? I just want some water," she says, helping herself to a glass and running the tap.

"That beeping. Stop the tap, listen," Ed whispers.

To his surprise, she does as instructed. "Oh, yeah," she says, uninterested.

"I can't find where it's coming from," he says. "I've checked all the appliances."

She looks at the bowl of popcorn, then takes a large handful, shoveling it into her mouth in one go, chewing noisily and letting bits of corn spit from her mouth as she speaks. "I'll help you find it if you make me a bowl, too," she says, eyeing the popcorn.

"Sure, you can take that one," Ed says, put off by her grubby little hand helping itself to his midnight snack.

She smiles triumphantly, grabs another greedy mouthful, then pauses, narrowing her eyes in concentration. "I don't think it's coming from here, you know," she says. "Is there a basement? I think it's underneath us."

Ed concentrates, his brow furrowed. "You might be right!" he says, shuffling over to one of the hidden cabinet doors. "There is a basement. I've not been down but maybe it's coming from there. I know Hazeline mentioned keeping other appliances downstairs." *Like the incinerator.*

He opens the door and flicks the light switch. The space is instantly lit up brightly—the opposite of a gloomy, unkempt basement in a film.

"Cool!" Ellie exclaims, pushing past him and hurrying down the stairs. "Maybe it's a games room!"

Ed rolls his eyes and follows her down the stone steps. The room itself isn't too big—smaller than the kitchen itself. There's the incinerator Hazeline mentioned in his interview, and a row of recycling bins and bags on a trolley, which Ed assumes someone uses to cart the waste into a car to drop off at a recycling spot. There's a small utility sink in the corner, sparkling clean with a drying rack bedside it and a stack of towels tidily folded beneath. And beside the sink is the culprit of the beeping noise.

"This is boring," Ellie says with a groan. "No pool table or anything."

Ed ignores her and heads over to the beeping freezer, a little light in the top-right corner flashing orange. He opens the freezer and recoils from the smell, gagging and covering his nose with his sleeve.

"Eurgh! Gross! What is that?" Ellie coughs, following suit and clamping her hand over her nose.

"Something's gone wrong, it's defrosted," Ed says, following the cord at the back of the freezer to the plug socket. He unplugs the freezer and the beeping immediately stops.

"What the hell is in there, a corpse?" Ellie retches, stumbling over to take a look. But she gags again and instead flees, leaving Ed alone with the rotting stench. He counts to sixty and plugs the freezer back in, relieved to find the light now flashes green and that there's no beeping sound at all. He'd better turn the temperature right down as low as it will go, and tomorrow they'll have to dispose of everything in it. With great willpower, he sticks his hand into the freezer and begins rooting around in search of the temperature dial.

There are dozens of frozen meat packages in there, part-defrosted so they're soft and squidgy, pink water licking the edges of what is raw. Ed holds his breath and plunges his hand in again, and finally feels the circular knob he is looking for. Scrabbling, he digs through the meat parcels so he can see the dial, twisting it furiously and yanking it to the lowest possible temperature. Then he moves the food back into place, his arm slimy and wet.

He's about to close the freezer when he pauses, frowning at one of the ziplock bags. He lifts it, inspecting it closely. It's a slab of red meat, almost like beef, but the cut is unlike anything he's seen before. Sliced precisely, it must be the work of a butcher, but the fat is yellow and bobbly rather than white. Maybe it's gone off? But even the red part is strange, a deeper burgundy than any beef he's ever seen, the texture slimy but smooth like a cow's heart.

He gags again at the smell, and throws it back into the freezer, slamming the lid closed before rushing over to the corner sink and scrubbing at his hands and arms with the soap, desperate not to bring the smell of the rotting meat back to his bedroom with him.

When he leaves the now-silent basement and emerges in the

kitchen, he sees that Ellie has left the popcorn bowl on the side, untouched. Ed can't blame her—his appetite is long gone now, too. He throws the popcorn in the bin and goes up to bed, where he turns off the TV and falls asleep wondering what sort of animal that meat came from.

MEAT MOURNING

The next morning, Ed meets Hazeline down in the kitchen for breakfast. He's making a simple *tamagoyaki,* the fluffy, yellow eggs carefully rolled using chopsticks again and again while being lightly fried, creating a chunky swirling tube of yolky goodness. He slices it into little curls and serves them with soy sauce for dipping and a selection of fruit, delicately stamped into stars. The fancier it looks, the less likely she is to notice how bland and simple the offering is.

She's halfway through her meal when Ed broaches what happened the night before, and the memory brings a sting to his nostrils as he remembers the decaying smell.

"Hazeline?"

"Yes?" she replies after a noisy, squelching swallow.

"I'm afraid I have some bad news."

She puts her chopsticks down, her left brow slightly raised. "Oh?"

"Late last night, I was down here with Ellie and we heard a beeping. I followed it to the basement and I'm afraid your freezer had malfunctioned. I'm unsure how long it was off for, and I switched it back on at the main and it seemed to fix the issue, but the meat inside . . . well, I think it will have to be disposed of. It won't be safe to eat."

"*What?*" she spits.

Ed's shocked to see Hazeline turn a mottled shade of red, her fingers twitching as though grasping for a better explanation. She's a billionaire, for Christ's sake—surely she can just purchase more meat? Even if the freezer were filled with prized *fugu* meat, it couldn't cost more than mere pennies for her to replace.

Hazeline shakes, her eyes darkening, before she bellows an almighty curse and throws her breakfast plate on the floor, the porcelain shattering. Ed, shocked, leaps backward, then scrambles for a dustpan and brush, murmuring apologies under his breath.

Of course, it's only a moment before Rodrick rushes in to see what's going on, with the newcomer Ellie tight on his tail.

"The freezer, Rodrick, the freezer!" Hazeline screeches, a shaking hand pointing toward the basement door.

Rodrick pales, eyes rapidly darting from Ed to the basement door to Hazeline, and Ed pauses sweeping up the shards of plate and slivers of wet egg to watch the altercation.

"It malfunctioned or something, says Ed!" She is almost crying, her throat bobbing beneath her thin, papery skin.

"Is the meat all off?" Rodrick whispers, looking to Ed with wide eyes.

"It stank pretty bad," Ellie says, leaning against the doorframe.

"I wouldn't feel okay about cooking it," Ed admits nervously, confused by everyone's overreactions to some bad meat. Perhaps it was imported?

"Well of *course* you wouldn't feel good about cooking it," Hazeline spits at him, and Ed shrinks back, continues sweeping with his head down. "For fuck's sake, Rodrick, what are we going to do?" she seethes.

"I'm sorry, was it special?" Ed asks tentatively.

Hazeline half laughs, half cries, slapping both hands on the tabletop.

Ed frowns, and Rodrick comes to his rescue.

"There is an extremely large and important dinner party that we host annually. The meat had been slowly collected for the occasion," Rodrick explains. "We added more to it yesterday evening. Something must have happened with the freezer when it was deposited."

Ed feels a stab of annoyance that this is the first he's heard about a fancy supper party, and wonders if Hazeline is using a catering company—or worse, a different chef. He imagines she pays double for an annual soirée.

"That fucking freezer company is going to get their heads chopped off when I'm done with them," Hazeline mutters bitterly. "I'll fucking buy the whole company just so I can sack them all!"

Ed blinks, and at the door, Ellie snorts with laughter.

"Let's go see. Maybe something is salvageable," Rodrick offers, placing a gentle hand on Hazeline's back and giving her a small squeeze.

She sighs deeply. "It will all have to be binned. You know that, Rodrick. We can't take any risks, can't make anyone sick."

"Perhaps we can postpone the dinner?"

Hazeline tsks and flaps the idea away with her wrinkled hand. "We can't do that. These people have diaries busier than a whorehouse in the trenches. We'll have to contact the charity, see what they can do for us. In the meantime, Ed shall have to go to the carcass auction as a backup."

"Carcass auction?" Ed swallows.

"It's annual. A big event in Tokyo, lots of the finest carcasses available to bid on. The best cuts of Kobe money can buy. Usually attended by bigwigs and restaurateurs," she explains drearily, her rage quickly dissipating and being replaced by some sort of meat mourning.

"I see. Well, I'd be more than happy to attend on your behalf," Ed offers. "I'll pick out the best of the best. Your dinner guests will be delighted, I'm sure!" He smiles.

Hazeline looks terribly defeated and doesn't bother trying to smile back. Rodrick leads her toward the basement door as though she's an invalid, murmuring gently to comfort her as he does so, their arms entwined.

When she gets down there, they must open the freezer and see the damage—the darkened, browned meat slabs—because Ed hears an almighty shriek of distress from Hazeline. At this, Ellie buckles with laughter.

"Imagine being so pressed over some burgers," she cackles.

Ed frowns at her. "I imagine those so-called burgers cost more than college tuition in your country," he says, and she quickly straightens up, laughter abating.

WELCOME TO THE MEAT MARKET

Ed is suited and booted, ready to go to the carcass auction.

"What a strange concept. I never had any idea this existed," Sayuri says as she straightens his tie for him. She smells clean, of soap, and her hair brushes the front of his face with the scent of honey. It's been a long time since she fussed over him like this, but since Ed's working more regularly she's been way more relaxed, sleeping better and being less snappy with him.

"Neither did I," Ed admits. "But I guess if you're not in the industry and stinking rich, why would anybody know about it?"

"True," she says. "Do you have an allowance for the day?"

Ed shakes his head, stepping back to check his reflection in the mirror, Sayuri beside him. "No, Hazeline's terribly stressed over the freezer mishap, so just gave me her shiny old credit card and told me to buy whatever coveted carcass everyone else seems to want the most."

"Oooh, her fancy credit card! Perhaps you can buy me a Birkin bag," Sayuri jokes.

"I'll grab one on my way home." Ed winks, kissing her on the cheek.

The truth is, he feels slightly nervous. He's never attended an auction before, but part of him worries that it will be as addictive as gambling. He'd be lying if he said he doesn't still itch every day at the thought of placing a little bet with some of his newfound salary, in the hopes that one good win will make all his money back and erase all of the problems his debt is still causing. After all, surely he's due a win after so many losses?

The thought that the rush of waiting to see if his bid has been accepted will be similar to the rush of waiting to see if his gamble has paid off is worrying. He loosens his tie a notch, clears his throat and leaves.

The event is nothing like what Ed imagined. He was picturing a British butcher shop, sweaty and stinking with sticky floors. Rather, the auction is in a huge exhibition center, usually home to fancy corporate events or trade shows. At the entrance is a huge sign which reads: *WELCOME TO THE MEAT MARKET.* Beneath it, a person hops from foot to foot excitedly in a pig costume, a little chef hat atop its head and an apron straining against its round potbelly. Ed approaches and the pig jumps up and down, waving its little hoofed hand at him.

Ed waves back awkwardly, wondering who is inside the pig suit.

"Want a photo?" a woman nearby in an apron matching the pig asks. "Post online, free chorizo!" She holds out a tray of blistered, porky discs.

"No, no," Ed declines, rushing on. Who the hell would want a photo of themselves with a human-sized pig?

Once inside, he's met with dozens of stalls advertising everything imaginable, from industrial metal butchering equipment to custom embroidered aprons to handcrafted Japanese chef's knives. Meat suppliers hand out tasters. There is even a table with the pig mascot in plushie form, the hat and apron worn by the majority of the toys but some of them dressed in a white T-shirt that reads: *I WAS AT THE MEAT MARKET!*

Ed shudders and continues weaving his way through the crowds to reach the auction room. Even his toddler wouldn't want that hideous pig toy.

Once in the auction room, it's substantially quieter. Everyone is wearing suits, same as Ed, and there are rows and rows of tables and chairs set up. Ed makes his way to an empty seat, set up with a computer screen, a folder featuring all of the available lots, and a remote control he can use to input his bids. The screen is currently waiting on Lot 1, showcasing a close-up photograph of the marbling, the official meat grading (A5, obviously), information on the supplier, the breed of animal, and weight, and a starting bid. All of the seats and tables are facing a glass wall, and behind it hang a dozen meat carcasses on display for the bidders to see in person. Ed picks up the wire-bound book of options and begins to flick through, distracted only when a woman sinks into the seat beside him.

She looks pig-like herself, with blond ringlets and a little rosy snub nose. She's breathing heavily, a T-shirt straining against her breasts which reads *Hot Girls Grill* in plastic diamanté.

"Are you American, too?" she asks him loudly, leaning over. Her voice is brash and echoes in the quiet room. Ed forces himself not to flinch away.

"No. British."

"Oooooh, I love a Brit. Say *wor-tuh!*" She cackles.

"No," Ed says, glancing down at her feet. She has a bag filled to the brim with pig mascot stuffies. One in the branded Meat Market T-shirt, one in the apron, and two holding up Japanese flags.

"I just love Mr. Piggy Hamlet," she says, picking up her bag and showing him all her wares. "We have loads of him back home in the restaurant windows. The customers love 'em!"

Ed, once more, tries not to flinch away from her. He can't remember the last time he felt snobby, or above someone, but something about this woman is so pitiable, so pathetically gauche, that he doesn't want anyone to assume they have come together—the two white people sitting beside each other. He shifts his chair ever so slightly away from her, nodding silently with a tight-lipped grimace.

She doesn't take the hint. "We run a barbecue joint down in Louisiana," she continues. "Best ribs in all the south! You ever been to Louisiana?"

"No," Ed replies.

"Well, you gotta come. And if you do, swing by Rib Tickler's and try us out. You won't regret it!"

Ed makes a sort of *hmm* noise, and finally she backs off, distracted by something on her phone.

He takes the opportunity to turn his body away from her and go through the auction catalogue. He knows which lot he wants immediately.

Hazeline told him she wants pork. She likes the sweet taste of it and wants to see how Ed will cook it for her. "You know, they say human meat is reminiscent of the taste of pork," she said, before bursting out into peals of laughter at Ed's horrified expression. But if it's pork she wants, it's pork she'll get.

There's a pig carcass up for grabs, produced at Yamatsuri Farm. It has impressive breeding and lineage and the farm's pork is supposedly famous for its perfect melding of soft meat and gentle, sweet fat. This is the pig Ed will buy today. It's one of the final lots, so he'll have a long stint of sitting and waiting for his moment, but this is a new experience and he is happy to sit back and soak it all in. So long as the American woman with all the carcass auction merch leaves him alone.

A STAGE OF CADAVERS

And the bidding begins! It's not half as exciting as Ed hoped. An auctioneer stands at the front, the window of carcasses behind him. He calls out and Ed watches the electronic display above him flash red numbers as people input their bets from their seats. Ed can't believe how much money people are paying for something so consumable. Once it's eaten, it's gone forever. So what are they really paying for? The momentary experience of taste? Or the ability to turn the investment into even more money, throwing in some cheap vegetables and up-pricing it as a dish for hungry customers with too much loose change? Perhaps the feeling of bidding in an auction is not so different from gambling after all.

The room is silent, and even the American woman beside him has quietened as she watches the numbers intently, waiting for her chosen lot to come up. The process is restrained, as Japan tends to be, with very little noise or commotion, even when people win their item of choice.

Ed watches as a Kobe beef carcass goes for twelve million yen, and thinks about all the things he would buy with that money. A new car, probably. Although getting a new car would mean no more work pickups from Nakamura in the fancy black Bentley, so maybe he can put off replacing his little Mitsubishi Mirage for a while longer.

Finally, his desired lot is announced by the auctioneer, who holds out an arm to showcase the pig hanging on a hook behind him. Behind the glass pane, darting in between the swinging carcasses, is a woman in a full body suit wearing a hair net and face mask. She presses an electronic instrument against the meat, which confirms for the audience that it is 1+ grade, the most prime quality of meat. The screen in front of Ed updates to display the information from the brochure, alongside the starting bid. Ed swallows. It's the same amount of money as what was in Kaori's university fund before he gambled it all away on a horse race. His heart begins to beat furiously, the anticipation of the win or loss making him excited. He tries to calm himself down. This isn't exciting. It's a guaranteed win; he has no limit to what he can pay and it's not his money, anyway. There's no personal loss. So why won't his body listen to his brain? Why is adrenaline coursing through him the same way it does when he sits at home watching the races on television, waiting to see if he's won?

He closes his eyes, breathes in deeply, and presses the button to enter his bid. Every time it increases, he presses again to confirm that he wants to remain in the bidding. It goes on, and on, the auctioneer getting more excited and Ed twitching with exhilaration as people begin to drop out. He keeps on bidding, and bidding. He thinks it may be just him and one other person now, and he wonders who they might be. But he won't risk looking away from the screen, from the numbers, to try to work it out. He'd never manage anyway; people are hitting the buttons on their remotes to place bids as discreetly as someone passing a bag of drugs under a table. Fingers barely moving. Faces not twitching. A legal game of poker happening before an audience of cadavers.

A bead of sweat breaks out on his forehead. He is loving this. And finally, the auctioneer calls an end to the lot. He's won. Of course he has. It takes everything in him not to yell with triumph, to sit and take the victory with polite grace. He sits through the final few lots with interest, watches as the American next to him wins a rib cage of beef, her fist curling and pumping silently with the success.

At the end of the auction, Ed goes to leave the building on a high when he is approached by another pig mascot.

"I'm not interested in any photographs, I just need to collect my win and leave," he says, holding his hands up, but to his surprise, the pig leans in toward him.

"Mr. Ed Cook? You are to follow me downstairs to the premium members' club."

Ed frowns. "You must have the wrong man."

"You're here for Mrs. Yamamoto, no?"

Ed pauses. "Yes."

"Then you must come. It is invitation only, and we have a package for Mrs. Yamamoto." The pig gestures and Ed feels as though he is in a strange dream as he follows the pig through the crowds, the coiled cotton tail bouncing with each step.

He is led away from the general public, through a door and downstairs into a dimly lit room, locked by a keypad. The pig removes its pink hoof hand, quickly enters the code and shoves Ed through the door. Everyone in the room turns to look at him. It's mostly men—dodgy-looking, suited and booted, with scars and cruel eyes. A couple of women are seated in laps, their arms around the men. It's like being in a hostess bar—worlds away from the meat market upstairs.

Ed pales when he recognizes a face he hasn't seen in a long time. But not long enough. It's Ikagi, and he's with two henchmen. Ed bows deeply, holding his breath as Ikagi strolls up to him. Is this all just a setup? Has the pig brought him here to be killed in front of an audience?

Ikagi's wearing a sharp, tailored black suit, sunglasses covering his eyes. Tattoos snake out of the sleeves and cover his hands, one featuring a dragon. The scaled tail curls up onto his ring finger, ending in a coil. "Edward Cook. What a surprise," he says, his voice silken. Behind him, one of his thugs cracks his knuckles. "To what do we owe the pleasure?"

"Please, I don't want any trouble. I'm here on behalf of my employer, to purchase some quality meat."

"Ah, your infamous secret employer who has for some reason sent you on meat runs." Ikagi smirks.

"Please, it's consistent work. I'm making all my payments," Ed whispers.

"That you are. I'm pleased, Ed. I want us to be friends, you know. I don't like being owed money any more than you like owing it," Ikagi says.

"I understand. I'm sorry. I'm working hard and will pay you back in full soon."

"That's what I love to hear." Ikagi smiles, the skin stretching on his face unnaturally.

"Well, I'll leave now. But I will have the next payment for you by the due date, I swear. I'm good for it," Ed promises.

"Good. I don't want to ruin one of my beautiful blades with your *gaijin* blood," Ikagi says, still smiling.

Ed nods, blood draining from his face, and goes to leave.

"Oh, and Ed?" Ikagi adds.

Ed turns.

Ikagi punches him square in the face, and Ed's eye socket cracks. He staggers backward, the men in the room parting and a couple of them gasping, averting their eyes from Ikagi as his two gang members clear the bystanders. Ed cowers on the ground and waits for another hit, but it doesn't come. He cracks one eye open, the good one, and finds Ikagi standing over him.

"That's for outbidding me. I wanted the pig carcass to roast for my nephew's birthday. Your employer is a very lucky man."

And with that, Ikagi walks away, leaving the room, Ed still on the ground.

He groans, turning onto his side, but nobody makes a move to help him. He sees a pair of feet approach him, and wonders if they'll put a hand out to help him up. Instead, a large, heavy, wet package lands on his shoulder and Ed jolts back on instinct.

"Relax. We're not with Ikagi. He's just an occasional visitor," the man says.

"What is this?" Ed rasps.

"For Hazeline Yamamoto. I hear you're her delivery boy," the man says, turning away from Ed and back to a group of men who appear to be playing cards in the corner.

Ed winces as he sits up and inspects the package. The blue plastic bag is damp, and inside he finds a load of ziplock bags, red meat squished into them messily. He scrunches his nose. What is this stuff? Why would Hazeline order this when there's an award-winning pig waiting to be butchered?

Ed stands, keeps his head down, and leaves the room.

LITTLE BLACK BOOK

"What happened to your eye?" Sayuri gasps as soon as Ed walks through the door. Kaori takes one look at him and begins to bawl. Rather than rushing to him, Sayuri goes over to pick their daughter up, murmuring to her and stroking her head gently. She looks to Ed, horrified.

"Someone was mad I beat them in the auction," Ed mumbles.

"You got hit in the face over some *meat*?" Sayuri gasps, now at the freezer pulling out a bag of ice and wrapping it in a towel. "Here, sit," she orders, gently placing the ice pack on Ed's face. He hisses at the sharp sting, and Kaori crawls over to him and grabs at his arm. Her face is blotchy and tear-stained, but she's forgotten about the drama already, distracted by the ice parcel on her dad's face. Ed pulls her in for a cuddle, his wife still holding the ice pack to his face. It begins to go numb, the blade of the cold ebbing away into a dull nothing.

"Did you call the police? Did anyone see?" Sayuri asks.

"No, it all happened so quickly. By the time I got up, the guy was gone. I didn't want to cause more of a fuss," he says.

"This is disgusting! How can someone behave in such a way! In the middle of Tokyo?" She shakes her head sorrowfully, and Ed feels a stab of guilt for lying to her.

"Hey, hey, I'm okay," he says, pulling her into his other side. "Here, look, my two beautiful girls are here taking care of me. What is there to be sad about?" He forces a smile.

"Did you at least win the auction?" she asks with a half smile.

"I sure did."

Kaori screams, slapping both of their knees at once with her chubby palms.

"What happened to your eye?" Hazeline gasps.

Ed sighs. He's now been through this charade with his wife, Nakamura, and Rodrick. Days have passed and the bruise has blossomed into a yellow, blackish puddle on his face. Nakamura spent the entire drive after the meat market feverish, asking him questions and glancing rapidly in the rearview mirror, as though expecting a fleet of Yakuza to be on their tail. Rodrick raised a single, bushy brow, and asked if this new look was *à la mode.*

"I walked into a post," Ed says to Hazeline lamely.

She narrows her eyes at him.

"Where's Ellie?" he asks, keen to divert attention away from his puffy eye.

Hazeline glances quickly at Rodrick, who is fussing over his bonsai as usual. He doesn't seem to notice, though he stiffens momentarily. Or does he? Ed's unsure.

"She's gone. She wasn't quite the right fit for us here."

"I'm not surprised," Ed comments. She was obnoxious, ungrateful, and rude. He can't imagine Hazeline would have put up with her behavior for very long, so it's no surprise she's been shipped back to the States.

"No?" Hazeline purrs at him.

Ed shrugs. "She was not quite the same personality type as your usual staff," he offers carefully.

At the table, Rodrick splutters a short laugh, covering his mouth and finishing with a brief bark of a cough.

"And what personality type do you think I hire, out of curiosity?" Hazeline asks, her mouth curving upward, her finger brushing her jawline pensively.

Ed chews on his lip. "Hard workers."

"Indeed." Hazeline blinks, darting another gaze at Rodrick. "I do have a good little loyal group of you, don't I? And you do all work hard," she acknowledges.

Rodrick spritzes the bonsai a little more enthusiastically, as though proving a point.

"I'd like you to follow me, Ed. I have something special for you to work with tonight."

He trails after Hazeline and follows her into the reading room where they first met. He hasn't set foot in it since that day all those weeks ago. It still smells of incense, still feels like a strange blend of feminine and dangerous.

"I also wanted to thank you for your excellent work at the auction. I know those things can get pretty competitive—dog-eat-dog, and all that jazz. But you managed all on your own! And really, it's a fine piece of meat. I can't wait to try it tonight." She smiles.

"It's no problem," Ed says.

"And thank you as well, for collecting my special delivery. In all honesty, I wasn't sure they would have it in time, so it was a welcome surprise."

An unwelcome surprise for me, Ed thinks, recalling the dark room and dodgy men peering at him after he was socked in the face by Ikagi.

"I don't usually order from them. I find them unpleasant and dirty to work with," she continues, wiping her hands together as though ridding herself of their reputation. "But after the freezer fiasco, needs must."

"What type of meat was it, that they got for you?" Ed asks.

"Tonight is going to be important for me. There are some influential people attending and I'd like them to have a wonderful time. They're very dear friends, and we go back quite a while," she says fondly, ignoring his question entirely.

"I will be sure to do my best to please," Ed replies, hint taken. He isn't to pry. He'll find out when cooking it, no doubt.

"We'll need to cover your eye—it looks terrible. Like I've hired some low-level Yakuza to work for me," she says, wrinkling her nose.

Ed flinches.

She seems to notice but continues on as though she hasn't. "I'm sure Rodrick can sort out a bandage for you. We'll just say you've had laser eye surgery or something. I'd love for you to cook some of the pork you won at the auction, and I have a special piece of meat which I've managed to source and would like you to prepare."

"The meat from the blue bag?" Ed asks.

"No, that has been put in the freezer for the right occasion. This is something else entirely. Much fresher."

She reaches for that little black book Ed remembers from his interview—her private recipe journal. It's still on the top of her book pile, unassuming and boring amidst all of the other trinkets and treasures. "I have a recipe here that will work for the cut," she explains, flipping through the book.

"Aha!" She pauses on a page, stabbing it with her finger. "Here it is." She dog-ears the corner of the page for Ed, before closing the book and handing it to him. "This is very precious to me. It's all of my favorite and most unusual recipes from over the years. If you can pull this off, I will be deeply impressed, and would like for you to cater my annual dinner party as a reward. It pays triple."

Ed's eyes light up. Triple! Enough to pay back Ikagi a chunk of his debt without much interest. "I'd be honored!"

She smiles. "Good. Well, you'd better do your best, then, like always. Now, let's get Rodrick to bandage you up. I'd try to cover it with makeup, but it's far too dark and would still show through. You must have really rammed into that pole," she adds, her eyebrows raised.

Ed knows he isn't fooling her. "I guess," he replies.

"Well, in future, watch where you're going, petal. You never know what creature you may run into."

Back in the kitchen, with half of his face and one eye covered by a medical bandage that Rodrick sourced from Nakamura's medical cupboard, Ed flips through the little black book. He first goes to the page that Hazeline marked for him to use this evening. The book is battered, clearly well loved and used. The contents are in Japanese, the writing small and scratchy in black ink. At the top of the page is a smear of something—a condiment perhaps? A reddish-brown tinge just below the first line, as though someone wiped a dirty finger across it.

The page is titled: *Special Liver.* The recipe is simple enough: it involves soaking the meat in milk prior to cooking in a skillet, and serving with onions and a thick sauce. The title seems misplaced; nothing about it is strange or unusual. Ed can't fathom why Hazeline has gone to the lengths of writing this recipe down—and why she's chosen to serve her esteemed guests such a paltry offering.

"Careful! Please, careful!" he hears Hazeline shriek from the front of the house. He heads out to see what the commotion is and sees Nakamura hefting a very large package into the back of a van. It's wrapped in what looks like a tarp, and Nakamura is struggling to get it in. Ed rushes over to help.

"No, please, get away! I can do it. You shouldn't have to do this, to be involved," Nakamura grunts, blocking Ed from the parcel.

"Jesus, what is that? A body?" He grins. "Come on, you look like you could use the help." Behind him, Hazeline watches with interest, arms crossed.

"No. It's *fine,*" Nakamura insists, getting the end of the package into the truck with one final huff. He quickly moves Ed out of the way and shuts the door.

"What is it?" Ed asks.

"What do you think it is?" Hazeline asks.

Nakamura looks at the ground.

"Looks like a body bag." Ed laughs.

"Quite!" Hazeline smiles back.

"I'd better go," Nakamura says, getting into the van. "See you later."

"Thank you, Nakamura! And give my love to Agawa!" Hazeline says with a wave.

Ed frowns, trying to remember why that name is familiar, but comes up blank. Instead, he goes back into the kitchen to continue leafing through the little black book.

He flips through the other pages, frowning slightly as he takes in the underlined titles. *Creamed Sole. Buttered Brain and Rice. Bone Marrow Broth. Crispy Skin with Dipping Sauce. Boiled Lung and Pickled Veg. Deviled Kidneys. Brave Braised Heart.* It's a bizarre mix of favored recipes, and nothing sounds appetizing in the slightest. On some pages, Hazeline has written little notes and highlighted them. *Less salt next time. Cook for less time—was overdone by 4 mins.* The tome is meticulous in its detail, with the cooking times calculated by meat weight and down to the minute. Why so specific?

. . .

Almost an entire day has passed. Nakamura has recently returned, and Ed is skimming Hazeline's recipe for deviled kidneys when Rodrick enters the kitchen, holding out two bags. "The meat for this evening," he explains, presenting them to Ed.

They're cold, and are clearly in the middle of defrosting. Ed takes the first, which is large and weighty. "We carved this from the auction carcass you won!" Rodrick says, and he even smiles. "It's pork ribs. Do you have a recipe that will work with these?"

"Yes, that won't be a problem," Ed assures him, thinking back to his British barbecues and the smoked ribs he'd slave over with his dad. "I'll use the smoker." He's been keen for an excuse to work with Hazeline's fancy, expensive smoker.

Rodrick nods. "I'll have it set up outside in the garden and prepared for you. There are a variety of woods for you to choose from in the basement."

"And what's the little package?" Ed asks, looking at the other bag, which is warmer than the first. The meat inside is a much darker red than the pork.

"This is the liver for Hazeline's recipe."

"Will it be enough for all the guests?" Ed asks, frowning as he takes it from Rodrick. It's in a ziplocked plastic bag, the blood pooling at the bottom in a gelatinous syrup.

"It will be served as an appetizer; they only need a small sliver each," Rodrick says.

Ed nods. He'll serve it with the onions on toasted ciabatta, like a weird bruschetta.

"What is it? Lamb liver?" Ed asks, examining the bag.

"It's imported all the way from America," Rodrick says vaguely.

NOBODY LIVES LIKE THIS

Ed sweats, wiping a hand over his damp brow. He lifts the heavy lid of the smoker and takes a bottle, quickly spritzing the pork ribs with the honeyed apple water before lowering the cover again. They smell divine, and are starting to go black and crispy on the outside, the fat hardening into a sweet, crunchy shell. He wipes his hands with a dramatic clap, feeling pleased with himself, and struts back into the kitchen, his chest puffed out. The liver is prepared as well, sitting in a puddle of milk as per the little black book, a strange ball of wet flesh in a white glaze.

"Something smells great!"

Nakamura comes into the kitchen through the back door, and jabs a thumb at the smoker.

"There should be plenty of leftovers. You should swing by when the guests have left," Ed offers.

"I may just do that, I love pork ribs." Nakamura smiles. "Fancy a smoke?" He holds out a packet of cigarettes.

Ed isn't much of a smoker, but used to dabble socially when he was out drinking with work colleagues, and he figures this is sort of the same. "Sure, why not," he says. After all, he's well prepped, everything is ready to go, and he has plenty of time before the guests begin to arrive. He follows Nakamura out to the garden and they head away from the smoker, past the pond, and halfway to Nakamura's annex.

"Here's good," Nakamura says, brightening and passing Ed the lighter. "I know it's far from my house, but I still worry about the smoke getting near Suki's room and messing up her lungs or something," he explains, taking a deep drag. "I tried to quit once, but then she got the cancer and it seems to be the only thing that helps me de-stress."

"I get it, don't worry," Ed says. Then, to his surprise, he opens up a little. "I'm that way with pachinko, but I've stopped playing now. Went cold turkey a few months ago—not because I had any willpower, really. More because I'd run out of money."

"Is that how you got into all the . . . bad business?" Nakamura asks, circling his pointer finger at the end of the sentence, and they both know he's referring to Ikagi and his men.

Ed nods, eyes on the ground.

"Don't worry, I won't tell Hazeline," Nakamura promises.

"It just became something I did to escape my reality, I guess, but I realized it wasn't helping me at all. But it was too late, and I was in way too deep."

"It's hard to give up things that make us feel good mentally, even though they're terrible for us physically," Nakamura agrees, flicking some ash onto the ground.

"It's true. The pachinko, the gambling . . . It may not have rotted my organs, but it has wrecked my family, my lifestyle, and I guess in some ways, my health," Ed admits, thinking of the current status of his eye. "I want to stop for good but I keep slipping up. It's hard, when there's money in my account and I need an escape."

"What are you running from? A bad marriage or something?" Nakamura asks, his voice genuine and conversational rather than nosy or demanding like some people might be. Ed appreciates the lack of judgment.

"No, not at all. My wife, Sayuri, she's great. The best, really." Ed sighs sadly. "I lost my job, and I was a new father, and I felt like I was failing her. I felt like I was a bad dad, a bad partner, and I had no clue what I was doing in any aspect of my life. I told Sayuri I was out looking for jobs, and at the start, I was, but every time I walked past a parlor I ended up going in. I thought of it as a little reward after dropping off my résumé, as a sort of pick-me-up when I was feeling bad about myself, or anxious. Eventually, I stopped handing my résumé out altogether, and just sat in the parlor all day long playing, pretending I was applying for jobs. It was easier than handling more constant rejections. They'd see me, a white man, and think I couldn't speak Japanese, or understand the customs. I'm too much of a risky hire out here. And when I was waiting to see if I'd won, it was the only time I really felt any actual emotion other than shame, or fear."

"*Majide.*" Nakamura shakes his head sorrowfully, stamping out his cigarette and immediately lighting another one. "You are burdened by your own expectations for yourself. It sounds like your wife did not put these pressures on you, but that you put them on yourself." He offers Ed another cigarette. Ed declines, taking in his words.

"I guess so. I guess I just feel like she took a punt marrying me so quickly, so I could stay here in Japan with her. And I felt like what she wanted in exchange was a lifestyle I haven't really been able to give her since we had the baby. If Kaori wasn't born . . . I know I shouldn't say that, but if she wasn't, we might not have struggled so much with me being out of work."

Nakamura lets out a groan and shakes his head. "What sort of lifestyle is it that you think your wife and child want you to provide?"

Once upon a time, Ed would have said just getting by comfortably would be enough. But now, he replies, "A lifestyle like this," gesturing behind him to the beautiful house.

"Nobody lives like this," Nakamura scoffs. "Not even Hazeline. You think she's happy here?"

"She seems happy," Ed says, surprised.

"The woman has been in mourning since her husband died. I heard her weep almost every day the first few months after I moved in. I think she felt kindred to me in a way, because she could not have a baby, and Suki and I won't have a baby. It must be hard for her to see you go home every day to your wife and child, the life she's been robbed of. Everyone has their struggles, just some are better at hiding them. Your wife probably just wants a kind husband who spends time with her and helps with the child. You're making good money here, with Hazeline?"

"Yes."

"Then you're doing enough. The only thing stopping you being a great husband, a great father, is your own self-doubt. If you start believing in yourself, appreciating what you have day-to-day, you won't need the rush of gambling." The second cigarette is stubbed out.

Ed smiles. "You're a bit young to be so wise."

Nakamura grins at him and shrugs. "With great trauma comes sage wisdom, I guess." He glances back at the annex behind them.

"I'm sorry. About your wife," Ed offers.

"Thank you. Hopefully she will live a long and happy life with me," Nakamura says. "Hazeline is giving us the best chance of that happening, anyway."

Ed looks to the kitchen and checks for anyone else around, but it's quiet.

"You like her?" Ed asks candidly. "I can't seem to work her out, even after all this time."

Nakamura shrugs. "I respect her. And I will be forever in her debt for what she has done for Suki and me. She's given us the gift of time. Who knows, maybe we'll even be able to have a family one day. If she gets better, maybe we can adopt or something."

Ed nods slowly. "You think Rodrick likes her?"

Nakamura barks out a laugh, shocking Ed. "You're kidding, right?"

Ed blinks.

"I would say Rodrick likes Hazeline. A bit too much, perhaps." Nakamura grins mischievously, shaking his head.

"Shh!" Ed hisses, eyeballing the kitchen pointedly. Rodrick has wandered over to the windows and is peering at them curiously.

Nakamura waves at him, and he narrows his eyes before retreating back into the house, leaving them alone again. They both burst into peals of laughter.

"Say, Nakamura. Do you know much about the people coming over tonight, or Hazeline's big annual supper event?" Ed asks, once they've finished laughing.

"Eh, not really. She has a lot of bigwigs come and go. Some come often, some never return. She's frivolous with her friendships, much more so than she is with her staff," he says pointedly. "Last year, that huge American tech guy came for the supper club. You know, the one who created that big social media app and married that young model?"

"No way!" Ed exclaims. "He came all the way here for supper with *Hazeline*?"

Nakamura shrugs. "I guess he really liked the menu."

There's a short pause, then both men burst out laughing once more.

Nakamura sighs. "I'd better get back to work. I have to clean the van to take it out again tomorrow."

"Another big delivery?"

"Nah, collecting this time. I have to return to Agawa-san to pick up the rest of our order." He wanders back toward the house without realizing what he's said, but Ed's brain is ticking over quickly.

Agawa. He frowns, trying to remember. Then it clicks. Chef Chungpu's voice rings in his head.

Best butcher this side of Tokyo. Nobody can beat Agawa-san's cuts.

Whatever was in that body bag, Nakamura delivered it and is having it returned, piece by piece.

EMILY OR EMMA

A wild screeching erupts in the kitchen—the sound of geese screaming. The first of Hazeline's friends have arrived. Two women, both white, both overdone with makeup and wearing silly heels that are out of place in the house. Hazeline is wearing her soft leather slippers, flat and lined with sheepskin. Despite being shorter than them, she looks like the leader of the pack, the most confident, the most sure of herself. The others are hiding behind masks, their Chanel and Gucci bags angling off the crooks of their arms awkwardly, the smell of designer perfume overpowering the usual scents of the house.

Ed stands at the sink, washing his hands and taking in the scene before him, desperately trying to push away his conspiracy theories relating to the body bag. After all, he has a dinner to cater.

"Emily, darling, it's been so long," Hazeline gushes, air-kissing the orange woman with big yellow hair upheld by pearl clips.

"Well, it would have been shorter if you lived in London with us instead of all the way out here in the jungle." The woman lets out a strange fake laugh that makes the hairs on Ed's arms stand up.

Hazeline stretches her mouth into a smile in response, but it doesn't quite reach her eyes as she stares Emily down.

"I mean, who can blame you? This house is beautiful, and so *big!*" Emily gushes, quickly correcting herself. Hazeline drops her shoulders just a fraction, leaning in to greet the other woman, a redhead wearing a dress so tight that Ed can see her belly button indent. "And you look just fabulous, Emma."

"The Botox and boob jobs help!" The woman winks and the three women laugh as though the funniest joke in the world has just been told. Ed squeezes his good eye shut to stop from rolling it.

The blonde places her bag on the ground, and behind them, Ed watches Momo silently sniff it before cocking a leg and peeing all over it. She's oblivious, and he snorts a laugh.

"Here, I have something for you," says the redhead, rooting around in her Gucci bag feverishly. "Just a little gift," she says. Ed watches with interest. She produces a little red velvet bag tied up with a ribbon. Hazeline's greedy little paws are held out, and she gasps in delight as she rips the ribbon off and pores over her new jewelry.

"Oh! Oh, Emma! It's just marvelous! Gosh, where ever did you find such a thing? Here, look, Emily," she says, holding out the necklace.

Emily glances at it and gives a tight-lipped smile. She is clearly put out that she, in comparison, arrived empty-handed.

"Rodrick?" Hazeline seems to realize for the first time that her housekeeper has made himself scarce. In his absence, she turns to Ed. "Ed, petal, come. Look at my gift! Would you be an absolute darling and take it to Rodrick, ask him to put it with all my special treasures? He'll know what I mean."

"Good lord! What happened to your face?" Emily or Emma—he's already forgotten who is who—asks, her hand clapped over her mouth.

"Laser eye surgery," Ed says.

"For just one?" she replies, nose scrunching slightly.

"He had a lazy eye. Terrible squint," Hazeline says.

"Oh gosh, how very brave," the other Emily or Emma says.

"Yes, Ed is a little trooper," Hazeline says, and Ed can see in her eyes that she's laughing at him.

"Here you go, off you run, make sure it's locked up in the special jewelry box!" she says, dropping the necklace into Ed's hands and turning to the women. "Now, girls, let's go catch up, shall we?" She nods to the garden where Rodrick has set up a small cocktail table for them by the pond, margarita glasses lined up and ready to go.

"Oh yes, let's!" Emily or Emma says, hopping in her silly little shoes with glee.

Ed finds Rodrick in the reading room, flipping through some of the recipe books. He jumps up guiltily—then, seeing it's only Ed, relaxes.

"I thought you were Hazeline."

"Hiding out?" Ed asks.

"I loathe her friends," Rodrick admits, and Ed laughs.

"I can see why. Momo pissed on one of their purses."

Rodrick laughs, and it's the first time Ed's heard it. It's a low rumble, deep but surprisingly warm. "She only sees them about once a year, but it's once too much," Rodrick says with a small shudder.

"They seem very different to Hazeline." Ed thinks of the way they so overtly flaunt their wealth, their facades all glamorous despite just going to a friend's home for dinner.

"Yes. They are. But they all have similar taste, I suppose," Rodrick says.

"Not in clothes."

"No, not in clothes." Rodrick laughs softly.

"Rodrick," Ed starts, tentatively. "Yesterday, the large package in the tarp that went to the butcher . . ."

Rodrick looks up. "The deer?"

"Deer?"

"We shot a deer in the woods," he replied.

"Oh. Of course. Never mind," Ed says, feeling, once again, idiotic. "Anyway, the friends, they gave Hazeline a gift. She told me to find you. She wants it put in her special jewelry box with her other treasures?"

To his relief, Rodrick looks like he knows exactly what this means, and heads to the back of the room to a large, antique dresser.

"Hazeline stores all of her heirlooms and special trinkets in here," he explains, taking a small key from his chest pocket and opening the drawer to reveal an array of items, many of which look antique. Silver spoons with beautifully carved handles and inscriptions, dried flowers captured in glass lockets, a strange taxidermy bumblebee lying in a velvet ring box, and brilliant jewelry of all colors and stones.

"Wow," Ed says, wondering who Hazeline will leave it all to, with no children of her own. Hopefully not her terrible friends. And what about Ed? What trinkets does he have to pass on to Kaori when she's older? Nothing of sentimental value, nor market worth. All he has is mass-produced plastic crap, devoid of any originality, story, or specialness. Why is it that he has become so used to spending money on ten plastic dolls, factory-manufactured and sold in Kiddy Land, instead of saving the money and buying one perfect doll—something truly special and harder to find? He decides that, from now on, he will take more time finding quality items for his daughter, thrifted treasures, instead of praying that a higher quantity of toys will help make up for his poor fathering skills.

"Are those teeth?" he asks, pointing at a set of earrings set in gold.

"Yes. Wolf fangs, I believe," Rodrick replies.

Ed pulls a face.

"Do you know about the Kalinago people?" the housekeeper asks.

Ed shakes his head.

"Hazeline's fascinated by them. They are fierce tribespeople of the Caribbean, and the word 'cannibal' originated from when colonizers discovered them. The male warriors would wear the teeth and bones of their victims as trophies, and wearing gold was a status symbol. I think these earrings are an homage to them."

Ed looks down at the new necklace for the first time, the one gifted by Hazeline's friend today, and is horrified by the bizarreness of the piece. It's a small, delicate gold chain, but on it is what looks like a piece of bone. It must be animal, though it looks like a small finger bone, and it's been painted gold and embedded with tiny little azure gemstones. Wire coils around the end of the bone, and a strange ringlet of black hair runs through it. Ed wrinkles his nose and hands the necklace to Rodrick, who takes it without comment. At the back of the dresser drawer is a small wooden box. Rodrick opens it and places the necklace amidst various other chains and sparkles, and it's while he's closing the box and carefully replacing it in the drawer that Ed notices one of the items in particular. It's a silver bangle, lying beside the bumblebee. But what catches Ed's eye is the inscription on the inside of the band, written in a careful, black script in English.

You are forever my heart. All my love, R.B.

Rodrick Bauer.

PENNY IN A VAULT OF GOLD

Ed wants to tell Nakamura that his suspicions are correct, about Rodrick and Hazeline. To gossip and laugh and share ridiculous theories about it all. But the doorbell rings, and Rodrick is somehow already there, greeting the final three guests. Ed hovers nearby, unsure whether he should introduce himself or wait for them to ask. Thankfully, Rodrick feels his nervous energy and takes control of the situation.

"Come through, everyone, please. Hazeline is outside entertaining. And this is our chef, Ed Cook, who will be serving you today." The girl drops her head in a tiny bow. The two men stand ramrod-straight, one eyeing him with a dangerous grin, the other looking through him as though he is just a ghost.

"Nice to meet you, mate," the first says. He is mixed-race, thin and wiry, a film director from London. Ed shakes his hand, grateful. "What's going on under there, then?" He winks.

"Laser eye surgery," Ed replies.

"Mad one!"

The second man does not introduce himself, but he doesn't need to. Ed recognizes him. He's a high-powered senator from the US.

He is stiff, shifty, and avoids Ed's eye, but he holds out his hand brusquely for a shake, mumbling something incomprehensible under his breath as he does so.

"And this is Miyuki," Rodrick finishes, gesturing to the small Japanese girl. Miyuki, of course! Ed thought he recognized her, but she seems so different in real life. She is one of the biggest J-pop stars of the moment, but whenever Ed has seen her on television, she's been a shiny, sparkling doll—laughing, flirting for the camera, popping a hip and throwing up a peace sign for her delighted fans. Today she's dead behind the eyes, serious and calculating. She nods again, and Ed mirrors it.

Rodrick leads them through to Hazeline in the garden, where a new round of exclamations and excitement begins, the men peacocking around the two women in tight dresses, Miyuki tilting up the corners of her mouth in the smallest of greetings, quickly picking up a margarita glass.

When Rodrick returns to Ed in the kitchen, he leans in closely. "That singer, the girl. She's a psychopath," he whispers.

Ed laughs, then, taking in Rodrick's serious demeanor, sucks it back in.

"For real?"

"Yes. Watch yourself around her. She 'accidentally' stabbed me with a fork once."

Ed is getting the dinner ready to serve when Hazeline splits away from her friends, who are still outside drinking and chatting. "Ed, petal. I'd like a quick chat?"

He immediately tenses, but follows her out of the kitchen and into the reading room.

"Did you put the necklace away as I asked?"

"Yes, Rodrick locked it away in the jewelry box in the top drawer," Ed says, relaxing.

"Good, good. Lots of lovely things in that drawer. Sentimental, too. Many precious gifts from my dear Botan. But always locked, so don't you go getting any ideas!" She wags a finger at him and laughs.

"I would never," Ed assures her, though he tastes the lie on his tongue. If it was six months ago, he would have rifled through the drawer and pawned her goods off for gambling money. But he's not gambling anymore. He's controlling his urges. He has no choice.

"Now, Ed, we've all played along with you so far, but I want the truth about what happened to your eye," she says, sitting down and looking at him expectantly, hands crossed in her lap.

"I told you, I—"

"—don't insult me. I know that wasn't caused from walking into a pole. You practically have a fist imprint on your face. I want to know who hit you, and why."

A silence drags out, Ed shifting his feet, watching his slippers wriggle on the smooth surface of the floor.

"I don't like secrets in this house, Ed. And I can't hire staff who have secrets."

The threat hangs in the room, weighing Ed down as he looks at her, wide-eyed.

"It would be such a shame to lose you, so close to the big annual dinner party," she goes on, inspecting her nails.

"Okay. Okay, I'll admit what's been happening," Ed says hastily, desperate not to lose this job. "I'm in debt. Great debt. From . . . well, from gambling," he admits quietly, a hot flush of shame curdling his insides. He is mortified. "But it's under control. I've been paying them back. I'll be clear soon."

"And who do you owe this money to? How much is it in total?" Her lips purse.

Ed tells her the figure, his voice a whisper. She does not flinch.

"Tell me who you owe."

"A man. A bad man, called Isamu Ikagi. But I'm paying him off and it will all be over soon, I promise—"

Hazeline holds her hand up and Ed halts, mouth still open.

"I will pay off your debts, Ed. I will send Nakamura and Rodrick to find him, and we will sort it all out."

Ed takes in a sharp breath and blinks stupidly, his jaw on a hinge.

"I don't want all this hassle distracting you, it's not a worry. You can just continue working for me until it's all paid off," she says with a wave of her fingers, as though the amount is just a penny in a vault of gold bars. To her, it probably is.

"But, I—oh, Hazeline, I couldn't . . . I mean, if you're sure?" he babbles, feeling as though a tight and painful bubble in his chest has just burst. To his great embarrassment, tears begin to stream down his face.

"Oh, don't now. Stop with all the hysterics," Hazeline says, flapping a hand in the air. "We will sort this all out, yes?"

Ed drops to his knees. "Thank you. Thank you, thank you so much," he weeps.

Hazeline stands, looks down at him pityingly. "Don't worry about it. Now, sort yourself out and come serve us supper," she says, marching out of the room swiftly and leaving Ed on the floor.

In that moment, Ed thinks that he would do anything for Hazeline, who has unknowingly not only cleared his debts, but saved his family. Saved him from himself.

CULINARY SINS

When Ed finally returns to the kitchen, he feels like his face may split from smiling. He feels like he's floating, salting his food with a flourish and even doing a little twirl on the way to the sink.

"What happened in there?" Rodrick asks him, eyes narrowed.

Ed taps the side of his nose and laughs. "Don't worry, nothing saucy." He winks at Rodrick, who blinks at him, startled, then begins to stutter and huff in indignation. Ed laughs again, then glides outside to collect the pork ribs from the smoker. The men instinctively pull away from the women to come over, the senator curiously peeking over Ed's shoulder, lingering beside him like a begging dog. Ed puffs his chest out, twirling the tongs in his hand like a showy bartender relying on tips.

"I've been dying for a peek under here ever since I arrived," the director admits, standing on Ed's other side. "Hazeline gave me a right telling off every time I wandered too near. So, what do we have going on? Smells lush."

Ed opens the lid of the smoker with a flourish. The ribs are black and glazed, the smell nutty and sweet.

"Cor!" The director folds his arms and leans back. The senator is nodding theatrically, his eyes fixed on the meat.

"Smoked with a pecan and walnut-wood combination," Ed explains, quickly removing the ribs and transferring them to a large platter. "They'll rest for a moment and I'll slice to serve, but in the meantime, the appetizer is ready for you."

Rodrick, who is hastily refilling drinks, overhears and ushers the guests inside to the dining table, which has been carefully laid with bamboo placemats, calligraphic name-cards, and flickering candles placed in recycled dark wine bottles. There is something charming and simple about the decor, reminiscent of students on a budget playing at grown-ups having a dinner party, but Ed knows better. These aren't six-quid bottles of wine from the Aldi discount section; they were handpicked and recommended by Japanese sommeliers for whatever meal Hazeline was serving, now cleaned and repurposed for decoration. The placemats aren't Ikea basics, but natural, dye-free bamboo handcrafted by artisans in Oita prefecture. True wealth, Ed is learning, is not flaunted. It is discreet, tasteful, and proud. To the untrained eye, the setup might look simple and affordable. To those with wealth, who know the price tags of the decorative wine bottles, the quality of the mats, the light scent of the soy candles—well, to them, it is exquisite and tasteful.

"I have to leave on some important business for Hazeline. You will have to serve dinner alone," Rodrick tells Ed quietly as he plates the liver.

"No problem," Ed says, distracted, trying to make the plates look fancy, the slivers of meat carefully placed on the toasted bread and decorated with the onions and mushrooms, the sauce drizzled in what Ed hopes is an artistic way to finish it off.

He brings the plates over to the guests, who all hush as he approaches. Is this what power feels like? Once everyone is served, he clears his throat and wipes his hands down his trousers. "This is

Hazeline's special liver recipe, served on a toasted garlic sourdough with mushrooms, onions, and a rich accompanying sauce. Enjoy." He bows, and to his great delight, Emily or Emma claps in excitement.

He returns to check on his ribs, to see if they're ready to serve, but discreetly listens in on the conversation.

"Cheers, everyone. To our culinary sins," Hazeline says, holding out her glass of wine.

"To our culinary sins," everyone echoes.

Itadakimasu, Ed thinks to himself.

Ed is slicing the ribs when he hears the first groan.

He looks up. It's the senator. Opposite him, Miyuki puts down her chopsticks, and closes her eyes as she chews slowly.

"Ugh. Ed. This is divine," Hazeline moans.

"God, you never fail to deliver, Hazeline," the director says, picking a bit of meat from between his teeth with a loud sucking sound.

"Well, enjoy. This is, after all, the main attraction," Hazeline says.

Ed frowns. Main attraction? What about his ribs? Surely *those* are the main attraction, not her bizarre milky onion liver?

"And so fresh! You can really tell," Emily or Emma says, taking a deep drag of her wine, the swallow loud and vulgar.

Hazeline smiles demurely, taking another tiny bite of her own portion and chewing slowly.

"And where is it from?" Miyuki asks. It's the first time Ed has heard her speak, and her voice is quiet, monotone.

"Well, actually, this was a bit different to my usual offerings. This one came all the way from Mississippi," she says. And then she turns, and looks Ed dead in the eye, smiling.

DESSERT

KNOW YOURSELVES

A chill runs down Ed's back, the hairs on his neck and arms static and electric as he looks at Hazeline. It looks like her eyes are twinkling, daring him to say something. A predator toying with its prey. He clears his throat, turns away from her watchful gaze and washes his hands, but they're shaking. Mississippi. Where Ellie was from. A coincidence, surely? A strange, creepy coincidence. Because what is it he's thinking here? That his boss, this tiny, graceful old woman, slaughtered and served up an American teenager for supper? He thinks back to when he told Sayuri about the lamb shank incident, her laughter, his realization at how ridiculous he sounded. This is the same, but on steroids. A cannibalistic heiress? Ed shakes his head, flicks the water droplets from his hands and dries them quickly on a towel. Ridiculous. She's winding him up.

He senses rather than knows that Hazeline has stopped watching him. Still feeling flustered, his body not yet caught up with his rationale, he begins to plate up the pork ribs. He ignores his heart beating painfully in his chest. His body seems desperate to go into flight mode, and every ounce of Ed's willpower is fighting against it, forcing himself to remain calm, to not let his imagination run away with him. Despite the blackened crust on the outside, the insides of the ribs are perfectly cooked, pink and juicy, and he serves them on top of a small mound of white rice, with Asian slaw on the side and a sprinkling of spring onions as a garnish. He brings the plates to the table and once again introduces the course, finishing with another small bow. The director is rubbing his palms together, greedily eyeing up his plate. The senator licks his lips. Miyuki looks bored. Momo is at Hazeline's feet, gazing hopefully up at his master, licking his lips. Emily and Emma have their phones out, snapping photographs of their food.

"No phones," Miyuki barks, to Ed's great surprise.

The redhead turns a shade of pink, then quickly shovels her phone back into the purse at her feet.

"Chill, it's not like we were taking photographs of any of our faces," the blonde says, rolling her eyes but putting her phone away, too. "Nobody will ever know that the pop princess was dining with us today."

"Regardless. You know the rules. No photos," Hazeline snaps.

A beat of awkward silence descends on the room, then the director tucks into his food and the quiet is replaced by the scraping of cutlery, the squelch of chewing, the glugs of more wine being poured.

Ed begins to clean up the kitchen. The final course is just a fruit platter and sweet *umeshu.* Another successful evening in his cooking career, despite his inner turmoil at the end of the appetizer.

"So, tell us, Hazeline, how is business?" the senator asks.

"Am I allowed to ask you the same question?" Hazeline bats her lashes at him.

"No politics at the table, please," Emma or Emily groans.

"Well, that's me and my updates out then!" The senator laughs. He has begun to redden from the alcohol, his eyes glazing.

"But really, how are things?" the director asks, looking to Hazeline.

"You know, could be better, could be worse," she replies.

"I'm assuming worse, based on the fact we're eating pork ribs right now," Miyuki says drily.

Hey! Those pork ribs are the finest money can buy! I got a black eye for those ribs! Ed thinks.

"We had an unfortunate freezer mishap," Hazeline shoots back.

"Christ! What a nightmare," the director says.

"Indeed. An expensive nightmare."

"But the ribs are delicious," the senator quickly adds.

"Yeah, Hazeline, *so* good," Emily or Emma gushes.

"What's the outlook for your famous dinner party, then? It's still happening, right?" Miyuki asks. Her tone makes her words sound like an interrogation, and once again Ed finds it difficult to pair the stern woman at the table with the smiling, flirtatious and giggly J-pop star he's seen in interviews.

"Yes, it's still happening," Hazeline says. Her tone is clipped. "I'll go to the charity this week and am sure we can arrange a way of ironing out the issue."

"Ah yes, the charity. How's that all going? You're *so* philanthropic, it's commendable," Emily or Emma says, leaning across the table toward Hazeline, who has the decency to look bashful.

"Yes, yes, well, you know. Those of us who are blessed with privilege must do our part to help those in need!"

"And I do *always* donate to charity," Emily or Emma adds pointedly, looking at each dinner guest in the eye in challenge.

"Of course, of course," the director agrees. "Always!"

"And attend galas and events to help raise money," the senator slurs from his seat.

"I give a monthly donation to children in need," Emily or Emma adds, nodding her head as though approving her own actions.

"Gosh, what a table of generous humanitarians we all are," Miyuki deadpans, her voice dripping with sarcasm.

"Well, it's better to do something than nothing at all!" Emily or Emma retorts. She looks offended, her Botox straining to give way to the slightest of frowns.

"Yes, and really, the single mothers' plight in Japan is terrible. Every little bit helps," Hazeline says.

Ed frowns. Single mothers? What does that have to do with anything? Is this what her charity work is about?

"It's true. I've read terrible things. So many poor women out there, they're really struggling. They have no support from the government, and they're ostracized by family and friends," Emily or Emma says.

"Let's not pretend we're here doing what we do out of the goodness of our hearts," Miyuki cuts in. "We could pay for a billion condoms and get them handed out. Hell, why not just castrate all the men?" She snorts, and the senator's mouth drops open in horror. "We could protest for more government aid. We could stop society discriminating against single mothers, making it difficult for them to rent homes. We could fight harder against the gender pay gap. Instead, we do what? Play at charity and host fancy dinner parties."

Ed frowns, confused.

Silence descends on the table, and Ed can see Hazeline trembling in rage from where he stands.

"If you don't want to be involved, you didn't have to come. Nobody is forcing you to be here," she hisses.

"You misunderstand me," Miyuki replies. "I'm perfectly happy to be here. I am having a fine time. I love the . . . exclusivity of the food you serve at your soirées, which is why I am always here. I leave stronger, more powerful. What I don't want to do is sit yapping, pretending that we are all doing a service to this country to make ourselves feel better. Know yourselves. Know who you are, accept it, and move on. Stop creating these false narratives of yourselves as altruistic saviors."

This time, the silence drags out even longer, the only sound a strange giggling from Miyuki. In his chair, the senator sways, muttering incoherently under his breath.

Emily and Emma stare fixedly at their cleaned plates, one of them picking viciously at the edges of her manicured nails.

The director has leaned right back in his chair and takes a long gulp of his drink.

Hazeline's mouth has pursed into a tiny, puckered grape, and her eyes have narrowed.

Ed can't bear the silence any longer, the awkward tension that Miyuki has drenched the table in.

"*Umeshu,* anyone?" he offers with an overexaggerated smile, holding the bottle up like a trophy.

PROFESSIONAL HELP

The guests are at the door, sharing slightly uncomfortable goodbyes, when Rodrick returns. He looks oddly flustered, beads of sweat at his hairline. Ed hears the car approaching the home before he sees the headlights. Nakamura parks up, and Rodrick stands politely to the side, allowing for Emily and Emma to scoot past him. They're drunk, stumbling slightly and giggling.

"Do you need a lift? Nakamura can take you to wherever you need to go," Hazeline offers.

"Our taxi is already outside," Emily or Emma replies, blowing a kiss to Hazeline. Ed watches them totter down the long driveway, legs spindly, heels tipping at strange angles, causing them to have a baby-deer-like gait. The senator left immediately after dinner, too drunk for a round of *umeshu.* It's only Miyuki and the director who are still here.

"I'll take a ride," Miyuki says. "I need to get back to the city."

"Nakamura will help you," Hazeline says, raising a hand to Nakamura, who is still in the car. He tips his head and exits the vehicle, opening the back door for Miyuki, who gets in without so much as a word of thanks.

"My car's parked just there, I'm sober," the director informs Hazeline. "Thank you for a wonderful evening," he says, leaning in and depositing a dry kiss on her papery cheek. Behind them, Rodrick jerks his head away. Then the director saunters off without so much as a nod to Ed, who fed him all night, nor Rodrick. Ghosts in a mansion.

As soon as the engine starts, Rodrick is right beside Hazeline, whispering feverishly into her ear. She nods, then bats him away like he's a needy puppy. Perhaps he is.

"Ed, petal. Just so you know, Rodrick has sorted out your little problem with Ikagi. He won't be a bother for you anymore."

"You paid my debts? Already?" Ed blinks.

Rodrick shrugs. "The Yakuza aren't so hard to spot in the streets."

Ed drops to his knees, bowing at both of their feet. "Thank you. Thank you so much!"

"Christ, get up, won't you. You'll get your knees all dirty. There's no need for any of that fuss. I haven't paid them off for you; it's a loan. You just owe me now instead. And lucky for you, I won't be distributing any black eyes," Hazeline adds, looking down at him with an arched brow.

Ed huffs a laugh and rips the bandage off his face now that they're alone again, giving his sallow skin some air to breathe.

"Astoundingly yellow," Hazeline comments.

"He must have really walloped you," Rodrick agrees.

"But never again!" Ed grins. "Never again!" he repeats, the realization sinking in as he fist-pumps the air in victory.

Hazeline laughs. "I'm going to bed now, it's been a long evening. Thank you for your hard work, both of you."

Ed and Rodrick both bow a good night, and then Ed sits on the front step of the doorway, looking out into the woodland. A new realization begins to dawn on him—something he hasn't thought too much about before. He stills, blinking rapidly.

"Is something wrong?" Rodrick asks, standing beside him.

"No, not at all," Ed lies. He doesn't feel comfortable sharing his concerns with Rodrick, and decides to wait until morning to catch Nakamura over a cup of coffee and speak candidly about his feelings. He's surprised to find that there is a strange emotion that must have been hiding in the center of his chest, and now that Ikagi has been paid back by Hazeline in full, the feeling is crawling out of its crevice and seeping outwards, trying to infiltrate Ed's happy mood.

The feeling is fear.

Ed slept restlessly, purposefully leaving his phone unplugged so it would run dry, cutting off his ability to gamble online. He's in the kitchen, preparing a quick breakfast for Hazeline. He has a feeling she'll be feeling slightly under the weather, judging from how much she drank, and has decided on some simple toast with sweet and creamy red bean paste to soak up the alcohol and restore her sugar levels. He knows he's made the right choice when Rodrick comes in, informing him that Hazeline will be eating in bed this morning, before taking it away on a tray with a jug of ice water.

And just on time, Nakamura swings by to get his morning coffee and read the day's to-do list. Every day, Hazeline and Rodrick lay lists out on the counter for all the staff. Nakamura's has information about any trips he's required to run. This morning, it looks very sparse.

"Not much on?" Ed asks.

Nakamura shakes his head. "Nope! One quick trip to the butcher with Rodrick to pick up some orders and that's me for the day!"

"The deer?" Ed asks.

"Yes," Nakamura replies quickly.

"What are you going to do with your time off?" Ed asks.

"I'll probably hang around with Suki. She's awake, and more lucid than usual. The medicines can make her drowsy but she's in good spirits today, so perhaps we will watch a show together, or I'll read a book to her or something," he says. "What about you?"

"Well, to be honest," Ed admits, "I was hoping to speak to you before I went home. You know Hazeline sorted out my debts last night?"

"*Majide!*" Nakamura's eyes widen. "All of it? With the Yakuza?"

"Yes." Ed lowers his head, chews on his lip.

"Did she find out because of the . . ." Nakamura gestures vaguely at his eye, the hand motion becoming bigger until he is circling his entire face.

"Yes."

"Well, this is great news!" Nakamura laughs, stopping when he sees Ed's pained expression. "Ed-san, this is good news, no?"

Ed sighs. "I will owe Hazeline now instead."

Nakamura darts his eyes to the empty kitchen doorway, then back to Ed. "Hazeline . . . Well, she asks a lot of her staff. Maybe sometimes too much. But she is also loyal, and will protect you and keep you around if you have proven yourself as one of her inner circle," Nakamura says, his voice low.

"No, it's not her I'm worried about," Ed says. "I think I spent so long trying to work out how to pay Ikagi back that I didn't give much thought to what would happen once he was actually paid. Now I will have money in my account, and no debts, and my life is not in danger. You understand?" he asks, raising both brows.

It clicks for Nakamura. "Ah, you are worried about the gambling?"

"Very," Ed admits, wringing his hands. "I even let my phone die so I wasn't tempted to play a quick round or two last night."

"But why? You have not gambled in so long. Why break that now?"

"Well, I wasn't gambling before because I had no money. If I gambled what I was making away before paying Ikagi back, I would have been in serious trouble. Every penny I made was either going to him, or to the food on my family's table. With Hazeline, she is less demanding when it comes to repayment. She won't add interest or anything, just wants me to slowly work it off. So it feels like I suddenly have more money than I've had in a very long time, burning a hole in my pocket. And that part of my brain that thinks *you could double it in seconds* is still there, whispering to me."

Nakamura shakes his head. "You can't, you have worked so hard. You must fight the urge."

"It's easier said than done. I don't know how to fight the urge. If I did, I never would have placed any bets with Ikagi in the first place."

"I think, Ed-san, that deep down, you know what you have to do."

Ed looks up at the younger man and knows what he means. He doesn't say it, waits for Nakamura to do it for him.

"You have to come clean to your wife, tell her everything, and get professional help."

"What if she leaves me?" Ed asks, his voice a whisper.

Nakamura shrugs, as though it doesn't matter in the slightest. "Then she leaves you, and you can only blame yourself. At least she will leave you knowing the man you truly are if you come clean and you're honest with her. But I don't think she will. You seem to love her very much."

"I do," Ed insists. "But she has pride."

"You know, Botan had a problem with alcohol, for a year or two. I heard about it through Rodrick. It happened before his cancer, when his family became estranged after he married Hazeline. They didn't approve of her. A mixed-race socialite," Nakamura says quietly.

"He was an alcoholic?" Ed asks.

"Yes. Drank himself into a stupor every night. He was sad. It's hard, I imagine, choosing between your wife and your family. I am lucky I haven't had to make that choice. But Botan did, and he chose Hazeline. It was hard, especially as the press were all over it. His parents were paying investigators to drag up the most sordid of secrets from Hazeline's past, having them all publicly aired to try to force him to leave her out of embarrassment."

"Poor Hazeline!"

"Yes, but she didn't care about any of it. All she cared about was Botan, how it was hurting him, and how, in turn, he was hurting himself. She managed to finally get him the help he needed, and he was sober until his death as a result of her involvement. She persevered; she didn't give up on him. Do you think your wife would give up on you so easily? Or will she love you as Hazeline loved Botan?"

"I'm not sure," Ed replies honestly, thinking of all the lies, all the late nights he crept home and slipped into bed after a bad day of betting—all the weeks unable to pay for Kaori's daycare. "But perhaps it's time for me to find out."

NO MORE SECRETS

Ed is playing with his fingers, sweat pooling slowly at his hairline. His knee is jiggling up and down, and it takes a moment for him to realize Sayuri has asked him a question.

"Sorry, what?"

"I said, can you help dry the dishes while I feed Kaori?"

"Oh, right. Yes." He gets up, body on autopilot, and wobbles over to the counter, tattered dishcloth in hand. His heart is hammering in his chest. *Tell her. Tell her. Tell her.*

"Is everything okay? You're acting very distracted," Sayuri says, holding a spoon up to Kaori's little pink mouth. Their daughter gobbles it up and opens her mouth again for more, a tiny bird after its worm.

"Erm, mmm. I—yeah. Mmm. Not really, I guess. I dunno," Ed mumbles, trying to swallow but finding a lump in his throat. He pours himself a glass of tap water, swirls the liquid around in his dry mouth for a moment.

"Ed?" Sayuri tries. "What's going on? Has something happened at work?" She puts the spoon down, widens her eyes. "You haven't lost your job again, have you?"

"No. No, no. Nothing like that," he says quickly.

"Ugh, thank goodness," she breathes out. "I don't know that I could bear to go through all that stress a second time, and you've been so much happier since you got this new job."

He pauses. "I have?"

"Sure. You're home a lot more, you've been playing with Kaori more. You're watching cooking shows instead of horse racing on the television, always thinking about how to better yourself and your cooking rather than being miserable out at the bars with your friends. You've just been more . . . alive, I guess." She shrugs, wiping a glob of goop off Kaori's cheek.

"Huh. I guess you're right," Ed says, looking down at his distorted reflection in the back of a spoon.

"So what is it?"

"Hmm?"

"What's wrong?" she asks, blinking up at him.

His shoulders sag.

Tell her. Tell her. Tell her.

"It's . . ." He's finding it too hard. He swallows. Perhaps it just needs to be blurted out, quickly, so it's less painful. Like ripping a Band-aid off. But no—that may be less painful for him, but it's disrespectful to Sayuri, who deserves more. She deserves an explanation and a real conversation about this. It can't be swept under the carpet.

"Could we . . . could we sit down and talk about it?"

"Oh? Yes, of course. It sounds serious," she says, and her voice sounds small.

"It is, I suppose," Ed says, leading her away from the kitchen table. They set Kaori up with a coloring book and some stubby crayons, sitting slightly away from her so they can speak candidly.

"I have something to admit to you," Ed begins, taking a deep breath.

"Oh my God. You're leaving us. You've met someone else?" Sayuri brings her hand to her mouth, shaking her head rapidly.

"No, no, no!" Ed says quickly, grabbing both of her hands and holding them tightly. "Nothing like that, none of those things. It's about money."

Her fingers in his grip clench lightly. "Money?"

"Yes. I have something to admit to you, and you're not going to like it. And it's very difficult for me to admit that I have been hiding something from you for so long, but I need you to understand that I am working on solving the problem and it's under control. But I need your help."

"Huh," she muses, almost to herself. "And you need *my* help?" She's frowning, her voice sardonic, but she keeps her hands in his, her body facing his with total attention.

"When I lost my job, you remember I was playing pachinko a lot?"

She nods, lips pursed.

"Well, I got pretty obsessed with it. Not with the game itself, with the feeling I got when I played it."

"Feeling?" She tilts her head. Sayuri has never understood the fascination with the game, grew up watching her granny play it while Sayuri waited by her side like a puppy, the sounds and lights of the parlor offensive to her senses.

"I don't know, like a . . . rush, I suppose? And so that was when I started gambling on the boats and the horses. The pachinko money wasn't giving me enough of a rush after a while, and I had to turn elsewhere."

"I see," she says slowly, waiting for him to continue, to see how far he is taking this conversation.

"But then soon, even those bets, they weren't enough, you understand? It wasn't enough for me. I needed more and more to feel alive and awake. So I ended up betting with some Yakuza."

Sayuri gasps, rips her hands from his, and curls them into tight little fists. "Ed!" she exclaims, then quickly darts her eyes toward their daughter, who is still coloring, singing gobbledygook to herself, oblivious. "You didn't!" she hisses, her voice quieter.

"I did." He lowers his head, and feels his eyes water slightly.

"All those bruises . . . The car being written off!" He watches as realization dawns, her face paling, her eyes glazing over, then hardening. "Those were all lies!" she hisses at him, leaning back.

"I'm so sorry. I am so, so sorry."

"So what? What are you saying? You owe them money? How much? Oh, God, are you in danger? Are *we* in danger?" She looks over at her daughter, her eyes wide with horror.

"I did owe them money. Not anymore. Hazeline paid them off for me."

"*Hazeline?* Your boss paid off the Yakuza for you?" Sayuri echoes, shaking her head in disbelief, bringing a hand to her cheek as though soothing the sting of a slap.

"Yes, I just have to work it off for her."

"Why would she do something like that for you? Don't try to tell me it's because you're a great chef. We both know it's not that," she says, her voice dripping with disdain. "You've survived this job so far by cooking omelets, salads, and barbecues. So why—why would she do this?"

"I think she's just a nice woman to her employees. I told you how she's helping Nakamura's wife, didn't I?"

Sayuri doesn't seem convinced, and crosses her arms.

"So now you just owe her? And how much is it? A lot?"

"It's a lot," Ed admits. "But Hazeline won't charge me interest like the Yakuza did."

"And this money you've frittered away of ours, how bad a position are we really in? How is Kaori's future going to be impacted by this?"

Ed blinks, surprised at his wife's intuition. She can't know about the college account being drained, surely? No, she's just putting her child first in the face of a crisis, as always. Instinctively maternal.

"It's manageable," he says eventually.

She sighs, slumps back into the sofa, rubs her forehead. The empty space in his palms where her hands were feels cold.

"Why didn't you tell me this sooner?"

"I was ashamed," Ed says, looking down. "Embarrassed. It's a shameful thing to have such little willpower, to have lost all of our hard-earned money. And even more so here, where gambling isn't even legal."

She's nodding in agreement, but won't make eye contact with him.

"This rush you spoke about," she begins slowly. "What do you mean? What is not fulfilling you in your life? Is it me?"

"No! No, Sayuri, not at all. You and Kaori are the reason I've managed to get out of this spiral. You're my reason to keep trying to do better," he says, racked with guilt that his wife would even consider this a possibility.

"I guess I just felt like a failure, for losing my job. I felt like I wasn't providing for you in the way you deserve. I also . . . I don't know how to behave around Kaori, and it makes me feel like I'm not cut out to be a dad."

He expects some sort of sympathy at this, but instead, his wife gives a loud *tsk.* "No parent knows how to behave the first time around. You think I knew how to be a mother immediately?"

"I never really thought about it. I guess I just assumed it came naturally to you. That you had some sort of parental instinct that I was missing. You make it seem so easy," Ed says.

"Well, it isn't. It's hard. I have no clue what I'm doing. Some days I want to lock myself in a room and cry because I don't know what my daughter wants, what she's thinking, if she even likes me!" Sayuri says, her eyes filling with tears. "And you think that you're the only one feeling that way and get to run off and hide at gambling dens instead? Lying to me about it all and still clinging on to so much pride that you rebutted my attempts to help you get a job?" She sounds vicious, a rage in her he has not experienced before.

"I never knew you felt that way. I thought it was just me," Ed says.

"Well, it's not," she snaps. "And maybe if you had bothered to ask me, to communicate, or to help me out a bit, neither of us would have felt like we were struggling." She sniffs, wiping her eyes with the back of her hand.

"God, I am so sorry, Sayuri."

She glares at him. "Why now? Why are you telling me now?"

"Because I need help. I need you to help me. I'm scared. Scared I'll gamble again, lose us even more. It's all I think about when I'm not at work." His lip wobbles. What kind of a man is he? He's clearly been a terrible partner to his struggling wife, and now he's asking her to take on the added responsibility of caring for his gambling addiction? What a waste of space.

She regards him carefully, then eventually lets out a long sigh. "You're a good father, you know. Kaori loves you. She is always happy when you come home from work. She loves how you play with her, when you tickle her and do things that I'm too afraid to do in case I drop her or break her somehow."

They both look to their daughter, who is scribbling away with concentration, the tip of her tongue sticking out as she frowns down at her work of art.

"I think I'm just putting too much pressure on myself," Ed says, thinking of his conversation in the garden with Nakamura. "I feel like I have to be perfect, the perfect husband, perfect father, and if I'm not, I'm worthless. Then, to try to feel something other than empty, I gamble."

Sayuri is silent for a long time, but he can tell that she's thinking carefully.

"You're kind, Ed. You're loving, and caring, and funny. But you're not intelligent, you don't notice things happening right in front of your face, and you're selfish," Sayuri says evenly. "To bring this home and expect me to fix it all for you, to make it all better, is selfish. Do you so desperately need a woman to step in and be your hero?"

She has never been so candid with him before. He isn't sure if she is referring to herself as the heroine, or Hazeline. It doesn't matter; either way, she's right.

"I just need help," he says sadly. "And I don't know who else can do it."

She gives a long, tired sigh. "Okay. Well, I think the best thing for us to do is for you to let me be in charge of all of our income and expenses for a while. Until you feel that you can easily go without gambling," she says slowly.

Ed nods, and to his surprise, immediately feels a weight off his chest.

"I'll take all the cash, we will transfer all the money and your salary to an account you have no access to, and go from there," she says, sounding confident in her ability to take control. As though she had this plan all along, and has been waiting to reveal it, to ease his burdens. Ed nods eagerly. "Yes. Yes, that would be a huge help. The less money I have, the better."

"And you need to get some help for your feelings, for why you're gambling, I suppose. Maybe therapy?" she suggests.

Ed isn't a fan of the idea, but is in no position to bargain. It's one thing admitting to his wife how pathetic he feels, another admitting it to a stranger. But it's the least he can do.

"Hypnotherapy can sometimes be effective for gamblers," he admits.

"Hypnotherapy? I think you will find it hard to find someone who helps gamblers in Japan," Sayuri hedges.

"I could use a British one, do it online over a video call?" Ed suggests.

Sayuri nods. "Whatever you think will work."

Ed feels a surge of love and appreciation for his wife. "Thank you," he says, pulling her close for a hug. "I'm so sorry."

"I hope we can come together now as a family. Be closer, communicate more openly. No more secrets," she says sternly.

"No more secrets," Ed agrees.

"And Ed? About Hazeline . . ." she says.

"Yes?"

"Just be careful of her."

"Careful?"

"Nobody with that much money or power does something purely from the goodness of their heart. Remember, she may be after something, too."

OISHII

"She says jump, I say how high." Ed shrugs, taking a drag of his cigarette. A week has passed since his conversation with Sayuri, and he's been spending more time at Hazeline's house than usual. She has offered him more and more work, pulling together casual meals for her to enjoy, and it's been low-stress, the money being sent directly to Sayuri. When he told Hazeline the change in bank account, she raised a brow, smirked, and said nothing. He wonders if she actually needs him this much, or if the extra shifts are her way of throwing him a bone, helping him pay off his debt even quicker.

"I'm the same way, don't worry," Nakamura says. "I guess, at the end of the day, I'd do anything for my wife, and that's just how it goes."

"Me too," Ed says firmly, stubbing his cigarette out for emphasis. "Except quit smoking?" He nods to Nakamura's hand with a wink. Nakamura shoves him playfully, and they both laugh, eventually going quiet and listening to the guppy pops of water from the koi fish in the pond.

"Fancy a snack?" Ed asks.

"Sure." Nakamura stands, and the two of them walk back through the doors into the kitchen.

Ed opens a cupboard, and pulls out a square Tupperware holding layers of white doughy mounds. "I made some curry bread this morning, there's plenty. We can both have one." He grins, heating up some oil on the hob and setting two of the floury parcels out on a plate beside it.

"Curry bread. *Oishii!*" Nakamura sighs. *Delicious.*

Ed quickly brushes the little dough packages with an egg wash, before pressing a light coating of panko breadcrumbs evenly over them on every side. The oil has begun to vibrate with heat when Ed places the two bread rolls in it, fizzing and spitting at him happily. A quick couple of flips with the tongs, and a few minutes later he is putting two ocher sausage-shaped rolls onto plates for himself and Nakamura.

They bite into them at the same time, and Ed closes his eyes. Crispy and crunchy on the outside; sweet, tart curry on the inside. "Mmmm!"

"So good!" Nakamura says, happily munching away beside him. "You cook this a lot?"

"No. Only a few times, really. My wife taught me how to. When I first moved to Japan, I loved curry bread so much. I got it every time I went past a *konbini.* Eventually, she showed me how to make it myself to save some money!"

"Perhaps your wife should be the chef instead," Nakamura jokes.

"She probably should, to be fair. If I'm honest, I didn't really cook that much before coming here."

"And if I'm being honest, I didn't really drive much before coming here either," Nakamura laughs. "I just had a license and was desperate!"

"Similar scenario for me. I knew how to cook, but nothing fancy. I've definitely taken 'learning on the job' to a new level. I'm surprised Hazeline hasn't noticed, and demanded something of higher quality."

"She probably knows. She's keeping you for a reason, even if it isn't your cooking," Nakamura says.

Ed goes silent, pondering this.

"But you like it," Nakamura says. A statement, not a question. "The cooking, I mean."

"I don't think I realized how much I liked cooking before. It's different, doing it here, for Hazeline. There are no constraints, creatively or financially. I can cook how I want, using whatever ingredients I want. It's not the same when I'm getting home after a long day at work, hurrying to find something I can make quickly and cheaply to feed my wife and child. Or when I worked back in Britain and had a strict, boring menu of bland fast-food dishes."

"I think you'll find that life here with Hazeline is different full-stop. It's free of any struggles at all. I feel calm all the time, even though my wife is sick in bed every day. It's not the same as it was when we were back at home, when I was losing hair over every new medical bill and had to plaster a smile on my face while I helped her to the toilet, pretending everything was going to be fine—when truthfully, I didn't know if it would be."

"Is this how the rich live? With such total ease in their day-to-day?" Ed asks, licking his fingers of the final panko crumbs.

"Well, ask yourself, Ed. As of right now, you're here, living in this house, too."

"But it's different for me," Ed argues. "I go home at the end of my shift, to reality. It's not like you and Rodrick, here in this nirvana constantly."

"It could be. It's not as if Hazeline is lacking in space. If you keep working for her long enough, I'm sure she'd eventually tell you that you're welcome to a permanent space here."

Ed blinks. He's never really considered that, but now he thinks about it, didn't the job ad mention a full-time, live-in role? He imagines Kaori squatting by the rocks, feeding the koi. Sayuri resting after a long hard day in the private onsen tub. Ed on the balcony, a glass of wine in hand as he reads a bedtime story to his daughter. Desire seizes his whole body like a coil and it takes him a moment to breathe out properly. "I'd love that," he admits quietly, as though afraid to jinx it.

"Dream big, my friend," Nakamura says, piling the two empty plates and taking them over to the sink. "We could be neighbors!"

"Ah, scratch that then, I'm out," Ed jokes.

"Jerk!" Nakamura grins, sauntering out through the garden doors and heading back to his part of the gargantuan home.

INVITE US IN

A few weeks have passed, and Ed and Sayuri are both trying to wrangle Kaori into daytime clothes when the doorbell sounds. Kaori squirms quickly, making the most of the distraction and slipping out of Sayuri's arms before joyfully running away in just her pants, her chubby arms waving in the air jubilantly.

Sayuri sighs. "You get the door, I'll capture the baby."

"Deal," Ed agrees, opening the door just as Kaori begins manically wailing and screaming in distress at being caught by her mother and forced into a jumper. He blinks in confusion.

It's Hazeline. On the tiny doorstep of his home. Behind her, Nakamura stands, looking sheepish, and he tries to mouth something to Ed, making phone gestures with his hands, but Ed is too stunned to take it in. Rodrick is by her side, as always, peering around the *genkan* with interest.

"Hazeline?"

"Yes, I was in the area and thought I'd swing by," she says breezily, looking past Ed and into his home.

A moment of silence passes, Ed utterly flummoxed by the intrusion.

"Well, are you going to stand there gawking or invite us in?" Hazeline asks.

"Ed? Who is it?" Sayuri calls from the bedroom.

"It's . . . it's my boss," he croaks out, gesturing for Hazeline to enter. She does so, Rodrick behind her and Nakamura closing the door.

"I tried to warn you we were coming. I texted you," Nakamura quickly whispers.

"I don't know where my phone is, I haven't used it this morning," Ed whispers back. "Why is she here?"

He's pulled from the hushed exchange with Nakamura by Sayuri emerging from the bedroom, a screaming Kaori in her arms. At the sight of three strangers in her home, his daughter's screams quickly downsize to confused, upset burbles.

"You must be Ed's wife," Hazeline says.

"Yamamoto-san!" Sayuri bows deeply, taking Kaori with her.

"Pretty thing," Hazeline comments about Sayuri, almost as though speaking to herself. "And who is this charming lady?" she says in a louder voice, smiling at Kaori, who has now hushed completely aside from a few sniffly hiccups. "Why so sad, little one?"

"This is Kaori," Sayuri offers, just as Kaori grabs one of Hazeline's necklaces and begins inspecting it to within an inch of its life.

"Good taste in jewelry," Hazeline says, putting her hands out and offering Sayuri relief. Sayuri glances at Ed, who is standing dumbly watching the interaction as though it's a TV show, before acquiescing and handing her child over to Hazeline, who begins jiggling her in her arms with surprisingly maternal instincts. Ed stiffens, something in his gut terribly uncomfortable at seeing Kaori in Hazeline's wiry, birdlike grip. He wants to yank her from those arms, cuddle her close and not even allow Hazeline to look at her.

Oblivious to her father's distress, Kaori makes some happy gurgles, switching between peering at Hazeline's face and examining the necklace.

"Rodrick, the gift?" Hazeline says, looking to her housekeeper, who immediately steps forward, gift bag in tow.

"What's this?" Sayuri asks, one hand to her chest as he holds the bag out to her. She leans into a bow, receiving it with both hands.

"Just a little something for the baby." Hazeline smiles down at Kaori.

Ed nods at Sayuri to open it, and inside the bag, nestled within tissue paper, is a beautiful music box. It's handcrafted from wood and there is a forest scene painted onto the sides, bears and wolves and monkeys dotted within the trees. When opened, there's a tiny mirror beneath the lid, and a small monkey springs up and begins to spin, a twinkly song playing.

"It's beautiful," Sayuri gasps. "We can't possibly accept this!"

"Please. Consider it a gift of thanks for letting me intrude on you today. Besides, every little girl deserves a special music box," Hazeline says.

Ed thinks back to his desire to leave Kaori with some trinkets of worth, and is thankful that Hazeline has unknowingly kick-started his plan.

"I always wanted a child. Botan and I tried," Hazeline says quietly, sadly, to nobody in particular.

Beside Ed, Rodrick stands up a little taller.

"We never managed, of course. I would have liked a little Yamamoto running around." She strokes Kaori's hair gently, as though fingering a silk robe.

"I'd like to think he would have been a great father, so unlike his own. Not rigid or afraid to show love. A man who put family before duty. But if I'm honest, I'm not sure that he would have been that way. We'll never know, will we?"

There is a beat of awkward silence.

"Please, let me get us some tea," Sayuri rushes, turning toward the kitchen counters.

"Make . . . er, make yourself at home," Ed says awkwardly, quickly sliding all manner of toys and objects off the sofa and onto the floor, opening up a space for Hazeline to perch, Kaori transferred onto her lap, now sucking on the end of the necklace. Ed hopes it's not one of the necklaces made from human teeth or bones.

Rodrick is discreetly wiping surfaces with his finger, occasionally closing his eyes in despair when it emerges fluffy with dust. Nakamura is dithering from foot to foot, tightly wound with nervous energy, and he keeps eyeing Kaori on Hazeline's lap with unease.

"I am honored for the visit, and apologize for being unprepared," Ed says politely, all the while thinking how rude it is for his boss to interrupt him on a weekend off and intrude on his family time. Hazeline looks wildly out of place in his small, shabby home. She seems bigger somehow, taking up more space compared to her tiny form within her spacious mansion.

"Nonsense. As I said, we were passing through and I realized you lived nearby, so I thought it would be worth stopping to see if you would like to join us today."

"Join you?" Ed echoes.

"Tea!" Sayuri announces in an overly cheery voice, and Ed notices she has brought out their nice tea set, the one they got as an anniversary gift from her grandmother, and which they only use on special occasions.

"Thank you, petal," Hazeline says, watching as Sayuri self-consciously pours out the tea for each guest. Kaori has become bored of slobbering over Hazeline's neck jewels and has turned her attention instead to Rodrick, yanking on his shirt from the sofa while he stands and pretends it isn't happening.

"Join you where?" Ed asks again.

"We are off to Minato City to visit my charity headquarters," she explains.

Ed glances at Nakamura, who returns the tiniest of shrugs.

"Charity headquarters, right," Ed says, unenthused.

"That sounds lovely! Wow!" Sayuri beams, and Ed can hear that her voice is false but to Hazeline she probably sounds authentic.

"Yes, I like all my staff to be involved in the philanthropic side of my life once they've proven certain loyalties," Hazeline says.

Ed notices that Nakamura is staring fixedly at the floor.

"What sort of charity work is it you do?" Sayuri asks, taking a sip of her tea.

"I work with single mothers in poverty." Hazeline gives her a humble smile.

"Really? Impressive!" Sayuri nods. "I can't imagine having to do this all alone," she adds, looking pointedly at Kaori who, distressed by Rodrick's lack of attention, has begun slapping his legs violently.

"Quite," Hazeline says, her eyes laughing at her lovesick butler. "Well, Ed? What say you? Busy day or time for a quick trip?"

"Erm." He looks to Sayuri, silently and telepathically begging her to come up with a polite excuse for him not to go, but she just smiles at Hazeline, and he's sure she's thinking about all the money they now owe her.

"You go, Ed. We'll be fine here for a few hours!"

"Right," he says.

"Wonderful." Hazeline beams, slapping both of her knees with her hands. "Nakamura-san, will you go and prepare the car? I shall just finish my green tea and let Ed get himself ready and we will be right with you."

Nakamura quietly exits their home, leaving Ed with no choice but to grab his jacket and belongings for the outing.

Hazeline stands, strolling around the room with Kaori hitched on her hip, slowly sipping on the tea she is holding with her free hand and pausing every now and again to inspect something as though at a museum. Occasionally, she lets out a small noise, oohs and aahs, and it makes Ed want to slap the mug right out of her hands. He's a normal person living in a normal home, not some sort of fascinating poverty-stricken sideshow.

"Is this you, Ed?" she asks, looking at a photograph of Ed back at his council house home in the UK.

"Yes."

"Whereabouts was it you lived in the UK again?" she asks.

"Slough."

"Ah, yes." She nods slowly, moving along and stopping at their wedding photograph. Sayuri is wearing a rented embroidered white bridal kimono, her hair in a sleek updo, with Ed beaming beside her in his own black groom's kimono. He remembers being desperate to show how willing he was to embrace her culture, and how he happily ditched the idea of a western suit to match her outfit of choice. In the photo they are sitting side by side at their ceremony, both holding a cup of ritual sake.

"Lovely. A beautiful photograph. And you, Sayuri, where is your family from?"

Ed bristles. He doesn't want Hazeline in his home, learning personal and private information about his wife. He doesn't want her near their daughter. He wants the two worlds to be kept separate, though he's not sure why. Is it embarrassment that he feels, or protectiveness?

"Osaka," Sayuri replies. Ed is relieved she has kept it vague. If she had said the specific ward, Hazeline would have recognized it as one of the poorest areas of Osaka, and Ed doesn't want her judging his in-laws or his wife.

"Shall we go?" he says, eager to get her out of his home.

"Ed!" Sayuri admonishes, startled by his overt rudeness.

"Don't worry, petal. I've just finished," Hazeline says, placing her mug down. "Thank you for the tea," she adds, lowering her head the smallest fraction.

"Kaori, please," Sayuri sighs, pulling her toddler away from Rodrick, much to his obvious relief.

Ed holds the front door open, desperate to separate his wife from his employer. His real life from his dream life. His shameful struggles from his slowly blossoming professional pride.

"Thank you for your hospitality. I will return him to you in no time." Hazeline smiles.

Ed's not sure why, but he feels a stab of fear about stepping into the car, sure that wherever it is that Hazeline is taking him, it will not be what he's expecting.

THE PENTHOUSE

Nakamura pulls up outside a skyscraper-style building. It's sleek, almost entirely glass, with huge window panes slotting together to form walls. Rodrick steps out of the car first, holding the door open for Hazeline.

"Are you parking up and joining us?" Ed asks Nakamura as he scoots toward the door.

Nakamura hesitates, then shakes his head. "No, I will wait for you all to finish up," he says. He avoids making eye contact.

"Is everything okay, Nakamura-san?"

"Yes, yes. I just prefer not to mingle or involve myself very much in Hazeline's work. I'll keep to driving."

Ed frowns, perturbed by this answer.

"Ed, hurry up!" Hazeline barks. He snaps to attention, exiting the car, leaving Nakamura behind and taking in his surroundings. The streets of Minato are busy, as always. If Hazeline's rural, traditional Japanese home is at one end of the scale, and Ed's modest and cramped apartment is somewhere in the middle, Minato is at the opposite end. It could be New York or London, all Japanese characteristics and architecture erased in favor of grandiose modernity. The buildings loom as brightly lit towers; the streets are spotless and the roads wide, peppered with fancy cars bearing shining logos, as opposed to the practical smaller models in Ed's neighborhood. The salarymen stride with purpose down the streets, frowning at phone screens, briefcases in hand, while the women have perfectly styled hair and walk in smart, tailored dresses, designer bags perched on their shoulders.

"Is this the office building?" Ed asks, looking up to try to make out how tall the tower is.

"Not exactly," Hazeline responds, gesturing with a flick of her fingers for him to follow. Rodrick holds the door open and Hazeline enters an extravagant, airy foyer. Immediately, the security guard stands and bows, greeting Hazeline by name before flitting a suspicious gaze at Ed.

"We weren't expecting you today, Yamamoto-san," the guard says.

"An impromptu visit," she replies in Japanese.

He nods and quickly presses a button, calling the lift down to the ground floor, and Ed follows Hazeline into the mirrored elevator. The security guard then presses the button for the top floor, keying in a code before nodding politely and exiting, leaving Ed standing awkwardly behind Hazeline and Rodrick. "Top floor, huh?" Ed says.

"The penthouse," Hazeline corrects.

Fancy. Though at this point, Ed expects no less. Hazeline Yamamoto is not exactly a third-floor type of person.

The elevator moves rapidly and smoothly, the numbered buttons lighting up one by one the only hint that they are even moving. After not very long at all, there is a quiet chime to announce they have arrived, and the doors open into an extremely grand and airy space. It's all modern, white, sleek, and chrome. The windowed walls look out onto a startlingly dramatic view of Tokyo. Most of the furniture looks custom-made, designed to fit in the space perfectly. Is this an *apartment*? He was expecting an office of some sort.

Ed is surprised to see a teenage boy lounging on the curved bouclé sofa, a controller in hand, headset on his head, ferociously clicking buttons with his eyes glued to the enormous TV screen, where he appears to be in some sort of fantasy battleground.

Hazeline chuckles. "Not even noticed us!"

Then comes a set of hurried footsteps, a young woman emerging. "Yamamoto-san! We weren't expecting you, I apologize!" She bows deeply, her pin-straight dark hair falling in front of her face as she does so.

"No need, it was a spontaneous visit. I wanted my new private chef to see what it's all about," Hazeline replies, holding her arms out widely.

"Ed, this is Honami. She runs the day-to-day here." The woman flushes prettily and Ed smiles at her, dropping his head in greeting.

"And," she turns to the boy, who is still oblivious to the company behind him, "you remember Koji."

"Koji-san!" Honami snaps, loud enough to give Ed a fright. It works—the boy turns around, and his eyes briefly widen in surprise at the small gathering that has formed a meter away from him without his knowledge. He quickly rips the headset off and bows to all of them. "*Sumimasen*! I did not hear you come in," he apologizes. "Nice to see you all again."

Ed feels utterly confused as to what is going on. What exactly is this place?

"The rest are out at the lake for water sports today. Koji was unable to go; he has a stomach bug," Honami explains, gesturing to the blanket setup on the sofa.

"Hmm. Yes, now you mention it, you are looking a little pale. Well, rest up. We need you fit and healthy!" Hazeline smiles, and the boy bashfully sits back down in his sick nest, the headset returning and his attention immediately back on the screen, fingers furiously smashing away at the buttons.

"Can I get you anything?" Honami asks, gesturing toward a huge, modern kitchen.

"Green tea would be lovely, just while I show Ed the setup?"

"I'll help make it," Rodrick offers, heading confidently over to a cupboard and opening it to reveal all the tea tins.

"You must be here a lot," Ed comments, noting Rodrick's familiarity.

"We visit when we can," Hazeline says. "Usually we bring gifts for the kids, but I assumed they'd all be out today. They're often out during the day, especially at weekends. We like to organize trips and outings, to museums, historical sites, and the like, to keep them occupied. We had organized a trip to Nasushiobara for this weekend. They're helping out staff at a local dairy farm and relaxing in the onsen in the evenings."

"That's a shame then, that Koji was unwell for it," Ed says, wondering when in the day Hazeline has time to do all of this so discreetly in the background.

"I'm sure we will organize another one soon," Hazeline says, walking Ed down a short hallway and opening a door to reveal a huge bedroom. Inside is a set of bunk beds, as well as a single bed. The room has gorgeous pink and gold starry wallpaper on one side, the others fitted with built-in wardrobes or featuring floor-to-ceiling windows. There are stuffed animals on the beds, including the lion that Ed recalls from their camping weekend visit propped up on the pillows, J-pop girl band posters taped onto the walls, fairy lights strung around the bunk bed ladder, and two small desks. One is covered in makeup, the other in cute animal stationery. To Ed's horror, there is even a poster of Miyuki and her band above one of the beds, Miyuki grinning bashfully, holding up a peace sign and wearing a small, pleated miniskirt.

"We have the lovely three girls in here at the moment. Aiko, you remember, is seven, Hana is eight, and Asuka is thirteen, so she's beginning to get into makeup and boys. She will probably want her own room, soon."

Ed blinks. It's the type of space he would die to give Kaori—minus the psychopathic pop star poster. She would probably be stunned into silence just looking at it.

A cream canopy is draped over the single bed, and he can see a tray of nail polishes tucked underneath it, beside a pink radio.

Hazeline closes the door and turns back into the hallway.

"That room is where Honami stays, or if she's back at home or on vacation, one of the other staff members who covers her. We won't intrude," she explains, pointing to another closed door.

"This room is Koji's." She opens the door to a room that is the polar opposite to the girls' room. A huge gaming setup is on one side, and extravagant Lego models and anime figurines are neatly lined up on display shelves. They have lighting discreetly taped underneath, lending the items a museum-display-style quality. An expensive-looking guitar is propped up at the end of the double bed, and underneath the bed are stacks and stacks of manga.

"He gets his own room—a boy his age, you know," Hazeline says, raising a knowing eyebrow at Ed, who clears his throat and looks away.

"Perhaps we shouldn't linger though, we don't want to catch whatever bug he's caught." She moves Ed around to another door.

"This is the last currently occupied room," she says, flinging the door beside Koji's room open. "This is Daiki's room. He's eighteen now, so won't be here much longer. I imagine we will move Asuka into his room once he leaves. There are a few empty rooms we were hoping to fill this year but no luck so far."

"Where will he go?" Ed asks.

Hazeline blinks at him. "Well, when they age out of staying here, become proper adults, they go on to the Hazeline Yamamoto internship," she says, closing the door to the room and herding Ed back the way they came. He thinks back to Ellie, of how they referred to her as an intern, too. "Usually we wait until they are in their mid-twenties, but there can be some exceptions made under certain circumstances."

"I don't understand—"

"Not now!" she interrupts with a snap, then she quickly rearranges her face into a beaming smile for Honami's benefit.

"Honami, petal. We're going to go and have our tea by the pool. Would you be a darling and stay to care for Koji while we go? Rodrick can bring the tray through for us."

"Oh." Honami pauses at the clear dismissal. "Of course, yes. Was everything okay? I apologize for the mess. As I said, we weren't expecting a visitor and Koji has been so poorly,"

Hazeline holds her hand up to silence her. "All was fine, Honami, don't you worry. We will just go and have our tea, then we will be out of your hair."

"Ah, okay," Honami says, relaxing slightly.

"There are some things I just want to explain to Ed about the charity," Hazeline tells her. "In private," she adds, raising her brows at Rodrick.

"Has Honami worked for you long?" Ed asks once she's out of earshot.

"A year or two. The charity staff tend to rotate a lot. We get a lot of young women looking to work after university, but after a few years they need to feel more settled, have a home of their own, a family of their own," Hazeline says in a blasé tone. "That's why there are many aspects of the charity work that we don't tell them about. Secrets reserved for my more long-term, loyal staff members. Like you," she adds pointedly.

Ed feels uncomfortable.

"I'm sure they can handle it," he says.

At this, Hazeline gives a very un-Hazeline-like snort of laughter. "Petal, you have no idea what these women can and cannot handle. They can barely stomach taking care of the kids full-time, let alone dealing with all the messy background details."

"Background details?" Ed asks.

"So curious." Hazeline turns to look at him. "So potently curious that I can almost taste it. Come outside, Ed, petal. Perhaps I'll tell you a little more, if you think you can 'handle' it."

Ed follows, even though his gut is telling him that whatever he's about to find out, it's not something he wants to know.

TO BE A PARIAH

At the back of the apartment, the glass doors slide open to a decked rooftop garden, a small swimming pool in the center. Rodrick carries the tray of tea and mugs to a small side table and Hazeline sits herself on one of the deckchairs. Ed is gawking at the view, the breeze lapping at his thin jacket. The pool is covered, but he can imagine it's quite the luxury in the humidity the summer months bring.

It doesn't go unnoticed that Rodrick goes to quietly close the sliding doors, leaving the three of them out of hearing distance, should Honami wander by.

"Apologies for the privacy, Ed. It's just that Honami and all the others who work for the charity . . . well, they raise the children and then see them off when they're adults, and that is the extent of their job. Think of Honami as an extremely well-paid, glorified nanny."

"I see," says Ed, not seeing at all.

"And of course it's not just Honami. There is a cook for the children, some young Tokyo University students who take them on day trips, language tutors for their English skills, all sorts of people involved in helping them live the best lives possible."

"That's wonderful," Ed says, glancing at Rodrick, who quickly looks away. "And where do they come from? Do they not have homes to return to?"

Hazeline sips her tea before answering. "Well, it's all terribly sad really. But they're all born to single mothers who are unable to care for them. Mothers below the poverty line. We only have the resources to take on a small number of children at a time, and spend a long time finding the right candidates."

"Candidates?"

"Yes. We handpick each case, because being part of this program is, really, a privilege. And it's about quality and suitability, not quantity. That is how we can provide them all with such a fantastic lifestyle. So, for example, Hana was born as the result of a one-night stand. Her mother was due to be wed, and the family didn't want the groom to find out about her indiscretion. It would have ruined her future—to be a single mother with no prospect for marriage. So we essentially purchased the child at birth."

"Purchased the child?" Ed frowns. "Like—like an adoption?"

"Sort of." Hazeline nods. "There are contracts to be signed; the mother can never look for the child, et cetera, et cetera. We give the mother a one-off payment, a goodwill gesture, and promise them that the child will grow up in luxury. And this *is* luxury, Ed," she says pointedly.

"Oh, I know! Even the best hotels in Tokyo aren't a scratch on this," Ed agrees.

"And it goes beyond the living situation. They get everything they could desire. And, for Hana, sure, her mother could have probably kept her, and worked out a way to make it pan out. She chose not to. But some mothers . . . Koji's, for instance. She really had no option. She worked at a hostess bar, had absolutely no money or anyone to go to for help. She didn't have the means to raise a child, so we helped them both. I believe that with the money we paid her for Koji she was able to leave hostessing, get herself some qualifications and a day job."

"That's brilliant," Ed says, doubting the words as they come out of his mouth. "But do the kids not want to know who their parents are?" He thinks of Kaori, of whether he would hand his daughter over to a stranger in exchange for cash. No. Not for all the money in Japan.

"Sometimes, but we just tell them they're deceased. It's easier to think their heroic parents died in a tragic accident and we saved them, than to believe themselves burdens, sold for a wad of cash like cattle."

"Burdens?" Ed frowns.

"To be a single mother in Japan is to be a pariah. They are shunned, Ed. It's terrible, truly. Myself, I can't begin to imagine the stress. No government support, terrible job prospects, it's a real struggle. In fact, nearly all of the poorest in Japan are single mothers. They are holding down the poverty line. It's awful. All because men can't keep their dicks in their pants. Or at least wrapped up."

Ed flushes, wanting to argue, but he is unable to form a coherent sentence.

"And so you raise them, and then what?"

Hazeline glances at Rodrick, then beams at Ed, ignoring his question entirely.

"Ed, petal, this is a terribly boring and depressing conversation. I've already told you more than even Honami knows, about their parents not being dead. Really, the reason I want you here is because I'd like you to know that after much deliberation, I'd be delighted if you would host my annual gourmet supper party. I have one every January to ring in the new year in style."

"Oh!" Ed says, slightly taken aback by the dramatic change in direction the conversation has taken.

"It will be feeding some of the most influential people in the world. It is a *huge* deal. You can't begin to imagine the clientele you will get to rub shoulders with," she says.

Ed's heart beats nervously in his chest. He's not good enough to cook for these types of people, surely?

"Are you sure? I mean, I don't feel prestigious enough . . ." He trails off lamely, thinking back to his burger-flipping days, picturing a young, dead-eyed version of himself holding an industrial fry basket beneath mucus-yellow oil. To think of him replacing the famous Chef Chungpu as Hazeline's annual supper club chef . . . it's terrifying.

"It's not so much about the food as presentation and things," Hazeline says dismissively. "I really do think you'll be perfect! And who knows? You may get more work offers off the back of it. Of course, I would expect you to put me and my own needs first." She looks at him pointedly.

"Of course!" he rushes.

"But still. I pay triple the usual rate for this event as it's so important to me—"

"*Three times?*" Ed interrupts, gaping.

"Do close your mouth," Hazeline says. "But yes. And as I said, it could bring all sorts of opportunities your way. Do you remember Chef Chungpu?"

"Yes." Ed nods, unsure how anybody could forget getting a private cooking lesson from a world-famous celebrity chef.

"He was nobody before my dinner party," Hazeline says, puffing her chest out slightly.

Ed thinks back to his conversation with Chungpu and just nods dumbly.

"I was traveling for business in China and found him in a struggling hole-in-the-wall restaurant. I saw his talent, and brought him in to be my private chef. He was with me for two years before going on to do bigger and better. We keep in touch, obviously," she adds with a modest smile. "He is still my go-to for lamb shank, as you clearly know."

A new life flashes before Ed's eyes. One where he's a celebrity chef, traveling the world on private jets, cooking for billionaires and their supermodel wives. A world where he comes home to his mansion and Kaori has everything she could ever need and more. A world where he can buy Sayuri the Birkin bag without a worry. A world where Ed Cook is *the* Ed Cook. Any questions he had about the charity are forgotten.

"I'd be honored," he stammers out eventually.

"I thought so," Hazeline purrs.

KENTUCKY FRIED CHICKEN

"Merry Christmas, love! We know you'll be waking up soon and we'll be fast asleep, but we've got the bubbly in the fridge ready for the morning. Santa is probably on his way to us now! Your dad's forgotten the fucking Yorkies so we're going to have to try to make them ourselves from scratch. Where's our son the chef when you need him, eh? Send our love to Sayuri and give Kaori a big kiss from Nanny and Grandad!"

Ed lets the voice message come to an end and smiles.

"Your family are okay?" Sayuri calls from the kitchen.

"Yes, they're fine," Ed says, getting up from the sofa to join her. He's put *Home Alone* on the television and Kaori is enraptured by it, giggling along despite not understanding what's happening. He wants to make sure she grows up with all the same classics he did.

They've set up a very small artificial tree in the main family room, and under it is a small but exciting pile of gifts. Most are from Ed's family, shipped over for them to have on the day. He saved to get something nice for Sayuri and Kaori, and to his great surprise, Hazeline handed him a large hamper with a big "thank you for your hard work" speech, which is currently set aside waiting to be opened.

When he first met Sayuri, she was embarrassed when he bought her a Christmas gift for the first time. It was a beautiful and expensive writing set that he'd noticed her looking at several times in the window of an artisan stationery store in the center of town. He knew that Japan was not a Christian country, but had severely overestimated how many people celebrated in the same way as westerners, and she'd not thought to buy him a gift in return. To help her feel less bad about accepting the gift, they went out to the park and strolled around in the cold air, sharing their ideas and thoughts on Christmas traditions. Every year since then, they have celebrated with a strange cultural blend, their own Christmas curated to suit their little family unit.

The day always begins with a Japanese breakfast, which Sayuri puts together for them. Ed insists on a morning celebration drink, and opts for some nice plum wine, which is easier and cheaper to source than prosecco—not to mention, much tastier. They have the tabletop tree, not having the interior space for anything bigger, and Ed plays Michael Bublé Christmas tunes all day which ring through the house joyfully.

For gifts, they do one gift each, and one for Kaori. Sayuri doesn't want her growing up spoiled, and having never gotten Christmas presents herself growing up, feels that one gift is more than enough for a child her age. Then for dinner they always have KFC, the same as nearly every other household in Japan.

"KFC?" Ed spluttered in the park when she explained it to him the first time. "As in, Kentucky Fried Chicken?"

Sayuri laughed and nodded. "It's tradition in Japan to have KFC. We preorder it and everything!"

"You *preorder* KFC? I don't understand, how did Colonel Sanders become a tradition for Christmas here?"

As it turned out, KFC had invested a huge amount of money into advertising in the seventies, positioning themselves as the must-have for a western-style Christmas dinner. The slogan was "Kentucky for Christmas!" The Japanese, not knowing any better, had fallen for it, and suddenly KFC was the trendiest thing to enjoy come December 25th. Ed was flabbergasted.

He watched in fascination that first year as Sayuri ordered their Christmas bucket—which they called the Christmas Barrel—online a few weeks in advance, then went to collect it on the 25th. There was a long queue. He was even more surprised to find that he enjoyed it a lot, and didn't miss the big roast with all the trimmings as much as he'd thought he would—especially when the time came and there was no washing-up to do. There was the obvious crispy fried chicken, but also a lasagne for some reason, along with chips, dips, and a special holiday dessert. Afterward, they fell asleep on the sofa, bellies bloated and Sayuri's head in Ed's lap, and Ed felt so blissful that he was sure that this was what he wanted every Christmas to look like going forward.

"Shall we do gifts now, before you go to collect the chicken?" Sayuri asks as the last of the pickled veggies are eaten from the breakfast spread.

"Sure," Ed says, standing to help her by starting on the washing-up.

"Don't, just leave it. I can do it when you go out." Sayuri smiles at him, her hand on his arm.

"Are you ready to open presents? Do you think Colonel Sanders has brought you something special?" Ed asks Kaori, scooping her up into his arms. This is a running joke; Sayuri mistakenly thought that the KFC logo was of Santa Claus, confused by the red design and white beard. Ed laughed when she told him, and ever since the joke has been that Colonel Sanders delivers the gifts as well as the chicken.

The three of them gather around the little tree, Kevin McCallister chasing the two Wet Bandits out of his home with an air rifle firing in the background.

"One for you, and one for you," Ed says, handing Kaori and Sayuri their gifts. He's bought Kaori a sort of build-your-own dollhouse kit, with large easy plastic blocks to use and small felt dolls to live inside. "It's supposed to be good for teaching them motor skills," Ed explained to Sayuri.

"Ah, yes, and we do want her to grow up to work in construction," she joked back.

She opens her own gift, and squeals with glee. "Oh, Ed! I love it! Thank you!" she says. It's a vintage silk headscarf he found for a good price in a thrift store, the sort of thing that is classy and he knew his wife would love. His own gift is a smart new tie, with tiny little chef hats printed on it, so discreetly that you wouldn't notice unless you really looked. "For the next time you have to go get beaten up at a meat auction," Sayuri jokes.

"I love it, thank you." He pulls her in for a kiss.

"Shall we see what the billionaire got us?" Sayuri says, reaching over for the giant hamper. It's filled with gifts, all wrapped carefully in gold paper. Ed wonders if Hazeline did any of it, or if it is Rodrick's handiwork. The first gift is the biggest and takes up the bulk of the basket. A traditional Japanese Christmas cake.

"Yum!" Sayuri smiles, holding it up and immediately placing it out of Kaori's reach. There are three smaller parcels left, their names printed on them. "She got me a gift?" Sayuri asks, frowning. "Why would she do that? Should I have gotten her something?" She looks worried.

"No. I don't know why she did this. Let's open it," Ed says, feeling immediately apprehensive.

His wife unwraps the little gift and finds a jewelry box inside. She looks at Ed, almost as though she's afraid to open it.

"Go on," he urges, even though a lump has formed in his throat.

She pops the box open and finds a necklace. It's a strange design—silver, with a central glass bead. Inside the bead is a strange wisp of dark red. "Wow. This feels very fancy," his wife says politely. Ed knows it's not her style; it's too large, too gaudy. "What do you suppose this is, in the middle? It doesn't look like a gemstone," she says, handing the box to Ed. He opens his mouth, then closes it, deciding better of saying anything. To him, it looks like blood.

"Open yours next," Sayuri urges, flapping her hands. He does so and finds a pair of gold chopsticks nestled in tissue. *Chef Cook* has been engraved into them in Japanese. "Wow," she breathes. "I think they're real gold! Plated, at least. They're beautiful!"

"They are," Ed agrees.

"What do you think she got Kaori? A car, perhaps?" Sayuri jokes.

Ed feels his heart thumping through his chest, but he tries to look casual as their daughter rips her parcel open in the most inefficient way possible. He breathes out a sigh of relief when he sees what it is. A wooden toy set. A bento box, with beautifully painted wooden sushi pieces, a fish fillet, egg halves, and chopsticks. Kaori immediately tips the box upside down, the pieces scattering, and begins trying to fit them all back in with absolutely no skill or luck.

"This was very kind of her," Sayuri comments.

"Yes," Ed says, looking at his wife's new necklace and trying to ignore the question of whether it really is blood within the necklace—and if so, whose.

UTTER MADNESS

A week has passed since Christmas, and all Ed knows about the supper club is that Hazeline wants more of her "special meat" cooked. He's not been sleeping, lying awake every night staring at the ceiling and imagining a series of different scenarios that all give him anxiety. What if he messes up the meal? What if they hate it, and throw their plates at him? What if Hazeline is so disappointed she fires him, and he resorts to gambling again? Too many scenarios, which at one time felt improbable but now have become almost certain in his mind. He wants to practice the meals ahead of time, make sure all the timings are perfect to avoid getting flustered on the day. Yet every time he asks Hazeline what they are having, she is dismissive, and just says something along the lines of "some special meat, I'm still sorting it all out."

Ed's making a coffee for Nakamura, who has just returned from driving Hazeline to an appointment. "Nakamura, have you been here long enough to have worked Hazeline's supper club soirée?" he asks.

Nakamura stands a little straighter. "Yes, why?" He shifts from foot to foot, as though needing the toilet.

"Do you know what they served? I need to start planning the menu, and Hazeline is not being very helpful. I don't even know where the bar of expectation sits."

Nakamura is chewing on his lip, eyes darting quickly from left to right. "Hmmm. Yes. Chef Chungpu cooked it last year, but not really sure what it was. I wasn't around much that evening; Suki was having a bad turn and I was taking care of her with the nurses," he says, but for some reason, Ed feels in his gut that this is a lie.

"You didn't have any leftovers?" he pushes.

"No," Nakamura says, but he won't meet Ed's eye.

"Hmmm. And you don't know what her 'special meat' is?"

At this, Nakamura visibly pulls back and away from him. "No, I'm sorry, Ed," he says quickly, grabbing the coffee from the machine and not even bothering to drop in his usual sugar. "I have to rush, but good luck, friend!"

Before Ed can respond, Nakamura has skittered out of the room with his coffee, and doesn't look back.

Ed frowns, but is determined. He can't sleep restfully until he knows what menu he is going to cook, and that he can produce it flawlessly. He wanders down to the basement, where Rodrick is unpacking a delivery of *umeshu* crates and putting all the bottles into a rack.

"Need a hand?" Ed asks.

If Rodrick is surprised by the uncharacteristic offer, he doesn't show it. "Sure," he replies.

The two unbox bottles companionably for a few moments before Ed takes the leap. "Rodrick, what is Hazeline's special meat that she wants me to cook for the supper?"

Rodrick pauses for a millisecond before continuing on with unboxing, his face frozen in a show of complacency. "Oh, it's like . . . some special imported cut, you know?"

"No, I don't know. That's why I'm asking."

"Oh, Ed, I don't really know much about food or cooking, to be honest. I'm sure she'll let you know what she wants you to cook ahead of time."

"Yes, but I need *enough* time! The dinner is one week away. I need to contact suppliers, make sure we have everything we need, practice the meal a few times—"

"I doubt you'll get enough of her special meat to practice with," Rodrick interrupts him.

"Well, yes, but that's why I need to know what it is! I can find a substitute cut to practice with."

Rodrick sighs. "I can't read Hazeline's mind. I don't know what the cut will be."

"Yes, but you know her better than all of us put together," Ed argues, and he sees Rodrick flush pink with pride. "I need to be able to cook a meal as good as what Chef Chungpu cooked!"

"Ah, Chef Chungpu! He will be one of the guests, I believe. I think he RSVP'd, anyway . . ." Rodrick frowns and looks to the sky pensively.

"Chef Chungpu is *attending*? And is going to eat *my* meal?" Ed staggers back as though he's been slapped. "Oh my God, I am so underprepared." He thinks he may hyperventilate. For Ed, a burger-boy-turned-fake-private-cook, to have to whip something up for a celebrity chef . . . Well, it's utter madness. He is going to fail and embarrass himself in front of the entire group. His name will become a joke. A literal pun—Cook can't cook!

"Are you all right, Ed? You look a bit green," Rodrick says.

"No! No, I'm not all right at all! I need to know what the hell I'm cooking. I can't show up and just fake this!"

Rodrick sighs. "I'm sorry, I don't know what to tell you. Hazeline hasn't shared her plans with me yet, and I'm not sure what was served last year. My memory's just not as good as it used to be."

"Rodrick, be serious. You're not that old. Why is everyone

avoiding telling me what the deal is with this dinner party?" Ed huffs, slapping his arms against his sides.

Rodrick ignores him and continues stacking, the sound of the glass bottles slotting into the wooden rack grating on Ed further.

"Fine, if you won't tell me, I'll find out from elsewhere." He turns and marches up the stairs to the kitchen again, moving more quickly than usual. He's surprised to see Hazeline out in the garden, sitting by the koi pond with a book. She's wearing a puffer jacket, and has set up a portable heater at her feet. He steels himself, and clenches his fists before heading her way.

"Ed, the door, please. You'll let the heat out," she drawls at him. He sheepishly turns, closes the door, then returns to her.

"Is there a reason you're interrupting my reading hour?" she asks, looking up at him from the pages of *Animal Farm.*

"I'm sorry. But I need to prepare for next week in order to cook the best meal possible. And to do that, I need to know the cut of meat you are providing me with," he says, trying to keep the anxiety from wobbling his voice. He feels a tightness in his chest, and to his horror, is worried he may cry. When was the last time he had a good night's sleep?

Hazeline sighs, and puts her book down on her lap to look at him properly. "It's just my special meat, Ed. I think probably a cut from a fattier part, I've not decided yet," she begins, but Ed's nerves drive him to interrupt her.

"Hazeline, please. If I do not have direction, I cannot host this event. I am not willing to do a bad job and sully my name, and the only way I can possibly pull off a meal of this caliber is to prepare for it properly, which means practicing ahead of time, ordering in the best products, checking quantities and weights." He is speaking quickly, Chungpu's face in his mind. "In fact, I *refuse* to cook without the required information in case I mess it up," he finishes, breathing slightly heavily.

Hazeline slowly raises a single eyebrow. "You refuse?" She laughs, as though it's a joke. "You can't be a very good chef if you are unable to improvise on the day."

I'm NOT a very good chef, and we both know it! Ed thinks.

"I am able to improvise. But I am unwilling," Ed says, standing firm.

"You can't refuse, Ed," she sighs as though he is a toddler having a tantrum. "You owe me work until your debt is paid off."

Ed drops to his knees in front of her, shame out the window, his desperation to succeed at the party overriding any pride left in him. "Please, Hazeline. Please just decide on a cut, and tell me what it is." He brings his hands together in front of him like he is praying.

The second brow joins the first in lifting toward her hairline, and Hazeline smiles as though delighted.

"Are you sure you want to know?"

"Yes!" Ed says, exasperated.

"Once you know, there really is no going back," she warns, still smiling.

"I want to know," he repeats.

"Well then, take a seat, petal, and ready yourself."

She gestures to the empty chair opposite.

DO YOU NEED A BUCKET

"The special meat is obtained through my charity work," Hazeline says, watching Ed carefully.

"The . . . the charity we went to the other week, you mean?" Ed frowns, confused. "But what does that have to do with meat? You mentioned an internship, is it sort of like an international meat merchant job?"

Hazeline darts a glance at Rodrick, who has chosen this moment to come by to collect the tray with her empty coffee mug. "I'll take this back through to the kitchen," he says, coughing discreetly. As soon as he closes the door behind him, Hazeline looks to Ed.

"Come on, Ed. Work it out. You're a big boy."

"I'm sorry?"

She sighs, as though deeply disappointed by him. "Where do you think they're going? All those young adults I so carefully raise?"

"Um, abroad?" Ed guesses, imagining Koji five years from now, working on a beach in the Caribbean, or on the beige-hued streets of Paris, crusty baguette in hand, learning to be a sommelier.

Hazeline barks a laugh, but it's cold and false. "Come on, Ed! Think of Ellie."

Ed frowns. "She was at your home. Surely you don't take all the kids into your home as interns? She didn't even do anything. What was she meant to be, an assistant?"

"Well, no," Hazeline agrees. "Ellie was an exception. She was a last-minute arrangement, and we're lucky she was because we had to make up for the freezer mishap."

"The . . . the freezer?" Ed asks. He suddenly feels a cold chill wrap around him, and pulls his jacket tighter.

"Yes. The others weren't ready, and Ellie was usefully irritating and could remedy the loss of my special meat. Perhaps if she had been less ungrateful, perhaps if the freezer hadn't broken, she would be here right now. Perhaps she would have spent the year learning to play an instrument, taking language classes, shopping in Shinjuku, and spending weekends helping the elderly—or taking camping trips, playing sports, or eating noodles cooked over a campfire with the others. But she's not, though she has been useful in another way."

"But . . . didn't you just send her home? I don't understand, what does the freezer have to do with anything?"

"Wake up, Ed!" Hazeline suddenly snaps, sitting up in the deckchair and smacking her hands on the wooden frame.

Ed flinches, and he feels as though his heart is beating in slow motion.

"Where. Is. Ellie. Ed? Think about it. *Think.*"

Ed brings his hand to the back of his head. Ellie was here. In the house. An internship. Her parents needed the money for medical bills. She was flown in from America, through that awful friend of Hazeline's. No trace back to Hazeline, she said. Nakamura collected her from the airport. The freezer broke. Ellie was gone. Then what? What happened after?

His mouth goes dry. The dinner party. The strange meat parcel. Rodrick's vague answer about the cut. Hazeline's annotated recipe book. The liver. He thinks back to the meal he cooked, Hazeline's sharp gaze as his imagination ran rampant. His shaking hands as he tried to wash them. *Imported all the way from America. Mississippi.*

Ed looks at Hazeline, his eyes wide, his heartbeat erratic. His stomach churns in a nauseous roll.

She smiles at him slowly. "Well done, petal. You got there in the end."

Ed's breathing is coming out ragged, and he's desperately trying to get a grip on himself. He's misunderstood. He has to have misunderstood.

"I'm sorry, I don't think I—"

"Come now, Ed. You know what happened to Ellie. The same thing that's going to happen to all those being raised by my charity, eventually," Hazeline cuts in. "When they're adults, of course," she adds, as though this is common sense. "I don't kill children, I'm not a monster," she continues artfully.

Ed looks to the door, considers making a dash for it. But where would he go? And, God, he owes Hazeline all that money. He thinks of Koji sitting inside that vast penthouse, playing video games. Of Hana, and her stuffed lion. He gags, and Hazeline shrinks back.

"Do you need a bucket? I can ask Rodrick to fetch one," she says.

Ed doesn't respond, just covers his mouth with his hand and squeezes his eyes shut until he sees a mishmash of shapes and colors in the darkness, wishing to rewind time back five minutes.

Then, the door slides open, and he opens his eyes.

"So you've told him?" Rodrick says, an eyebrow raised at Ed, who is now bent over his knees and is shaking his head rapidly.

"Yes. I don't think it's gone down particularly well," Hazeline replies.

Ed raises his head. Looks at them both, wild-eyed. They are both acting so casual about this, so *normal.*

"You . . . you're telling me you *eat* them? You're eating *people?*" he finally grinds out, clasping the edge of his chair to stop from falling right off. This is the moment. The moment they will burst out laughing and tell him that, of course not, that is lunacy, where did he even come up with such a gag?

Hazeline pouts and shrugs. "Not often. An annual treat."

Ed leans forward, retches again. "What the fuck?"

"Do you need a sick bowl?" Rodrick offers.

"I already asked. He said no," Hazeline says.

"Who knows?" Ed rasps, his mind reeling, considering every person he has met through Hazeline, all the people coming and going from her home. "Who knows about this?"

"Well, myself and Rodrick, obviously," Hazeline begins, holding her fingers out as counters. "Nakamura, the traffickers." Ed thinks of Nakamura's kind face, of the cigarettes they've shared and chats they've had. This time, he does vomit, though only a bit of stringy bile comes up. He hasn't eaten yet, or his stomach would have heaved itself empty by now. Hazeline pauses her list to watch his gags with interest, and when he's finished, she continues as though never interrupted. "And some of the dinner guests, the ones who came for Ellie's dinner and the ones who attend the annual supper club. And . . . that's about it!" She looks to Rodrick for confirmation, and he gives a curt nod.

Ellie's dinner. Ed grips on to the side of his chair, knuckles whitening.

"Honami-san?" Ed chokes out, thinking of the young charity worker with the pretty smile.

"Nope. None of the charity staff know what happens to the children once they leave. And I'd like to keep it that way," she says pointedly, lowering her head to look up at him meaningfully.

"What the fuck," Ed whispers to himself, still shaking his head. "You're sick, you know that? This is fucking . . . fucking sick!"

At this, Hazeline narrows her eyes at him, irises dark pinpricks. "No, Ed. Do you know what's sick? Society letting children and mothers rot through poverty. Mothers being unable to feed their babies. People dying because they cannot afford healthcare. Children begging or becoming drug mules because they don't have the money to keep up with their school friends. Society is sick. The government is sick. I'm just the only person doing anything about it."

"You're mad," Ed whispers. "You're all fucking mad."

"Why? Because I pay mothers to ensure they have a good, safe life? Because I spoil the children rotten? Would you not rather live twenty years in absolute luxury than sixty years where every single day is a struggle? Where you feel like a burden to your mother, a money leech? I'm doing God's work here, Ed!"

"But you're killing people! People with their whole lives ahead of them!"

"Wrong," sings Hazeline. "The only reason they have a life worth looking forward to is because of the upbringing I have gifted them. If I left them where they were born, they would have nothing but decades of struggle or criminality to look forward to. I'm not stealing something from them if I am the one who gave it in the first place. I gift them education, and opportunity, and mindful exploration. All things they'd never experience without me."

"And you kill them," Ed says bitterly, tears in his eyes.

"Everyone dies one day, Ed. You will die. I will die. And all we can hope for is a quick and painless death. Which is exactly what these young adults are receiving. Utterly painless. They don't even know what's happening. A quick little jab in their sleep and away with the fairies. Another priceless gift from me to them. They say money can't buy happiness, but it can, Ed. It buys happiness, it buys comfort, it buys pleasure and chances."

Ed tries to slow down his breathing. He can somehow taste his tongue. It feels rancid and heavy in his mouth.

"But why not just do what you promise? Send them on internships? Why do you have to . . . to *eat* them?" he hisses.

She shrugs, as if he's asked her what her favorite movie is. "Why not? I told you before, about how I've felt since Botan died. I'm fucking starving, Ed. Since he's been gone, they fill me."

She leans back in her chair, crossing her arms as though daring him to argue with her.

"Not enough food in the house for you?" Ed chokes out bitterly.

"I gifted them total escapism from the terrible lives they were destined for," Hazeline says coldly. "These are children whose parents are devoid of any maternal instinct, you understand. They were not ripped from their weeping mother's loving cradled arms. They were tossed at us in exchange for cash and closed mouths. Sold like a pair of tired, battered, secondhand shoes. Expensive to fix up and not worth the trouble. I gave them a life of stability, comfort, love, and luxury. And, in return, they satiate me. They become a part of me. They nourish me and love me back, forever. I imagine if I had my own child, perhaps I would feel more fulfilled, but this seems to fill the void inside me. The thought of them rotting in the ground is obscene to me. Absolutely horrific." She shudders. "Why would I bury someone I have cared for for twenty years, when I could have them with me, always?"

"You sound batshit crazy," Ed hisses, still glancing at the door and trying to work out a way to escape. Rodrick is standing by it, straight and tall, utterly emotionless.

"Well, Ed, petal." Hazeline spits out the term of endearment so close to Ed's face that he has to wipe a speck of saliva away. "Seeing as you don't seem to care for the truth, or for my personal explanation, let me give it to you plainly and simply, in a way that even your embarrassingly decrepit little brain can understand."

She leans in, cups a hand to his ear, and whispers into it.

"It is cheaper to eat the poor than to feed them."

INDEBTED TO A MEGALOMANIAC

Ed feels hazy, as though he's hallucinating or is having some sort of out-of-body experience. He can almost see himself hyperventilating in the zen garden, Hazeline watching him, one eyebrow raised in morbid interest, Rodrick fanning him lightly with one of her many crane-decorated hand fans. He can't feel the frigid winter air. He can't feel much of anything, his body frozen in horror and his mind unable to process the information it has been spoon-fed.

"Perhaps he needs some water," Hazeline suggests, her voice lazy.

Moments later—or hours, perhaps—a cup of water is placed by his feet, directly in his eyeline. He is still hunched over his knees, awaiting the arrival of vomit, though it doesn't come. He looks at his warped reflection in the water, his eyes bulging and wild.

"Ed, how are you feeling?" Hazeline asks, leaning forward and placing a gnarled claw on his knee. He flinches away, despite the genuine concern in her voice. "Come now, try to sit up."

To his horror, he finds himself following instructions, his body desperate to protect itself from this woman through subservience.

"Now, Ed, I know this is a lot to take in, so let's sort out getting you home so you can mull it over."

"Mull. It. Over?" Ed whispers.

"I don't want to have to remind you, but you do owe me rather a lot of money, so I do still expect to see you for your shifts. And we do need to continue preparing for this dinner party, after all."

"Dinner party?" he echoes, mouth hanging open.

"Yes, Ed!" She claps in his face, as though hoping to snap him out of his stupor. "The annual dinner party! The soirée! The main event! The entire reason this conversation came to fruition."

"I can't cook at that!" Ed exclaims, finally finding his legs and trying to stand, albeit wobbly on his feet.

"You bloody well will!" Hazeline gasps. "Need I remind you, you're paying off your debt. And beyond that, should you decide to go blabbing to anybody about what we're up to here . . . Well, I'm sure the police will be mighty interested in you as well," she says, her voice lowering.

"Excuse me?"

"You heard. Your illegal dalliance in gambling. Ties with the Yakuza! Your stupid friend with the dragon tattoo on his hand is no stranger to the police, I'm sure. Not to mention, you pan-fried Ellie's liver and served it on a silver platter."

"You wouldn't," Ed says dumbly.

"Oh, I would. I'll take you down with me if you so dare try. And I'd imagine my money can pay for much better lawyers than yours can," she adds haughtily. "Imagine, poor little Kaori, growing up with an incarcerated criminal father."

Ed slumps back down into his seat, all the adrenaline and fight-or-flight instinct rapidly leaking from his pores and leaving him desperately exhausted and deflated. He's stuck. Once again, he's made a bad choice and involved himself with a bad person and is utterly trapped by it. Only this time, it's not his life on the line. It's other people's.

He runs his hands through his hair, grabbing at the roots and lightly pulling to try to feel something other than the mix of emotions running through him. It doesn't work.

"Right. Well, now that we're all on the same page, do go home and rest up. I hope you feel much better soon," she says dismissively, as though sending him home with a common cold.

Rodrick appears by his side, heaves him up by his arm and then politely escorts him away from Hazeline and toward the front door.

"This is madness. Rodrick, you must see that it's madness," he pleads with the housekeeper as soon as Hazeline is behind them.

"I used to think so too, before I understood everything she was saying," Rodrick says, and there's a hint of pity in his voice. "She's right, you know. She really is helping, in her own way."

"You're deluded. Love has blinded you!" Ed hisses at him.

Rodrick blinks at him as though he's a toddler acting out in a wildly disproportionate manner for the occasion. "Doesn't love blind us all?" he asks.

Ed snorts miserably.

"Perhaps not a love of Hazeline," Rodrick continues. "But a love of life. Or money. Or opportunity. Everyone is blinded by something they love. Even you, Ed."

Ed allows Rodrick to silently walk him to the car, which he enters forlornly before closing the door.

For a long time, he sits there in silence with Nakamura, staring at the back of the leather car seat. He can feel Nakamura watching him in the rearview mirror, but can't bring himself to make eye contact with his friend. Is he really his friend? *Can* Ed be friends with someone who knows of such horrors and turns a blind eye? Though, perhaps Ed is just as bad. He knows within his gut that he is going to have to do the exact same thing, at least until his debt is paid off and he can run far away from Hazeline and all that he has learned. He can't have this debt, and the fear of Hazeline finding him, following him for his entire life. Is this what it has come to?

How did losing his sales job and playing pachinko end up in human sacrifice and being indebted to a megalomaniac?

And really, can he trust anyone at all? Nakamura seems so kind, earnest, and funny. How can he have allowed Ed to get wrapped up in all of this alongside him?

"Ed?" Nakamura's voice is quiet and tentative. Ed takes a deep breath and looks up. He sees Nakamura's eyes in the mirror, his brows raised in concern. "I'm sorry."

"Sorry for what? Not warning me off? Or not telling me that Hazeline is a psychopathic blackmailer? Or for being complicit in killing and *eating people*?" Ed asks bitingly.

"I *tried* to warn you! Several times, in fact! But yes, all of it," Nakamura replies, head down. "You couldn't find out until she was ready for you to know. I had to stay quiet to keep my job."

"Oh, your *job*! Well, in that case, all is forgiven. Thank God you can continue to ferry people around in this fancy fucking car!" Ed raises his voice.

Nakamura flinches. "I have to keep the job to keep my wife alive."

Ah. Ed had forgotten about Suki, lying in her soft hospital bed, being pumped with drugs and having her every whim cared for, courtesy of the Yamamoto bank.

He wants to say *fuck your wife, you coward,* but he can't. Because he knows that he would do the same thing in Nakamura's position. Hell, his position is even less life-or-death, and he is already complicit through ignorance, about to become just as tightly embroiled as everyone else in this prison home.

So instead he says nothing, and finally Nakamura starts the engine, and the long drive back to Tokyo passes in utter silence.

When they pull up outside Ed's home, he looks at it through the window, and suddenly the cramped, messy space he was so eager to escape is the one place he thinks he may find some comfort. He leaves the car without another word to Nakamura, and enters his apartment.

Sayuri is instantly there, giving him a brisk kiss on the cheek and talking to him about her day, the new steps that Kaori has taken, but Ed can only hear the buzzing in his head.

"Ed? Are you okay?" she asks, frowning at him and putting her hand on his forehead. "Ed! You feel all clammy!"

"I have a headache. I don't feel well." He manages to force the words out, and he doesn't recognize his own voice.

"Ed! Okay, get to bed. Come, Kaori is napping, you lie down and I will go and get you some medicine and ingredients for a hearty soup." She instantly snaps into caretaker mode, taking his jacket off for him and searching for her purse.

Ed nods, unable to give her any sort of proper response, and climbs into bed where he lies there, staring at the ceiling, listening to her calming chatter until he hears the door close and realizes she has left to pick up supplies for him. He turns his head, and across from the bed sees Kaori lying in her cot, snoozing, her breaths soft and gentle. He stands, goes over to her, and for a while just gazes down at her. She looks so innocent. He tries to imagine a world where money would be more important to him than her, but he can't. Tries to envision a cost someone would have to offer him to give her up, and is utterly unable to. Her toes twitch as she dreams, her tiny pink fingers clenching lightly. He picks her up carefully, trying not to wake her, and carries her to his bed, laying her down beside him.

Then, he holds on to his daughter and cries, quietly sobbing into her soft onesie, trying to allow the smell of her, clean and linen-like, to comfort him.

Everyone is blinded by something they love. Even you, Ed. Those were the words Rodrick said, and Ed knows it's true. He loves his daughter. He would do anything to keep her safe.

WICKED AND DISTURBED

Ed has been cooking all day. Chopping, slicing, sautéing, and frying. Last night he prepped. Marinated. Diced. Defrosted. He has done all of this without touching the special meat that Rodrick silently placed in the fridge for his attention, the package tightly wrapped in cellophane. But the dinner is quickly approaching, and he is beginning to grow concerned. He has to cook it; there is no way out of this that he can see. His hands shake as he flings onion into a pan, and when he washes them afterward he squeezes his fists under the cold water to try to stop the trembling.

He must not think about what is in that fridge. He cannot. He has to survive the day so that he can go home to his wife and child, put this behind him. If he continues as he is, he should be out of debt with Hazeline before next year's dinner. Then he can resign, and never see her again. Perhaps get a job in another restaurant with her recommendation. Live a peaceful life, comfortable and safe.

Is that what he wants, though? Even as he tells himself it is, he feels a pang, knowing that deep down, he wants more. But not if this is the cost. Not if it means forgoing his morals, taking from others to climb to the top. No, he is not that man. He cannot be that man.

And yet, he is. At least partly. Because he opens the door of the fridge, and without any inspection, hauls the huge meat package over to the counter. It is cold, damp, and heavy in his hands, and he holds it away from his body, as though it is a leaking bin bag. With a deep sigh, he places it on the countertop and stands there for a moment, his hands resting on the edge of the counter, his eyes squeezed shut and his face tilted down toward his feet. He takes in a deep breath. Then another. A slow breath out. *I touched it.* He rushes to the sink, runs the water until it's scalding, and forces his hands to remain underneath the rushing tap until they turn pink and sore. He coughs out a ragged sob, then quickly composes himself. He just has to get through the evening.

The next hour is a blur in his mind. He prepares the meat as instructed in the little black book. He pauses several times to compose himself. He is shaking at the beginning. Then he convinces himself it is pork. That this is all a joke, a silly test of loyalty. But just in case, he repeats Hazeline's words in his head, so many times that he can almost hear it as a tune. *All we can hope for is a quick and painless death. Would you not rather live twenty years in absolute luxury than sixty years where every single day is a struggle? I gave them a life of stability, comfort, love, and luxury. Quick and painless death. Life of luxury. Quick and painless. Painless. God's work. A gift.*

The more he repeats these phrases to himself, the more he tries to convince himself that it is, really, no different to any other cut of meat, and the easier the process becomes. Is he inadvertently killing a part of himself in that pan, too? Or was it always lurking beneath the surface, this ability to dissociate from societal standards and commit something so unthinkably wicked and disturbed?

The doorbell rings.

"Quick, quick! Music, Rodrick!" Hazeline calls out through the house.

The blaring of "Dies irae" from Verdi's *Requiem* begins to echo through the speakers.

The guests have arrived. It's dinner time.

GREEDY

Initially, Ed keeps his head down and avoids mingling with the guests in any way. It's easy enough to do; despite all of them swarming in the dining area mere feet away, nibbling absentmindedly on his carefully made canapés handed out by Rodrick, they barely spare him a glance. He is, after all, just one of the help. And as the room fills and more and more people arrive, Ed finds he has the space to look up, to soak it in, to stare down and judge each and every guest who has accepted the invitation to this sugar-coated massacre.

He spots Miyuki, the J-pop singer from the earlier dinner, though she ignores him completely. The American senator has also returned, and is guzzling wine at an alarming pace once again. Ed feels like he has fallen into an alternate reality as he shares breathing space with some of the most powerful, influential, and richest members of society. There are tech founders—doubtless flown from Silicon Valley, where they have been profiting in the millions from people's carelessly given private data. An AI engineer known for creating the "software of the future," as the *Financial Times* called it. A British MP, his chortle low and Etonian. A-list superstars more recently known for dating women half their age. A Chinese heiress and her cousin. A Japanese media mogul. Two Arabian property developers. A sheik. A collector of e-commerce businesses. A search engine founder. Two fashion designers. Four Chinese cryptocurrency aficionados, who don't seem to be mingling with anybody else. One lucky stock market trader, a Rolex watch on his wrist. A nuclear weapons distributor. The mastermind behind the number one sportswear brand. A diamond mine owner. A software inventor. Two American medical insurers. And, of course, Chef Chungpu, who was greeted to cheers of delight and recognition by nearly everyone in the room. It's a bizarre melting pot of races, genders, languages, interests, and business sectors. The one thing they all have in common is status—and, clearly, taste.

As Ed wipes down the kitchen surfaces, he picks up glitches of their conversations. It's all vapid, materialistic, and boring, as most small-talk tends to be. But he can't scratch the jealous itch that comes on hearing some of the topics.

"Just come back from the Bahamas, it was a quick one, but trying to really prioritize taking the time to enjoy life and switch off, you know?"

"God, you look gorgeous. Even better than last year! Have you had your teeth done?"

"New girlfriend I saw in the tabloids, a Victoria's Secret girl, right? You lucky dog, you!"

"I've left my fiancé, but kept the ring, of course. It's six carats!"

"One of those famous vloggers was trying to get an invite tonight, I heard. Can you imagine the delusion, thinking they would be able to attend? How absolutely fiendish!"

"Did you take the private jet? No other way to fly, of course."

"Oh, yes, I swung by there the other day, friends with the owner. Caviar to die for!"

"Such a shame your wife couldn't make it, send her my love!"

That last one was accompanied by a huge eye roll to indicate that the very last thing being sent to the wife was any sort of love.

Ed is fascinated to notice just how small he feels, without anyone so much as looking at him. They may as well have lined up to spit on him, for how their tactless conversations have made him feel.

Still, he forces a polite smile onto his face as Rodrick shows them to their seats. A long, rented dining table has been erected to face the zen garden, which has been lit up by candles and fairy lights. Ed was informed earlier that they would be eating their starter at the main table, and the main course would be enjoyed al fresco, at the stroke of midnight. One of the camping firepits has resurfaced, and Ed imagines them all holding hands, dancing around the flames like witches beneath the glow of the moon. The table plan was devised by Hazeline over the course of the week, and everyone's assigned seat is signposted by a name card slotted carefully into an elegant silver stand. In the background, the classical music is still playing, but instead of giving the setting a fine dining atmosphere, Ed feels it adds a sinister sense of creeping menace, the violins sounding rushed and choked as the guests await their plates.

"Ladies and gentlemen." Hazeline stands, taps the edge of her glass with a knife to bring the conversations to a brief pause. "I'd like to introduce my chef, Edward Cook." She holds her arm out toward Ed, who stands awkwardly in the kitchen, an island between him and the diners. He gives a little bow, and tries not to make eye contact with anyone as they all politely clap for him. He sees Chef Chungpu lower his head to him, and throw him a subtle wink. Conspirators. Ed feels a hot flush of shame.

Ed clears his throat and introduces their first course. "For your starter, I present an octopus and chorizo salad, served with avocado, lemon, and a blend of spices."

Some murmurs of interest, then the moment is over, Hazeline is seated once more, and they are all served their starters which they tuck into. Ed warms when he hears murmurs of admiration, and a few enthusiastic "delicious!" and "*oishii!*" comments above the chatter. They like his octopus and chorizo salad.

In that moment, all his fears and concerns abandon him, and he luxuriates in the fact that this table full of people who are seated in the finest dining establishments on a daily basis are enjoying *his* entrée. Ed Cook's octopus salad is a hit! He smiles to himself and continues listening in for more words of praise.

"Melts on the tongue, doesn't it?" someone says. Ed stands a little straighter, preens his hair.

But, of course, the conversation quickly pivots back to themselves, and their various ventures. He barely notices Rodrick slip something into the oven.

"Really, I'm desperate for someone experienced in coding to help," the sportswear brand guy is saying.

The software developer smiles. "Don't even worry about it, call me on Monday and we can hook you up with the best of the best."

"Honestly, you *must* join us skiing in Val Thorens," the Chinese heiress says flippantly. "As my guest, of course. I'll send a jet!"

She's speaking to one of the fashion house directors.

"I actually have a huge event coming up. It's going to be televised across America and I love Chinese cuisine. Won't you cater it? Here, take my card," one of the A-list stars is saying, passing a cream business card to Chef Chungpu.

It's a peacocking of power and connections, everyone angling to see who at the table can benefit them in some way, forging false friendships to cover hidden desires. Ed wonders if they all know what they sound like. Corrupt and nepotistic. Is this what true wealth brings? Humans acting as gods in other's futures?

He is so busy eavesdropping that he doesn't notice Hazeline standing until all the other guests have gone silent to allow her to speak. Most of the plates have been scraped clean. What's happening now? He turns to Rodrick for support, but for some reason the housekeeper is fussing with the oven again. Ed's chest begins to constrict. Is she going to move them all outside now? What is Rodrick doing? It's not time for the main dish, Ed isn't ready for it to be time!

The lights dim, so that all they can see is what is lit by the flickering of candlelight. Hazeline begins to speak. In the background, the music is turned down so all can hear her. It's Bach's Toccata and Fugue in D Minor. Though Ed doesn't know this. All he knows is that it's making him feel even more afraid, the frenzied organ a backdrop to her words.

"I'd like to thank my new chef, Ed Cook, for the wonderful starter. I can see we've all enjoyed it!" she says, raising her eyebrows at the guests, who all politely laugh. A small round of applause begins and Ed shuffles on the spot nervously.

"Rodrick, if you please," Hazeline calls. He watches as Rodrick comes toward the table, the contents from the oven now transferred onto a single golden plate. He brings it to Hazeline solemnly, and the entire room is hushed, eyes on the sparkling ceramic and what it holds.

"Ed, come here," she orders.

Slowly, as though his feet are stuck to the floor, Ed drags himself over to the table.

"Bravo, Ed," Hazeline says.

"Bravo!" the table echoes.

Ed heats and fidgets.

"I would like to invite you to join us for this course. This plate was made especially for you. I had Chef Chungpu prepare it for you ahead of time, and it's just been reheated so it's perfect," Hazeline says, gesturing at Rodrick, who brings over a chair for Ed.

Ed glances down at the plate, sees a strange, dark meat, and instinctively knows that it is not from any four-legged creature. No, this is something else entirely. Something wrong. He looks into Hazeline's eyes and sees the challenge.

No.

"No, no, I couldn't possibly," he says, starting to feel sick.

"You'll hurt Chef Chungpu's feelings. He went to a great deal of trouble to design this dish just for you," she says, nudging the plate slightly closer to Ed. He doesn't look at it, instead looking at Chungpu, who nods encouragingly.

"Please, Ed, I'd love to hear about your previous experience," the diamond mine owner says, leaning over, wiping his mouth with a napkin.

"I'm actually looking to open up some new restaurants. Are you interested in running your own space?" one of the investors adds, reaching into his chest pocket for a business card.

"M-me?" Ed stammers, blinking quickly.

"I love your boldness," the man affirms, reaching over the diamond mine owner to hand Ed a card. "You could run the whole gig. Choose your city. Whatever you want!"

"While working for me off-hours," Hazeline adds, wagging a warning finger at the man, who smiles at her bashfully. "No pinching my chef!"

"Also, I *love* your accent," one of the pretty Chinese girls says, fluttering her lashes at him. "What part of England are you from?"

"Oh—er, I, uh . . ." Ed fumbles over his words, barely noticing as Rodrick carefully pushes him down onto the seat. Instinctively, Ed tucks himself in beneath the table beside Hazeline.

"And please, tell me where you learned Japanese fluently? I need to train some of my staff," an investment broker calls out from down the table.

Are these people actually *interested* in Ed?

He's flushing furiously, stuttering out answers to the questions being thrown at him. He looks down at the plate. Scallops, carefully seared to golden. A creamy, rich, cauliflower purée. Pickled mustard seeds and carefully selected sprigs of micro basil as a garnish. And amidst it all, the special meat.

He pushes the plate away, leans his body back from it, turns his head to the side.

"Eat, Ed," Hazeline orders, her voice low.

His heart is beating loudly. His mouth is dry. His stomach curdles.

"I can envision you running a restaurant well, you know," the investor cuts in again, waving his fork at Ed enthusiastically.

Ed picks up his chopsticks, hands shaking, and takes part of a scallop, goes to rub it in the purée. "All of it," Hazeline says through her teeth, smiling wickedly.

Ed pauses. His gut roils painfully, nausea lumping in his throat. "I . . . uh, I'm not really very hungry."

"Eat, Ed. Eat, or leave," she says coldly.

He puts his scallop down.

"Are you scared? Scared that if you get a taste, you'll crave more? Hunger beyond need? Are you afraid that you will become ravenous, until there is nothing left for you to consume?" she says to him quietly.

"No," he replies.

"Or do you think you're better than us? More moral than us, perhaps? Because you're not, Ed. You're just as desperate as anybody else. So *eat up,*" she hisses at him viciously.

He looks down at his plate, and for the first time he looks at the meat properly. The skin has been roasted, and is golden and crisp, but he can still see it. He knows that this piece was chosen specially for him, for him to know what he was going to eat. *Who* he was going to eat. On the skin of the meat is a tattooed dragon, its tail curving into a small swirl.

Ikagi.

Ed breaks out in a fresh sweat, pushes the plate away, begins to stammer. His chest constricts. "This is . . . is this? . . . But when did . . . ?"

"Don't you like it, Ed? It was specially prepared, just for you. No need to thank me, although I have solved all your problems and gotten you a lovely meal to boot. Two birds one stone, and all that malarkey," Hazeline says, her mouth beside his ear so as to be heard over the background conversation. Ed is horrified to find himself feeling ever so slightly relieved. Ikagi is gone, for good. He looks down at the plate again. The last time he saw this dragon, it was attached to an arm that was hurtling toward his face and blackening his eye.

"The hands are underrated, petal. You can suck the deliciously fatty marrow right out of the finger bones," Hazeline says candidly, as though discussing the best way to carve a pineapple.

Ed's stomach rolls into itself once more, and he feels his face whiten.

"Ed, look at this," the investor says, holding out his phone. "This is the commercial space in Tokyo!" Grateful for the distraction, he reaches out for the phone and looks. It's a gleaming restaurant space in the center of Roppongi. "Can you imagine yourself running a kitchen there?" the man asks him with a wink.

Ed hands the phone back silently. He'd like to think he argues with himself for a long time, but in reality, he makes the decision quicker than he wants to admit.

He reaches for his plate before he can change his mind, forgoing the chopsticks, grabs a fistful of food, and takes a bite.

Hazeline leans in, so that only he can hear.

"You've earned this, Ed. It feels so good to be a little greedy sometimes."

REVELRY

Ed is throwing up in the bathroom. He ate the entire portion and was revolted by himself. It was delicious. A flash of the tattoo—wrinkled and blurred, barely visible among the charring of the skin—comes to mind, and he retches again. There is nothing left to empty out but bile. He wipes his mouth with the back of his hand, and with a great sigh heaves himself up from the floor and washes his hands. When he looks in the mirror, he does not recognize himself. He is not a father. He is not a husband. He is an animal. For what type of man could do what he has just done? He can try to justify his actions by saying it was revenge against Ikagi, that his death will help the streets of Tokyo be a little bit safer, but he knows that would be a lie. He did it because he wanted a seat at the table. Is this what Chef Chungpu had to go through, to get to where he is today? Who killed Ikagi?

He thinks of Rodrick and Nakamura in the annex that day when he thought he could hear a chainsaw, and holds a hand out to the wall to steady himself, his legs weakening. *God almighty, what have I done?* He stands in the bathroom for five minutes, or five hours, he's not sure. When his chest has finally stopped constricting and his legs feel strong enough to propel him forward, further from what he's done, he emerges from the bathroom cautiously. The music is still playing in the kitchen, but the room has emptied out. Around the table, which Rodrick has already cleared, are piles of discarded clothes.

In confusion, Ed looks through the glass panes into the garden, and he sees that the guests have all changed into robes, long and white. The wineglasses have been exchanged for large goblet-esque vessels, and the drinking has become frenzied. Some of the women are dancing, strange movements with their eyes closed and hands above their heads, swaying slowly and jerkily as though they are puppets on knotted strings. A group of men have gathered and are snorting a white substance from a tray, their eyes dark and bottomless, jaws grating feverishly. Hazeline is lounging beside the pond, the flames of the fire dancing off her skin. Her robe has slipped slightly, revealing a breast, pale and small. Nobody cares. The atmosphere is erotic and strange, their carefully constructed facades fading away into something more feral.

For the next hour, Ed stands and watches from the decking, caught between two worlds. He is still fully clothed, and does not make a move to join the outdoor partying. But he also does not make a move to retreat inside, or to flee. One of the Silicon Valley guys offers him a cigarette, his eyes glazed and his smile lazy. Ed accepts it, smokes it quickly, and nods occasionally as the man speaks at him at length about his newest project. Then he leaves Ed in the shadows, and returns to the debauchery. By ten to twelve, their masks of composure have slipped further still. Miyuki has stripped entirely, her robe cushioning her bare feet, and she is standing on a rock by the pond singing to an invisible audience—an eerie, melancholy tune. The American senator is slumped against a tree trunk, so drunk he can barely see straight, Chef Chungpu beside him, hand-feeding him milk bread to sober him up before the main course. The media moguls have been arguing about business, their hair messy, faces red and flustered, robes whipping in the wind to reveal their penises, sad and wilted from the drugs, contradictory to their furious bravado as they raise their voices, beating their chests like apes.

The AI engineer stands alone, laughing to himself occasionally, remnants of a line of cocaine beneath his nose. Two of the women have entered the pond and are sitting there chatting as though in a jacuzzi, a film star between them, his arms around them both. And then Rodrick appears, and he rings a golden bell, and everybody stands, silent, eyes dead and skin goose-pimpled. It's time.

Beside the firepit is a strange pot. It's made of cast iron, but is wide and tall, like a cauldron crossed with a pig trough. In it, Rodrick empties out the roasted special meat Ed prepared for the main course. Hazeline stands in front of everybody, and once again, speaks. Her words are slightly slurred.

"Our main meal was provided to us by my charity, and prepared by Chef Cook."

This time, when everyone claps, Ed stares blankly ahead and feels no pride. He thinks of the charity kids, and wonders if it's someone he has met in that pot. The oldest boy was over eighteen, wasn't he? Daiki? He brings a hand to his neck and finds it cold and clammy. He pulls his hand away and looks down at it, and for a moment, the flickering lights of the fire make his hand look clawed, like a beast's. He looks up. The MP is rubbing his hands delightedly, his eyes glazed and wild.

"And so tonight, under the light of the moon and at the stroke of midnight, we feast. I'd like a moment of silence for the offering, and to remind everyone to only enjoy their fill. To feel the power in each bite, be thankful for the experience, but to stay strong enough to remain in control of yourself. Take only what you need, as always."

She bows her head, and around the garden, everybody follows suit. Ed hears the insects in the leaves grating their crooked legs together.

The music has now been turned up, so loud that it's practically echoing through the forest—or are his senses amplifying everything? He isn't sure what is real anymore. This feels like a nightmare. Ed watches as some of the people remove their robes, a silent and sinister affair. Others keep them on. All of them make their way toward the metal trough. Ed doesn't want to look, but he also cannot look away.

Hazeline is the first to lean toward the meat, her breasts low and her back curved. She lifts a piece of meat from the tray, holds it up above her head like a trophy. "*Itadakimasu!*" Hazeline screams, a call for all to begin their meal.

Everyone clambers forward, animalistic and savage, backs hunched and toes curled. Hands reach into the trough and claw at the meat. He sees bloody sauce drip down one of the women's wrists, onto her Cartier bracelet. Robes are stained pink and brown as fingers tear messily at the offering.

There is a strange and eerie quiet as jaws rip away, and the wet sound of chewing is only interrupted by groans and grunts, primal and uncontrolled. Many of them close their eyes as they chew, masticating with nodding heads, frowning in agonized enthusiasm. Ed thinks of a nature documentary he saw once, where a pack of starving wolves hunted down an elk and ravaged its body together, trotting away afterward with bloodied maws and paws. He retches once more, but is again empty, and instead just hacks up the flavor of the cigarette he has smoked, the taste of tar thick on his tongue.

They make quick work of the food. By the time the trough has been cleared away, Ed realizes he has not moved an inch in over half an hour, and is still standing in the same spot on the decking, staring out into the darkness. It feels as though his soul has left his body, and he is now unable to move at all. The guests have outdone themselves, and many are lying around, rubbing their bloated bellies, full and exhausted. Rodrick keeps passing by him, carrying things into the kitchen and tutting pointedly at Ed's lack of help.

Let him clear the mess alone, Ed thinks to himself. *I won't touch that trough. I have sullied myself enough tonight.* He wonders when they will leave, if they will continue on until dawn breaks, driven by the drugs and the excitement of their illicit banquet. But instead, to his great surprise, they all put their robes back on, stains and all, and return to the kitchen to reseat themselves for the third course. The dessert.

"Ed, you must join us for just a moment. Here, at the table," Hazeline instructs. Ed finds he still cannot move, and one of the guests takes him by the shoulders and walks him to the table, sitting him down among them. They're talking to him, telling him things about restaurants and opportunities, but his head is too fuzzy and he can't concentrate enough to make out the words. He is seated there, dressed in his fancy chef's uniform, while they are covered in dirt, grease, and muck, twigs caught in matted hair, makeup streaked down faces, eyes dark and pupils blown. In the middle of the table is a long bone. It is huge, perhaps a rib bone, with one end slightly knobbed.

Hazeline stands. The corners of her lips are stained with what looks like blood. "I have something to announce this year, before dessert. As you all know, we had a very unfortunate mishap with the freezer. And I have not been able to restock at the charity as often as I would like. It takes a great deal of time to source the right applicants, as I'm sure you can all understand. We have a few years before the next batch will be ready to fuel us, and I am not certain that I will be able to find the right candidate between now and then. If I don't, there must be a contingency plan. We cannot skip a year."

Murmurs of agreement around the table. "Maybe we can find someone from our country," one of the Chinese guests begins.

Hazeline holds up a hand. "I have said before, the risk in importing is too high. I am unwilling to host here with foreign sacrifice."

More murmurs.

"That is why I have decided that, this year, we will play a little game. Inspired by the Aztecs."

At this the murmurs come to a halt. Ed is sure his heart stops as he remembers the story told to the children by the glow of the campfire.

"Game?" the senator asks nervously.

Hazeline nods at the rib bone in the center of the table. "Spin the bottle meets Russian roulette. I came up with it myself," she chuckles. "Whoever the bone lands on will have the great honor of being the sacrifice for our next meal."

At this, the table descends into a furious uproar.

"This isn't how we do it!"

"I'm not taking part. This is madness."

"What the hell is this, Hazeline? Your idea of a joke?"

"Why should we be the sacrifice? We are bringing good into the world, it's a waste!"

"We are the only humans who have consumed others. This makes us stronger, wiser, more powerful. Imagine how much we would pass on if *we* were to be consumed," Hazeline bellows.

"This is fucking insane." The MP shakes his head in astonishment.

"You're barking up the wrong tree here, Hazeline." The stockbroker stands, waving a warning finger toward Hazeline. Rodrick appears behind him and puts his hands on his shoulders, firmly pushing him back down into his seat.

"You are all *animals*!" Hazeline shouts, slamming her hands down on the table and shocking the guests into quiet. "Disgusting vermin, only willing to take and not to give! I have fed you and fed you, kept you safe, kept your warped pleasures hidden from society, and this is how you thank me? By refusing the courtesy of offering the same pleasure?" She spits. "Please. None of you are brave enough to admit you're afraid to die. That's the truth of it. But this is how life works. If you take, you must eventually be willing to give back. If not, you're just . . . just . . . GREEDY! Immoral, greedy barbarians! So shut the fuck up at my table, and play by my goddamn rules!"

With that, Rodrick spins the bone, and Ed watches as it wheels before him, before all of them seated at that table, and waits to feel the fear of it landing on him. The fear doesn't come. Perhaps it's what he deserves. Everyone has gone quiet, eyes on the bone. When it finally stops, bulbous end pointing at its mark, Hazeline smiles.

DIGESTIF

SAYURI

Sayuri was working at the café when Honami popped by. It was late, and Sayuri was getting ready to close the shop. Kaori was with the childminder, and Ed was, most probably, at the pachinko parlor. He thought she didn't know, but she wasn't stupid. She saw the receipts, she knew he was playing games all day instead of looking for a job. She was just biding her time, trying to work out how best to approach the conversation. But each day that she held her thoughts in, that she waited for him to confess—only to be disappointed—the resentment grew.

"Come to check in on your poor old manager?" Sayuri teased, pulling out a chair at the counter.

Honami had been one of Sayuri's employees, a pretty and eager young thing who worked hard and was good with customers, until she'd gotten a much better, much fancier job. "Nowhere better to get a delicious cheesecake," she replied with a smile.

Sayuri grinned at her and began to cut her a piece of cheesecake. "On the house. It'll be stale by tomorrow, anyway," she said, serving it up for her.

"Thank you," Honami said. "I actually dropped by to talk to you about something."

"Oh?" Sayuri was curious.

"Well, it's just, I heard that your husband lost his job?"

Sayuri flushed and darted her eyes away. How embarrassing. Had she become the talk of the town? Was everyone shaking their heads at her sad, gambling husband? She knew there were whispers when they'd gotten married, her friends had worried that he wouldn't uphold Japanese etiquette or values. His current unemployment—and lack of desire to resolve it—was only proving them right.

"I'm sorry, I don't mean to overstep," Honami said quickly. "It's just that, my employer, she's looking for someone, and so I thought I'd mention it to you in case it's of any interest. It's a chef's position, but I don't think they need too much experience, and I'm sure if you've taught him your skills in the kitchen, he'll get on just fine!" She held up her plate of cake for emphasis.

Sayuri bit her lip. "He . . . he doesn't really enjoy cooking, I don't think. Though I appreciate you thinking of us."

Honami darted a look around the café, but there were no customers, the shutters already half-down. The teenage employee who had replaced her had on a pair of headphones and was bopping to music as she swept up the cake crumbs around them.

"Look, between you and me, my employer is a very influential person. You've heard of Yama Uba?"

Sayuri gasped, bringing her hand to her chest. Everyone knew of Yama Uba, particularly in the poorer part of Osaka where she'd grown up.

"Yama Uba is an urban myth!" she said.

Honami shook her head solemnly. "She's not. She's my boss."

There had been rumors the last decade or so about a woman known only as Yama Uba, who bought children from their mothers and scurried them away to another place, never to be seen again.

Children would be warned to be good, or their parents would sell them to old Yama Uba. But beyond those rumors, there were others, too. Stories of people getting jobs with Yama Uba, and becoming rich beyond their wildest dreams.

"Who is she?" Sayuri whispered, leaning toward Honami.

"I can't say. I'm sworn to secrecy. There are legal contracts involved. But she pays well. Very well," she added, pointedly glancing down at her designer handbag.

"I've heard that some people who work for her end up disappearing. There are stories of terrible accidents happening at her home, away from witnesses, and that she pays off the victim's families when this occurs to keep them from prying too much," Sayuri says.

Honami shrugs. "Just rumors. After all, I'm still here, aren't I?"

That evening, Sayuri tried to speak to Ed about the job. She got as far as saying that her friend had told her about a role before he interrupted her, held his hands up, and said that he didn't want her to get him out of the mess he was in. "I don't want you paving my way in this country any more than you already have. I can't take your friend's job as charity, it's embarrassing!" he said to her. She could see she had wounded his pride; his entire frame seemed hunched and ashamed. She apologized, and went to bed, her back facing him.

But then, one day, her phone alerted her with a text notification. The joint bank account they had for Kaori's university fund had been emptied.

She was at work and gasped, retreating to the back room for staff and opening up the apps. She checked once, checked twice, and eventually rang the bank, who confirmed that all the money had been withdrawn by her husband.

She messaged Ed, asking what he was up to. He replied, saying he was handing out CVs in Minato City.

Her phone shook in her hands. He was lying. She knew he had gambled that money away. The money for their daughter to have a better life than the one Sayuri had had growing up.

She took the rest of her shift to calm down, to make a plan of action. She wanted to leave him. She wanted to go back to Osaka, to her parents, Kaori in tow. But she couldn't, because that didn't resolve the problem of giving Kaori a better life—one of financial stability. If Sayuri left Ed, she would not be entitled to child support the way she would if they lived in Britain. Japan had no mandatory requirements for child payments. She would have to provide for both of them on her café manager salary.

So instead, Sayuri made a plan. She called Honami, and told her that her husband needed this job, and she wanted Honami to help him get it. But they needed to be smart about it. It needed to be Ed's idea. He couldn't know that Sayuri was behind it.

And so Honami printed the ad in the paper. Later, Sayuri made sure that it was left on Ed's desk, face up, so that he would come home and find it. Honami told her employer to look out for his application, and that she recommended him personally. Sayuri spent the week hating Ed, unable to bear being near him. Every time she began to feel sorry for him, she would open the bank account and stare at the zeros, the fury returning.

She knew that there had to be some truth to the rumors behind the disappearances of those working for Yama Uba. There was never smoke without fire. Some people worked for her and flourished as a result, like Honami—or Chef Chungpu, who often referenced his old employer on his cooking show. Some people worked for her and vanished, never to be seen again. But the families were always better off, one way or another. Whether Sayuri was going to be the rich wife of Yama Uba's newest employee, or the rich widow of a husband lost to some strange, vague accident during his working hours—either way, she and Kaori would be cared for. If Ed was willing to sacrifice their marriage, and their daughter's future, for male pride and a gambling problem, Sayuri was willing to give him up. The irony of marrying with the end goal of a financially stable life and ending up with a husband who was draining her bank balance more than if she'd been a single mother was not lost on her.

She didn't think it was greedy of her, to essentially set her husband up with a dodgy boss in exchange for cash. After all, don't you have to have an excess of something before you can be greedy?

GLOSSARY

Burakumin—Historical lower class of people in Japan based on religion or occupation
Daiso—Similar to Poundland shops in the UK or dollar stores in the USA
Donburi—Rice bowl with various toppings
Engawa—A covered corridor with wooden decking which runs around the outside of a building
Gaijin—Foreigner or outsider
Gampi paper—Handmade from gampi bushes
Genkan—An entryway porch area of Japanese houses to take your shoes off
Hafu—Term for someone who is half-Japanese
Irasshaimase—Welcome!
Itadakimasu—Said before meals and roughly translates to "I humbly receive"
Izakaya—Little casual bars
Kani salad—Crab salad
Kanpai—Cheers!
Kintsugi vase—A vase which has been broken and repaired with gold
Konbanwa—Good evening
Konbini—Corner shop, such as a 7-Eleven, with popular food options
Majide—Modern exclamation, translates roughly into "for real?"
Mizubachi—Traditional antique Japanese water pots
Oishii—Tasty
Omurice—A type of omelet filled with fried rice and meats

Onigiri—Rice balls with fillings
Sensei—Teacher
Shabu shabu—Hotpot dish of thinly sliced meats and vegetables
Suzume—Sparrow
Ume—Plum
Umeshu—Plum wine, very popular in Japan and very delicious!
Yakisoba—Fried noodles
Yunomi—A ceramic tea mug with no handle

ACKNOWLEDGMENTS

As always, this is harder than writing the actual book, but I'll do my best to be efficient while not forgetting anybody.

The first and biggest thank-you to both of my editors, Jesse Shuman and Emily Griffin, who have each pushed me creatively and brought the most incredible enthusiasm and passion to both the UK and US markets. I thank my lucky stars every day that I get to work with you both.

My fairy godmother agent, Camilla Bolton, who took a punt on me with this book but believed in me and trusted my vision. Thank you for understanding what I was trying to do and supporting me expertly every step of the way.

Big thanks to both my UK and US teams at Penguin—it takes a whole host of people to create a book, and I am thankful for everyone from marketing and PR through production and copyedits. An extra shout-out to Zahraa Neseer and Carlos Beltrán for my beautiful cover designs—you created something cooler than I ever could have imagined.

Jack Barmby, my best friend and weird little brainiac, who taught me about Burakumin and encouraged me to make Hazeline as freaky as my heart desired. You're my favorite person.

Kate Murray for your bizarre little Ed rhyme via WhatsApp when I was spitballing ideas, which evolved into Hazeline's poem in her introduction scene.

Ken Kazu, who I met one time in a pub and described chorizo as little "porky discs." I thought it was hilarious, and he let me use the phrase in the book.

ありがとうございます Honami for letting me use your name and being the best Japanese teacher.

Alice Slater and Lucy Rose for being early readers and supporters of this book. The two coolest, most feral literary girlies on my side feels insanely wild and I am so appreciative of your support.

Always—Steven, my husband, for constantly massaging my ego and telling me how brilliant this book is, and Betsy, my angel baby, darling, gorgeous girl. Without our daily dog walks, I wouldn't have had half of the weird ideas for this book.

Last, thank you to that cheap bottle of red wine that I tanked, which led to me drunkenly changing a sex scene mid-write and turning it into the lambshank-in-bed scene: my favorite in the whole novel.

ABOUT THE AUTHOR

CALLIE KAZUMI is the author of *Claire, Darling* and a British Japanese writer who started work on her first book after being given Stephen King's *On Writing* by her father. She lives in London with her husband and their Bichon Frisé, Betsy.

X: @callieuntitled
Instagram: @callieuntitled